SUGAR
POP
MOON

SUGAR
POP
MOON

JOHN
FLORIO

SEVENTH
STREET
BOOKS™

59 John Glenn Drive
Amherst, New York 14228-2119

Published 2013 by Seventh Street Books™, an imprint of Prometheus Books

The characters and events portrayed in this book are fictitious. Any similarity to real persons, living or dead, is coincidental and not intended by the author.

Cover image © Bernice Abbott, *Changing New York* series 1936.
Photography Collection, Miriam and Ira D. Wallach Division of Art,
Print and Photographs, the New York Public Library,
Astor, Lenox and Tilden Foundations

Cover design by Nicole Sommer-Lecht

Inquiries should be addressed to
Seventh Street Books
59 John Glenn Drive
Amherst, New York 14228–2119
VOICE: 716–691–0133 • FAX: 716–691–0137
WWW.PROMETHEUSBOOKS.COM

17 16 15 14 13 • 5 4 3 2 1

Library of Congress Cataloging-in-Publication Data Pending

Florio, John, 1960-
    Sugar pop moon : a Jersey Leo novel / John Florio.
        pages cm
    ISBN 978-1-61614-795-2 (pbk.)
    ISBN 978-1-61614-796-9 (ebook)
    1. Bartenders—Fiction. 2. Prohibition—Fiction. 3. Distilling,
Illicit—Fiction. I. Title.

PS3606.L665S84 2013
813'.6—dc23

                                                                    2013010148

Printed in the United States of America

For the outsiders

CHAPTER 1

1930

*N*obody forgets running into an albino. At least that's what Jimmy McCullough said the day he put me to work at the Pour House. He looked me straight in the eye and told me a four-eyed geezer could spot a bleached coon like me from a mile away.

"Stick to misdemeanors," he said. "Because you're sure as hell gonna get busted."

I've since found out he was right.

I'm Jersey Leo, a walking cup of coffee with a splash too much milk, a steaming mug of cocoa with one too many marshmallows, a sideshow attraction in a circus that rolled into town when Prohibition started eleven years ago.

Business at the Pour House is booming—the bar is jammed and it's not even six o'clock. All the regulars are here because they've got nowhere else to go: New York City is trudging its way through an afternoon snowstorm, not to mention a yearlong blizzard of pink slips.

The Pour House is fairly large; it takes up a doublewide brick row house at 323 West Fifty-Third Street. The building stands out from the blocks of decaying tenements and aborted dreams known as Hell's Kitchen. It has its own walkway and stoop, not to mention a bouncer waiting to pat you down right inside the door. A dining room fills the front half of the place and holds eight polished mahogany tables. A pair of pocket doors separates it from the barroom, a square space with an L-shaped bar running across the back and right walls. It's a far cry from a fancy nightclub, but the Pour House is friendly, familiar, and always open. Most of our customers are regulars—the place has them hooked by their wallets, their tongues, and their souls.

Me, I'm here for a different reason. Whether or not I like Jimmy doesn't matter. The classifieds are awfully thin nowadays and I'm pulling in thirty-five bucks a week. I haven't checked but I'm fairly certain there aren't a lot of want ads for a chalk-white albino with yellow hair and no real skills to speak of.

I'm pouring shots of moonshine behind the bar when Larch walks through the front door. He has one of those foreheads that wrinkles at the top of his nose and leaves him with a puzzled look on his face, kind of like a kid leaving his first algebra class. But Larch isn't a mathematician—he's a cop. He spends his day behind the wheel of a squad car, raiding speakeasies like this one. It just so happens that he likes me and loves rye, so, as far as he's concerned, the Pour House is above the law.

The tip of Larch's nose is as red as a radish and the brim of his fedora is hidden under a dusting of fresh snow. A busty woman with blood-red lipstick and a Clara Bow bob holds his elbow. She's no movie star, but for a barfly like Larch, she's not bad, either. I've never seen Larch's wife and I'm sure that's still the case.

Diego is working the door. He's new to the place but he can sniff Larch's badge. He lets Larch in without patting him down.

"Hey, Snowball," Larch calls out. Everybody in the place knows me as Snowball and there's simply no undoing it. "We're hungry and we're thirsty," he says. His words are gobbled up by the sound of singing voices and clinking glasses at the bar.

Larch and his date stop in the dining room and sit down at a table for four. It wouldn't matter if they took the table for eight, because the entire room is empty. Everybody is crowded at the bar, waiting for me to take their money and splash a fleeting moment of happiness into their glasses.

"Gimme a second," I yell to Larch, knowing he isn't here to say hello but to enjoy a free meal—along with some whiskey to wash it down. I don't mind covering Larch, but Jimmy hates when he thinks anybody is taking advantage of him, even if it's a steady customer who can land his ass in jail.

"It gets my goat when a freeloader like Larch comes in here," Jimmy told me the first day I showed up for work. "He thinks it's easy to run this place, but I've got to grease palms, kiss butt, and bang heads just to keep it open." Jimmy sounds like a businessman, but the only business he really understands is the kind nobody talks about.

The good news is that Jimmy's not here tonight. I'm in charge and I'll keep Larch and the rest of the force smiling until he gets back on Wednesday. I'll put a cap on it, though. I can't afford to cross Jimmy again. He caught me pouring freebies for a street cop a couple of weeks ago and docked me two weeks' pay. Next time I may not be so lucky.

I walk over to Santi. He's squatting on one knee behind the bar, chipping down a block of ice with a screwdriver. He's wearing a white kitchen apron, his hair is slicked straight back, and clusters of tiny pimples dot his forehead. Santi once told me he wished he were white and not Spanish, but I set him straight. In my book he's one lucky Joe. He can spend the day walking through Hell's Kitchen, letting the sun toast his olive skin. I'd gladly take on any skin color—brown, white, yellow, purple—if those rays would stop feeling like a sizzling waffle iron. Anything beats being a nation of one, which is what I am.

Santi looks up at me, his screwdriver poised in midair. "Larch is thirsty," I tell him.

"Of course he is," he says. "It's free."

I tell him to keep Larch happy.

"I'll bring him the sugar pop moon," he says.

"Good idea."

We just got the stuff this morning and I can't wait to try it out. This isn't amateur street moonshine. I won't serve that swill—it'll burn a hole right through your gut.

Santi hustles off to the basement.

"And bring him two glasses," I shout out to him.

Santi is seventeen, six years younger than I am. I met him because his father, Old Man Santiago, owns the Hy-Hat, a social club up in

Harlem where I spend most of my off-hours. Santi used to follow me around the club like a puppy on an invisible leash. When I found out his old man was broke, I got the kid a job bussing tables here at the Pour House. I hope the money doesn't hook him. He's too smart to spend the rest of his days working for the likes of Jimmy.

Larch is sitting at the table next to the Christmas tree, which some wiseass has decorated with a pair of bloomers. I get Diego to take my place behind the bar while I walk over to Larch and his lady friend. She takes a long look at my kinky hair and red-rimmed green eyes. Then she stares at the pink blotches that stain my skin. A confused look comes over her face. To her I'm nothing but a nigger who's been dipped in bleach.

"Jersey," I say, giving her my birth name. I'd tell her that I got the name because my father won the state boxing championship on the other side of the Hudson, but she probably wouldn't believe me. I'm hardly the stuff of heavyweights. I stand almost six feet tall but weigh barely a buck sixty-five, most of the weight coming from a soft midsection and a pair of broad, bony shoulders. Luckily, my suit hangs loosely on my frame, as if it were draping a wire mannequin at Gimbels.

"Everybody calls me Snowball," I say, figuring Larch has mentioned me before.

A glint of recognition flashes in her eyes. "Oh, Snowball," she says. I extend my hand to her but I can see she doesn't want to touch it. I pretend not to notice.

"How's it going, Larch?" I ask. "Anything I should know about?"

"Nah, you're clean," he says.

I'm sure he feels powerful in front of his date, but the truth is that a pass from Larch wouldn't mean a thing if the Feds ever came down on me. The Feds are much tougher—and way more expensive—than a beat cop in Hell's Kitchen.

"There's a new chef downstairs," I say. Larch knows the kitchen is in the basement; we've gone down there once or twice for late-night snacks after the chef has gone home. "Try the steak."

"Sounds good," he says, smiling. I'm standing and waiting, but I can't take his order because Clara Bow is picking through the menu as if it's a special edition of the *Herald Tribune.*

Santi steps out of the bar crowd with two glasses in his left hand and a bottle of moonshine in his right. The glasses are already iced up and he puts them on the table.

"A splash of recreation for the officer," he announces as he pours two fingers into each glass.

The kid's got a brain—he's the chess champion at the Hy-Hat—but every once in a while he'll spit out a sentence that'll make your head spin.

He slides Larch a shot of shine. "Enjoy the fortitude."

Larch smiles before slugging down the moon. It barely hits his tongue when his lips pucker and his face twists. He spits the booze onto the white tablecloth.

"What the hell is this? Piss?"

"That's sugar pop moon," Santi says. He couldn't sound more offended if he'd distilled it himself.

I pick up Clara Bow's glass and sip the shine. It's awful. As much as I want to spit it out, I swirl it over my taste buds and hold it for a few seconds. It could be iodine mixed with sugar water. Whatever it is, it's not the real thing—and hack moonshine could kill somebody.

I spit it back into her glass.

"Please tell me this isn't the moon from Philly," I say to Santi. I just bought eighty cases of the stuff.

"That's it, that's the sugar pop moon," Santi says, staring at the bottle. I'm sure he's running the odds on whether I got taken. I already know the answer.

Santi's scared for me. I just spent $4,800 of Jimmy's money on this shine, and if it's all cow piss, I'm in deep trouble. Jimmy's still on me for throwing the boys at the precinct free cases of rye, so he'll surely think I scammed him by switching suppliers and pocketing the extra cash. Jimmy doesn't like it when his boys get cute. Ask Satch Jenkins. He used to bus tables here at the Pour House and he took Jimmy for a single case of whiskey. The poor slob disappeared—then resurfaced two weeks later selling newspapers in Times Square, unable to shout "Extra!" because Jimmy had taken out his tongue.

"Santi, bring Officer Larch a couple of beers while I figure out what's going on."

"Immediately," Santi says and heads to the bar.

My underarms are hot and clammy as I make a beeline past Santi and trot down the cement stairs behind the right pocket door. I walk through the kitchen to the back of the house; then I lift the broken wooden palette off the tiled floor in front of Jimmy's office. Muscling open the hatch, I carefully make my way down the three drop-steps and land in the dank subbasement. Santi calls this place the ratacombs on account of the furry creatures crawling around. I see one scamper across the floor but I let it go. It's good that the little bastards are down here; they keep uninvited punks from venturing too far into the space.

The ratacombs are dark and the musty air cools the beads of sweat that are forming across the back of my neck. I light the lamp under the hatch. To my left is the underground stairway that climbs up to Jimmy's office, but I head for the metal utility door that's camouflaged to look like part of the brick wall. Jimmy keeps the liquor piled up in a dark hole that is part of the neighboring row house, 321 West Fifty-Third Street. In one of his usual fits of paranoia, he bought that house just to have a place to store the stash. "Off-premises," he calls it. He even had some fancy law firm on Fifth Avenue create a paper trail that put both places in his cousin's name, so if the Feds were ever to stumble upon the liquor next door, they'd have to pin it on Jimmy's cousin. And Jimmy's cousin is dead.

The door is heavy, but I push it open and make my way to the stash. I rip open two cases of shine, pull a brown bottle from each, crack their paper seals and taste them. The first is counterfeit for sure. The second is even worse. I go through four bottles before finding a decent one.

I'm screwed. I bought this stuff off of a guy I don't even know, a crook named Denny Gazzara. It's not like I had a choice. Owney Madden's boys wouldn't drop their weekly shipment with me. They drove up in their polished Studebaker, tailed by a truck full of whiskey just like always, but the big guy with the cauliflower ear said he wouldn't hand off the booze unless he met with Jimmy first. When I told him Jimmy was staying out of sight until the heat from last week's raid dies down, he leaned out the window and told me flat out, "This load ain't for niggers." The joke is that I'm practically as white as he is, but I guess that never occurred to him.

Looking back, I'm thinking Gazzara could have had a mark on me right from the start. I was riding the train down to Philly when he grabbed the seat to my left. He settled back, took out some ledger sheets and began marking them up with a short, sharp pencil. It's unusual for a white businessman to ride in the back car with the colored folk, but I didn't question it at the time; I was too busy enjoying the fact that somebody was willing to sit next to me. He seemed like a regular Joe College—all decked out in a fancy suit and polished leather shoes— except he had the face of a street urchin. A dark scar crossed his right earlobe, making it look as if it were caught in a slipknot. And his eyes were two different colors. The left one was brown—as dark as a chestnut—and the right one as green as a young blade of grass.

He'd only been sitting for a few minutes when he put down his ledger and started chatting me up. I'd heard his name before, so I wasn't surprised when he mentioned his operation. He said he was cranking out cases of moonshine made from beets. Sugar pop moon, he called it. Then he took out a flask and let me try some. Whatever he gave me was damned good stuff, far better than the street shine that's been making its way around Hell's Kitchen the past few months. This moon tasted better than our house whiskey; it was rich and smooth with a bite of rhubarb.

I didn't give it much thought. I didn't have to. I needed to stock the place and start pouring some booze or Jimmy would have me bussing tables again. I agreed to sixty dollars a case—nearly as much as Jimmy pays for his best liquor—and then I practically begged Gazzara to get me eighty cases before dawn.

His boys delivered to the Pour House at three o'clock in the morning. Santi and I each taste-tested a different bottle that we pulled from a random case. It was the same stuff I'd had on the train—Santi liked it, too—so I paid the runners. Not wanting to get busted by the

Feds, we rushed the cases into the Pour House and stacked them by the bar. Then Santi and I lugged them downstairs, through the kitchen, and into the ratacombs one at a time, so nobody, especially not Denny's boys, would know where we kept the stash.

The runners must have known which bottles we would taste. The cases are probably flagged, but I don't bother searching for the marks. My albino eyes aren't worth a single bottle of this rotgut. I'd be lucky if all they did was shimmy back and forth, but they make the world look like a watercolor caught in a light mist. It doesn't matter—I don't need to read these labels to know there aren't many good bottles in the batch.

If I tell Jimmy I gave his cash to anybody but Owney Madden's goons I'm as good as dead. I've got to replace the shine or return the money before Jimmy gets back. My first thought is to hijack one of Madden's trucks and steal the booze, but I'd never get away clean—it wouldn't take Madden long to track down an albino smuggling a truck-load of liquor.

I walk upstairs into the dining room. It's filling up and I need to start taking dinner orders, but I've got bigger fish to fry.

Santi pulls me next to the fireplace. "All of it's bogus?"

"Enough of it," I say and look in on the bar. Everybody's happy. Two middle-aged drunks are singing along with the radio. "Body and Soul." The redhead next to them is swaying in place, holding a martini in her hand. Life sure is easier when you're drinking booze and not serving it.

"You have to straighten this out," Santi says.

Over Santi's shoulder, I see Larch smoking a cigarette and using his empty plate as an ashtray. I'd ask for his help but I don't need a cop, I need a miracle.

"And you have to start at the root of the circumstances," Santi says.

I get that he's talking about Gazzara and he's right. To get Jimmy's money back I've got to shake the bastard down. And since Gazzara isn't coming up to the Pour House, I'm going to have to go down to Phila-delphia and walk into his warehouse—in the middle of a town where my only protection, the name Jimmy McCullough, doesn't mean shit.

CHAPTER 2

*L*ike every other storefront in Harlem, the Hy-Hat Social Club is decorated for the holidays. Old Man Santiago must have spent the morning stringing lights around the window and hanging a glowing Santa face above the door. Inside, wreaths line the walls and red ribbons hang from the brass lights overhead.

I'm sitting with Santi at a booth in the dining room, trying to sort out Denny Gazzara's bait-and-switch. Through the double doors on my left, where four ping-pong tables are lined up, I can hear Old Man Santiago showing Billy Walker how to backhand a slam, which is a joke because the old man couldn't hit a lobbed grapefruit. The place is hopping; the bouncing ping-pong balls sound like Peg Leg Bates rattling the stage at the Cotton Club.

I started coming here when I was eighteen, a freshman at City College. I loved it from day one. I would show up after school to shoot pool and then come back after dinner to work with Old Man Santiago and Pearl in the kitchen. Nobody here ever seemed to notice I'm albino. In this place, I'm just another oddball.

It was a hot July weekend when Old Man Santiago told me he was shutting down the place for good. He was on his knees, cleaning out the inside of the icebox. A canvas work apron covered his flat chest and large belly; sweat lined his thick upper lip and soaked the wispy gray hairs on the top of his head. When he closed the icebox, his bony shoulders dropped and he sighed.

"There are other clubs, Jersey," he said, measuring his words as if he were a father telling his son he was walking out on the family. "You'll move on from this place."

I didn't get it, probably because I didn't want to get it. He seemed to have enough money to keep the place open; we all paid dues so we were never short on ping-pong paddles, pool cues, pop, hot dogs, whatever we wanted. It took Santi, who at the time was a twelve-year-old kid in knickers, to tell me that the dues barely covered the rent and his old man had been floating us with the little cash he had left over from his tailoring business. I guess Harlem wasn't missing enough buttons to keep things going. That's when I decided to help the old man out. He practically raised me—at least during the evening hours. I can't deny that once I found the Hy-Hat, I spent more time there than I did with my own father.

That next evening I threw on my nicest jacket, spit-shined my black oxfords, and took the subway to the Three Aces Restaurant in Hell's Kitchen to see Jimmy McCullough. I stood in front of him, my knees shaking inside my baggy pants, and told him I needed a job. Everybody up in Harlem knew what Jimmy did for a living. He'd show up every Sunday, walk from juice joint to juice joint, and collect bags of cash from the bar owners in exchange for hooking them up with bootleggers like Owney Madden. He was always decked out in a tailored suit and spats, his face clean-shaven and his short sideburns waxed into place. We'd never seen Jimmy raise his hands to anybody, and his droopy brown eyes could almost make him seem tired and innocent, but there was no question as to who pushed the buttons. At the time, I just figured that the poor suckers who got the brunt of Jimmy's stick deserved it.

"I'll hijack trucks, I'll do whatever it takes," I told him, clasping my hands together and practically praying to him. He was my only hope at saving the Hy-Hat. "Just don't tell my father or Old Man Santiago."

"I don't hijack trucks," Jimmy said, standing in the glow of the neon sign in front of the Three Aces, swigging from a bottle of cherry soda. "It's distasteful." As the last word came out, his lips, blood red from the pop, twisted with disgust.

He brought me into the restaurant, which was more crowded than the A train on a weekday morning. He had his own booth in the back; its padded red upholstery was so new it smelt like a freshly oiled baseball glove. He ordered me a cola and gave me a short lecture on how to be an upstanding outlaw. Being Jimmy, he also had the balls to give me advice on being a respectable albino.

"I don't care how white you are, you're still a nigger," he said, looking me over and shaking his head. "You know that, right?" He waited for an answer. "You know you're a nigger."

I wanted a job, so I nodded enthusiastically.

"That's right," he said, almost as if he needed to be sure himself. "You're a nigger." He spread some butter on a hunk of bread, bit into it, and kept talking as he chewed. "The cops don't like coons. And they won't give a buffalo shit that those splotches on your fucked-up face are as white as Sister Hannigan's ass."

I laughed because I thought it was funny—at least the part about Sister Hannigan—but I've since found out that Jimmy always talks about Sister Hannigan's ass, or her tits, or, when he's really riled, her twat. Maybe she taught him in grammar school or something.

"You better smile if you even sniff a cop. Kiss their asses with those pink mambo lips of yours."

"Yes, sir," I said, my knees still shaking under the table but a smile stretching the corner of my mouth. If he was telling me how to duck the cops, he was going to give me work.

"I'll tell you something, kid," he said. "Those bleached nuts of yours must be the size of coconuts for you to come down here and ask for work. You wanna work for me, you're welcome to it. But let me tell you something. If you ever think about screwing me for as much as one red cent, I'll kill you in ways you can't imagine."

That night he gave me a loaded snub-nosed revolver, a pair of brass knuckles, and a grunt job at a watering hole behind a butcher shop on Ninth Avenue. For months, I'd hurry out of class and roll kegs in and out of the stock room. He paid me well, so it wasn't long before I'd quit college, come clean to my father, and found my own place to live. The Feds eventually shut down the bar, but I'm still working for Jimmy and still using the money to keep the Hy-Hat in ping-pong balls and ice cream cones. And I've never stopped smiling my pink ass off whenever I cross paths with a cop.

Tonight the Hy-Hat is as busy as ever and I'm in the back booth. The kids keep this table open for me because it doesn't have a reading lamp. My eyes are grateful.

I lean against the wooden backrest, which rises two feet above my shoulders. The table is littered with pretzel salt and I make a mental note to tell Old Man Santiago to be sure the kids wipe the place down after closing time. I suck some pop and wait for Santi to answer me.

"What's my move in Philly?" I ask him again. I don't want to drag him into my mess, but a chess champ has got to be better than I'd be at planning this out. "I figure I'll make a ruckus. If I can rile him up, maybe he'll start looking for me."

Santi nods in agreement. "You don't have many other options."

"I also don't have time. Jimmy's back on Wednesday."

"That gives us six days," Santi says.

"It gives *me* six days," I say. I feel like Santi's older brother; I'm not about to let him catch a beating in Philly. "You have to watch the Pour House."

"Let Diego run it," he says. "You'll need me down there. The minute somebody needles you, you'll lose your sanity."

"I'll be fine," I say, even though he's got a point. I fly off the handle at albino wisecracks, and it's a safe bet I won't make it out of there without somebody taking a potshot at me. "I'll come home the second I settle up with Gazzara."

"That might not be so easy," Santi says. "I suppose there's a shot you could negotiate some kind of mutual reciprocity. But if Gazzara's half as mean as Jimmy, he'll cut your nuts off."

"He can't be as bad as Jimmy. Nobody is."

"True," Santi says.

The way he looks at me reminds me of how he used to say he wanted to be like me when he grew up. I'll always love the kid for that, probably because he's the only one who ever said it.

"You're going down there without any backup at all?" Santi asks.

"I can handle Gazzara alone," I say. And I almost believe it.

But I hate to go without the kid. If I were to leave him here, I'd be dumping the only ally I've got left. Pearl is already gone. When I went to kiss her last week, she backed off and scrunched her face. "We're friends, Jersey," she said. "That's it."

I didn't know what to say, because she'd gotten awfully friendly the night Old Man Santiago left us alone to close the Hy-Hat. We spent an hour in the kitchen, necking. "You don't taste albino," she'd said, which, if I hadn't been so deeply in love, would have really gotten my goat.

When she pulled away from me, I felt like screaming and vomiting at the same time. I wanted to drive my fist through my own face and watch myself in the mirror as the blood poured out of my unpigmented skin. Ever since I was a kid in Hoboken, I've known that no woman would have me if she thought our kids might turn out like me. I'm not saying that's what flashed through Pearl's mind, but I'd have sure felt better if I'd been able to offer her a full set of genes.

I shoved her out the door, but as I pushed I was hoping she'd cry out that she couldn't live without me. She didn't. I watched her walk down 122nd Street and almost begged her to take me with her, just so I wouldn't have to be alone again.

Santi is staring at me, hoping I'll change my mind.

"I've got nothing to lose, Santi," I say. "But you do."

Again, we don't say anything. We sip our sodas.

Santi puts his glass on the table. "I'll lay low," he says. "And I'll only stay until you find Gazzara. Then I'll come back, I promise."

I know him, he's not going to let up until I cave. "Okay," I say. "But I'm doing all the dirty work."

"I'll just be there for backup," he says, but he doesn't look me in the eye when he says it.

"I mean it, Santi. You're not part of this. Besides, I can take care of myself."

Santi nods, but he knows I haven't been in a fight since my father taught me to box nearly a dozen years ago. Maybe I can still throw some punches, but the only real heat I'll be packing is a dusty revolver, a pair of brass knuckles, and a mouth that's far bigger than the bleached coon standing behind it.

"Don't worry about me, Santi."

I lean back in the dark and hope the kid can't read the fear in my face.

CHAPTER 3

I park the Auburn on Market Street across from the Broad Street Station. Santi's asleep; he nodded off as we were passing Trenton. His feet are pressed up against the dashboard and he's using his overcoat as a pillow. I nudge him on the shoulder and he stirs, rubbing his eye with his fist.

He squints up at the Excelsior. "Is this the hotel?"

"Yep. And that's where Gazzara got off the train," I say, pointing across the street. "Let's check in and find a bar." I'm figuring if anybody is going to know a bootlegger, it'll be the owner of a speakeasy.

I step out of the car and the cold December air feels like a plague of mosquitoes stinging my chapped cheeks. I'm wearing my chesterfield, so I pull the lapels up to cover my neck and jaws, then tug on my fedora to protect my exposed forehead.

A few seconds later Santi steps out, his hair still mussed. He's cold but his skin is immune to the raking chill of winter. He throws on his overcoat and we hurry along the bluestone to the hotel.

It's been dark for hours, but a few working stiffs are still heading home from their offices. This city seems busier than Hell's Kitchen, but I'll bet the job market's not booming down here either. A lamplighter is lifting his long pole to reach the corner lamppost. He's wearing a plaid jacket and woolen cap, but I can see his hands shaking in the cold. The poor guy has probably been freezing his nuts off all week for a lousy twenty bucks.

"You look like you could use a drink," I yell over to him.

"You're telling me," he says as the gaslight flickers to life. "I'm frozen stiff."

On the far side of the lamppost a Santa rings a bell for the Salvation Army. I'm pressed for time, but I can't help myself. I unzip my leather bag and grab my flask. I'm about to pass the booze to Santa when he sees my patchy skin and winces behind his phony white beard. Fuck him. I throw the whiskey back into my bag and walk over to the shiny glass doors that lead into the Excelsior.

A doorman in a red hat and matching jacket hustles up to Santi and me. As he gets closer he stops in his tracks. I'm assuming the place shuts out colored folk, but this guy's not even twenty, so I ignore him and keep walking. The name Jimmy McCullough won't go far down here, but I've got another ace to throw down.

I take off my hat and shake the cold out of my bones. The space is so huge it dwarfs the people inside of it. It's two stories high with a pair of matching staircases that extend down from a small balcony on the mezzanine level. Between the stairs sits a towering Christmas tree done up in white lights and red bows.

A white-haired gentleman with a long face and bright blue eyes sits at a desk to the right of the tree. He's reading the *Inquirer*. His dark gray flannel suit and brick-red necktie scream out that he's in charge.

We walk over to him as his radio plays a brass choir's rendition of *Hark! The Herald Angels Sing*, a stark contrast to the newspaper's headline about an occult killing in Rittenhouse Square. I suppose he finds the music calming but the photos of mangled bodies make my stomach roll. The blood looks like splattered engine oil.

Santi looks at the oak moldings that stretch across the ceiling. "Nice place," he says.

"Indeed, it is," the gentleman responds, giving us a look that says we don't measure up.

I spot a nameplate on his desk that reads *Robert Baines*. "Good evening, Baines," I say. "We need a couple of rooms." To let him know we're flush, I add, "Your best."

Baines looks me over. He probably can't figure out if I'm black, white, or plaid.

"Can't help you," he says, turning his attention back to his newspaper.

"But Denny Gazzara told me you could." My breath tightens and my mouth goes dry. "He said to mention sugar pop moon."

Baines's white eyebrows rise on his pink forehead. He's listening, but he's not convinced.

"You are Baines, aren't you?"

Baines scans me from head to toe. I'm trying to look calm but I'm jumpy as hell. He must realize I'm not an undercover Fed because nobody with a sane mind would hire me to be an undercover anything.

"All I've got are the suites," he says, opening the desk drawer and pulling out two room keys.

The bellhop comes to take our bags; I hand him my coat and hat and tell him to take them to my room. Santi does the same.

"We're looking to wet our whistle," I tell Baines as he hands us our keys. "We've been driving all day and we're dry."

"You might try the drugstore on Twelfth Street, just past Lubin's Palace," he says. "Maybe pick up some cream for that skin of yours."

"Thanks," I say as I start for the elevator. The drugstore is a front, for sure.

"Hey," he says.

I stop and turn around.

"They're serious over there."

"So am I," I say.

The bellhop has our bags so Santi and I follow him into the elevator. He puts Santi in room 1213 and I get 1214.

When I open the door, I see I've got the honeymoon suite. The place is pure elegance, the white carpet is lush and the windows overlook the Philadelphia skyline. A bouquet of roses is on a nightstand at the foot of a brass bed. I toss the flowers into a blue glass wastepaper basket next to the doorway. Then I dump my bag on the bed, pull out my flask, and down a double shot. The whiskey burns going down but the sting in my chest makes me feel like I know what I'm doing. There's a small marble sink outside the bathroom, probably intended for a young bride to freshen up; I use it to splash some warm water on my face and soothe my skin. I dab my cheeks with one of the hotel's fluffy cotton towels, and then go next door to get Santi. I'll take him to dinner and then bring him back here before I head over to the drugstore. Gazzara doesn't have to find out that my only backup is a seventeen-year-old Spanish kid who plays a top-notch game of chess.

❖

The drugstore isn't anything fancy. Standing behind the counter is a wrinkly old man with a few strands of curly white hair sprouting from the top of his head. He's wearing a lab coat but I don't spot a single vial of medicine in the place. There are six tall glass jars on a wooden shelf but they hold only hard candies; the other boxes are filled with kids' toys, like high-bounce balls and slingshots. The only medical implement I see is a thermometer. If this guy's a druggist, I'm a sunbather. When I reach the counter, he dons a pair of thick brown eyeglasses and takes a closer look at my face. I don't say anything; I let him stare.

"I don't think we've got anything for you, son," he says.

"I think you might," I say. "My problem isn't my skin, it's my tongue. I'm dry as a bone. Baines from the Excelsior sent me. He said you have some liquids I'd be interested in."

When I mention Baines he nods knowingly. "In that case, head on back," he says, pointing toward a door marked *Employees Only*.

I enter a small office. A typewriter sits on a desk along with a pile of blank paper and a stack of carbons. On the far end of the room is a closet door. I look behind me just to be sure I'm not being set up. If I'm going to catch a bullet, I'd rather not be standing in a bogus drugstore when it hits.

Everything seems copacetic, so I pull open the closet door and find three short steps leading up to a heavy red velour drape. From the other side of the curtain I hear voices. They're cheerful voices. Speakeasy voices.

Hiking the stairs and passing the curtain, I walk into the exact scene I'd hoped to discover: a speakeasy the likes of which would attract Philly's top bootleggers. Gazzara must help stock the bar because it's too big for local upstarts.

I push my hat back on my head and take a look around. The room is three times the size of the Pour House. In the front, there's a lounge area with three couches, an armchair, and a piano player who's pounding out a rag I've never heard before. Against the back wall is a curved bar with a mirror behind it. In front of the mirror, three shelves hold various liquor bottles lined up like soldiers at roll call. They glitter the way good whiskey should—just looking at them makes my mouth water. I make a mental note to tell Jimmy to hang a mirror behind the bar at the Pour House. I'm assuming, of course, that the next time I see Jimmy he won't be sticking a blade into my spleen.

Two bouncers stand like pillars on each side of the entrance. The one on the left has a face shaped like a cube and a chest as round as a barrel. His partner has meaty cheeks but a muscular neck that seems to reach past his jaw and stretch up to his ears. Whoever put these thugs at the door did it for show. They're big, but they don't look like they've had many brawls other than an occasional ruckus with a college Joe who's had too many whiskey sours.

I unbutton my overcoat and spread my arms so they can pat me down. They won't find anything—I knew enough to leave my metal back at the Excelsior.

I walk toward the far end of the bar, where a heavy fellow is pouring red drinks into stemmed glasses for a couple of drop-dead blondes. He's got his shirtsleeves rolled up and the look on his face says he considers himself a chemist. A dozen rummies are gathered at the center of the bar, drinking beer, so I have to inch my way through the pack. When I reach the bar I wave my hand to get the tender's attention and he walks my way.

He's got a hard edge. His eyes are the rusty brown of tree bark. His cheekbones are sharp and defined, his narrow lips pulled tight. I figure the only way I'm going to get anything out of this piece of stone is by striking first, but he hits me where I live.

"What are you, an albino or something?"

"I'm both," I tell him. "I'm an albino and I'm really something."

I've got to calm down—it's only going to get rougher from here.

The tender's jaw tightens and he wipes down the top of the bar with a stained white towel.

"What do you want?" he says.

"You got any sugar pop moon?"

He stops cleaning the bar and looks over at the goons by the door. Suddenly, I wish I were with Santi back at the hotel.

"I got all sorts of moon," he says.

"Sugar pop moon is made with beets—right here in Philly."

"You want a drink, I'll get you a drink. I don't have any of that sugar pop garbage."

"Fine, give me a whiskey," I say and put a couple of bucks on the bar.

He reaches for the whiskey bottle and I feel something pressing up against my back. I turn and see it's the bouncer with the bulging neck. His breath stinks of old cheese.

"Everything okay here?" he asks me.

"I'll let you know when I taste my whiskey." My heart is pounding; I hear it more loudly than my own voice.

"I'll be at the door if anything goes wrong," he says. His cheese-breath is so close to my nose, my eyes are tearing.

"I'll give a whistle if I need you."

He leaves, but not before giving me a look that says he'd like to go a round or two with me.

My whiskey is on the bar, so I down it. It stings my tongue and heats my gut—and gives me the balls to push harder. Gazzara's not about to come looking for a wallflower.

"Hey, bartender."

He comes back with a bottle in his hand. His fingers are so hairy that a couple of strands pop out from under his wedding band.

"You ever hear of a guy named Denny Gazzara?" I ask.

"You ever hear of shutting your mouth and drinking your whiskey?"

I almost tell him that if I shut my mouth I couldn't drink my whiskey. Instead, I ask him again about Gazzara.

"Never heard of him," he says. A smile crosses his face and his cheekbones actually seem to get sharper. "But then again, even if I did, I'd deny it." He fills my glass.

"Good thing," I say, swigging the shot and then leaning across the bar so only he can hear me. "Because he told me he's going to fuck your wife. And when he's done, he's going to bang on you so hard, you'll wish that smug face of yours was made of concrete."

His eyes widen. I know he's not scared of me, so he must be terrified of Gazzara.

"That's right," I say. I do my best to look him dead in the eye but my goddamn pupils are shimmying again. It doesn't matter—he's focused on my lips, no doubt afraid they'll keep moving.

"He's going to fuck you, your wife, your family, and anything else you love," I say. "Then he's going to bash in those teeny white teeth, and while you're spitting out blood and maybe even pieces of your fucked-up tongue, he's going to open up your money box, take all your cash, and piss in your bottles of moon."

A dropped jaw has replaced his arrogant smile.

"But I guess you don't have to worry about Denny," I say. "Because you don't know him."

I straighten my fedora and turn around and walk out. The tender must be shocked because he's not budging.

Before I reach the door, I stop by the goon with the rotting tonsils. He looks me over and chuckles.

"Denny doesn't think I'm so funny."

He stops laughing and straightens his back. I've got my eye on his hands—if he clenches his fist I'm racing for the door. But he crosses his arms and returns to his military pose.

"That's better, musclehead. Just stand there and do nothing. Like a lamp post."

I walk out through the drugstore as the piano player barrels through "Ain't She Sweet." The old guy with the eyeglasses is sitting behind the counter. I nod to him.

"Hello, again," I say.

I walk over to the counter and pick up a pen by the register. On the back of one of his business cards I write my name—Snowball—and the telephone number of the pay phone at the Pour House.

"Give me a call if you get any wonder cream," I say before pulling up my lapels and walking out into the night.

I head up Twelfth Street but don't look behind me until I reach the jeweler's near Market. When I see the street is clear, I lean against the storefront and let my knees go weak. My breath is wheezing and I take a moment to steady myself.

My bet is that Gazzara will know soon enough that I'm in town, unless he confuses me with another albino bootlegger who came down to Philly to catch up with him.

I reach Market and see that Lubin's Palace is showing *Animal Crackers*. I'm tempted to buy a ticket for the late show. I love the Marx Brothers and I've got some time to kill while I wait for Gazzara to track me down. But I keep walking because Santi's back at the hotel, probably scared out of his wits that I've been shooting off my mouth and making things tougher for both of us. I don't know where he comes up with this stuff.

⌁

I'm about to enter the Excelsior when I hear a woman's voice. "You're cute," she says.

She's standing at the corner and steps into the circle of light beaming down from the streetlamp. The "you're cute" was directed at me, which is only one reason I know she's a hooker. She's a platinum blonde, like Jean Harlow in *Hell's Angels*. I put her in her early thirties. She's pretty, but she looks tired. Her skin is pale, even whiter than mine, but makeup is helping her out. She's wearing loads of rouge and her lips are covered in ruby-colored lipstick. I can just imagine how I look, every exposed inch of skin as red as her lips, my entire face tenderized by the icy Philly air that I imagine she considers refreshing.

If Pearl were waiting for me in New York I'd walk away. But I'm on my own and a hooker just might lead me to Gazzara. Besides, when you look like I do it feels good to hear you're cute, even if you're paying somebody to say it.

"Where're you headed?" I ask her.

A flowered red dress peeks out from her open black woolen coat. It hangs just below her knee and I can't stop looking at her legs.

"I know a cozy little cellar club, honey. You can buy me a drink, if you don't mind breaking the law."

She should only know.

"Sounds good to me," I say. Any place crooks, moonshiners, and gangsters socialize is the kind of joint Gazzara would be interested in. Going with a woman only makes it better.

I think about running upstairs to tell Santi where I'm headed, but opportunity doesn't wait for a loyal man.

"Let's go," I say. I'm gazing at those gams again.

She puts her arm around me, and for a brief second I feel like Gary Cooper. We walk along Twelfth Street, our breath turning to smoke in the December night. A bum asks me for a dime and I give him the three that I've got in my pocket.

She tells me her name is Margaret and asks me mine.

"Jersey," I say, even though I should be spreading the name Snowball around town. I just can't bring myself to say the name that Jimmy gave me, not when I could give her the one I'd be using if I'd inherited my father's rich, brown skin. For once somebody is calling me Jersey, and I'm enjoying it too much to stop her.

"Jersey," she says out loud, making a show of listening to the name as it rolls off her tongue. "Cute name for a cute boy."

She leads me to an apartment house on Tenth Street. The building looks industrial. It's four stories high, square, brick, and has arched windows. There's an alley on the right side that separates it from a butcher shop. Margaret walks into it and pulls open a steel door next to a green dumpster that's still buried under frost from last week's blizzard.

I follow her down a hallway to the back of the building. The place is clean and lit by a lone brass fixture that hangs overhead. It's warm inside so I take off my fedora as she knocks on a metal door and then pulls it open.

The joint is decorated like a typical underground cellar club: not much furniture and lots of bar. Here, the counter is opposite the entrance and four small booths line the left wall. There's nobody in the place except for a bartender mixing drinks and two flappers seated on stools in front of him. The one on my left has short, straight black hair. Her friend has shiny red hair that curls into big looping *O*s and she's got a slender black cigarette holder between her lips. There's an exit door on the right wall, probably an escape route, and next to it, one of those music boxes. No music is playing, though. For a cellar club, the place is eerily quiet.

Margaret walks up to the tender, a gray-haired hulk with round beefy arms, and whispers something to him before pointing at me with her chin. He looks me over and nods. Then he puts two glasses on the bar and fills them with shine and ice. She picks them both up and hands me one.

"I've got a spot where we can be alone," she says and leads me to a door next to the bar. We walk inside a small room that's furnished with nothing but a tiny brass lamp and a bare, stained mattress—both are resting on the floor. There's a window tucked in the corner but it's filthy. At this angle, nobody could look in and see us. I can't even see out.

I feel soiled just being here, like a hobo in need of a charity fuck. I can afford better than this. I make a decent amount of money, even though it comes to me through the bloody hands of Jimmy McCullough.

"We could have gone to my room at the hotel," I say.

"You didn't invite me, honey."

When she steps near the lamp, I can see that the makeup covering the bags under her eyes is so thick it's starting to crack like the plaster walls around her. She shuts the door and nods toward an iron coat hook screwed into the back of it.

"For your clothes," she says.

I hang my chesterfield and hat. Then I down a swig of moon and put my drink on the wooden floor—it sits in a cluster of stained rings left by a succession of glasses just like mine.

Margaret gulps her shine and reaches for the hem of her red dress.

"Don't," I say.

"Why else are you here?" she asks.

It's a good question. Unless she's about to tell me where Gazzara runs his outfit, I can't imagine us chatting and holding each other's interest.

"I don't know," I say. I sound like a pantywaist.

"C'mon, Sugar," she says, lifting the bottom of her dress. She hikes it all the way up to the spaghetti straps that stretch over her shoulders. "Come and bring me those lucky white bones of yours."

She looks so pathetic, standing there showing off her bloomers, that I down the rest of my shine and walk over to her. It wouldn't be right to leave her high and dry, holding her dress in the air, slapped in the face by an albino.

I close my eyes and do what I came here to do, repeatedly telling myself that she likes me. When we finish I sit up and button my shirt. She turns her back to me for privacy, which I find a little odd considering what just took place. She stands half-naked in front of the window, pulling her bloomers back up around her hips.

"Well, I'll be going," I say to the back of her head. She's already taken my money and I'm not expecting a receipt.

Margaret doesn't turn around and it hits me that something's up. My tongue goes dry and the rims of my ears burn.

I reach for the door but it flies open before I can grab the knob. Two Spanish-looking hoods wearing long woolen overcoats rush into the room. The small one has dark skin, waxed hair, and a thin mustache. The taller one is older—he's pasty white and has dark crescents under his eyes. And he's holding a foot-long cleaver.

"His legs, Hector. Get his femurs," the little one is yelling.

Hector lunges at me, swinging the blade at my legs. I grab his wrist with both hands and try to shake the knife loose.

Margaret rushes out of the room and the little guy charges me. He throws his arms around my waist and pushes me toward the window. I trip on the lamp and the three of us fall to the floor; my back lands on the mattress and the two of them tumble on top of me. The little one is on his knees. He's leaning down on my shins, pinning my ankles to the floor. I try to free my legs as I shake Hector's fists, which are now holding the cleaver between my legs. If I let go he'll slam me right in the nuts.

I wrestle my right foot free and kick at the little guy. I connect squarely with his face and he falls away. He's holding his nose with both hands and blood is dripping out from underneath his palms.

"My nose, my fucking nose," he chokes out as he clutches his face. "Fucking albino."

He points at my knees. "Get his legs!" he screams as blood runs from his nose to his chin.

Hector looks at him in shock. I take Hector's hands—and the cleaver in them—and bang them as hard as I can against the plaster wall. The silver blade falls out of his grip and bounces on the mattress before clanging on the floor. He squeezes his right hand between his knees as the little guy lunges for the cleaver. Hector is wide open—I could whack the back of his head with my elbow but I don't. Instead, I grab my overcoat and hat, stumble out of the room and head for the exit. The tender is gone and so are the flappers, no doubt paid by the cleaver boys to disappear.

I race out of the joint, my heart slamming its way up my chest and practically out of my mouth. I run down the hall and burst out the front door onto Tenth Street. The icy air scorches my skin and whips my eyes but it's a welcome pain. It's the sting of safety.

I run back to Market Street, my footsteps echoing into the night, and right then I swear to myself I'll never be dumb enough to get lured into a trap like that again. But I've got all of their faces burned into memory. The tender, the flappers, Margaret, Hector, and the little guy. I owe each one of them, just like I owe Gazzara. And I'll be back, because I like to pay my debts.

❧⊱⊰❧

The Auburn's headlights shine onto Route 25 as we hightail it out of Philly. Santi has been asking me the same questions since I got back to the hotel and found him pacing the lobby.

"Isn't the femur your leg bone?" He's trying to picture what went down at the cellar club, which is about thirty miles behind us.

"I don't know," I say, still trying to make sense of what just happened.

Santi's shaking his head. "They were going to chop off your legs? For messing with a bartender?"

The kid has no idea how far I pushed things.

"That's the short version," I tell him.

I turn on the radio and Rudy Vallee's singing "I'm Just A Vagabond Lover." I know every note because Old Man Santiago has the record at the Hy-Hat and I play it every time I'm there. Whenever I listen to Rudy Vallee I pretend I'm white—normal white—and as rich as J. P. Morgan. I picture myself on a yacht sipping daiquiris with Pearl. She's stuck on me and nobody is out for my femurs.

"What's your move now?" Santi asks. "We've got to map out a sensible plan of strategy."

I can't imagine how to fix this mess before Jimmy gets back. I'm in even deeper now, because Gazzara is obviously more than a small-town hood and I've spun him off his nut. I turn up Rudy Vallee and run through my options.

The one move I haven't considered is coming back to Philly with more muscle, but I'd have a tough time finding anybody crazy enough to join me. None of the boys at the Pour House will want to cross Jimmy. And I won't ask any of the tougher kids at the Hy-Hat; the whole point of the club is to keep them off the streets and out of trouble.

I hate to admit it, but the one person who could help me out of this mess is my father. He hasn't been too happy with me since I started working at the Pour House, and he certainly won't like hearing the name Jimmy McCullough—but if I present the situation the right way he just might stand by me. The champ knows what it's like to be behind the eight ball. He never took any guff from anybody, not even when the mob came down on him to take a dive. He did more than refuse: he knocked the guy out and walked away smelling as clean as freshly laundered towels.

I don't have many other choices. Calling my mother isn't an

option; she left after I was born and hasn't shown up since. I've never laid eyes on her, but from what my father tells me, she never had to fight to survive. She was born into money. Big money. And she's white.

CHAPTER 4

1906

*D*orothy Albright trailed her father down the aisle of the Third Regiment Armory, joining the crowd of businessmen surrounding the boxing ring at the front of the arena. Dorothy had pinned her hair up on the crown of her head and refrained from dabbing rouge onto her cheeks, but she was still a rose in a butcher shop.

She had been to the armory a year earlier to see one of her father's prizefighters take his lumps from Marvin Hart, the heavyweight champion at the time. The place hadn't changed—it reeked of sweat, tobacco, liniment, and greed. Beer stands were set up alongside the cheap bench seats in the back, and vendors worked the ringside aisles, hawking Cracker Jack and pretzels. Clusters of older men in sweat-stained work shirts gathered by the rear fire exit. They puffed on cigarettes as they talked in clipped sentences about the odds of the fight—and what they'd do with their winnings.

It had taken three hours to get to Camden from Hartford, and there were hundreds of more acceptable ways Dorothy could have spent her day, let alone her evening. There was no Bible passage that addressed it directly, but she knew two brutes fighting for public entertainment went against the Lord's word, somehow.

To say that she saw the world differently than her father did was an understatement. He'd been talking up this fight ever since the *Newark Evening-Star* had agreed to back the statewide tournament four months ago. He could barely contain himself when speaking of how his latest investment, Barry Higgins, would soon have the championship belt of New Jersey wrapped around his flat Irish midsection.

Back in grade school, Dorothy had admired her father, particularly when he spoke of respecting all people, regardless of their skin color. According to him, he'd always fought for the downtrodden. He even told her a story of how, when he was a young boy, he'd taken a few beatings at the hands of neighborhood teenagers for befriending the Negro, Tom Jeffries, who worked at his father's general store. But now, Dorothy realized that her father's tolerance wasn't enough to make him an upstanding citizen. He simply wasn't the straight arrow he presented himself to be. That's why she railed against him, hoping a run of bad luck would convince him that his gambling businesses weren't only illegal but built on temptation and moral weakness. His enterprise was the devil on Earth.

But Dorothy did have a reason for being at the armory, and she didn't dare mention it to her father. This would surely test his tolerance: she'd developed a fondness for a doughy knot of muscle named Ernie Leo, who was not only a Negro, but also Higgins's opponent. She'd been praying for weeks that Ernie would buck the odds and walk away with the prize money—and force the Higgins syndicate, particularly its prime operator, to rue the day it ensnared itself in professional prizefighting.

The overhead lights snapped off as Dorothy and her father found their seats. The only bulbs that now shone were the black torpedo lamps trained on the ring. Inside the ropes, Ernie shadowboxed in his corner. His skin was as dark as his leather boots, his legs muscular and sturdy. His feet looked heavy, as if they'd grown roots below the canvas. Above his beefy shoulders, sweat shone on his round face. Beads trickled down his pulpy ears, his short, fleshy neck, his puffy bottom lip, and the cleft in his chin.

Dorothy had met Ernie during one of her father's scouting expeditions at that dreadful gym in Hoboken, the place he'd take her when trying to prove that boxing was the result of discipline and endurance. The athletes did work hard, but that didn't prove anything. Most were lummoxes—their brains were as dense as their physiques—and every one of them was a pawn in her father's operation. Ernie was no exception, but he was sweet and decent. And she knew he was smitten because she'd caught him stealing glances at her in between rounds on the brown leather dummy bag. She'd imagined feeling him inside of her, smothering her with muscle, sweat, and pleasure. It was her greatest sin, her weakness of the flesh, and she'd struggled for all of her twenty years to keep it under control. Father Jennings, the pastor at Saint Anthony's of Padua, had told her months ago that he smelled this weakness on her, and she couldn't deny it. It oozed out of her every pore. Still, when Ernie hit that dummy bag, walloping it with his gloved fists and peering around the side of it, she felt a tingle stirring beneath her corseted waist as her sin grew deep within her loins and clamored to be set free.

On the day Ernie signed to fight Higgins, she'd sat with the fighter on a bench outside the trainer's room, intoxicated by the spicy smell of his liniment. Had her father seen them, he'd surely have lit into Ernie. He didn't abuse Negroes the way his cronies did, but that didn't mean he had any use for Ernie other than as a stepping-stone for Higgins. And he certainly didn't want Dorothy gumming up the works. She knew him well enough to know he'd have probably yelled about miscegenation, as if he didn't create his own laws whenever he needed them. He'd have been so busy barking at her, she might have missed hearing Ernie say that he considered himself more than a rented dunderhead.

"I'm not going to lose for nobody, not if I can help it," Ernie said. "I won't sell my pride. And I'm not gonna give up the prize money, neither."

It made sense that the twenty dollars meant more to Ernie than the title did; he couldn't be making more than ten cents an hour sweeping streets in Hoboken.

Now he stood in the ring, lumbering in a small circle, punching the fetid air in front of him.

"Higgins will be out soon," Dorothy's father said, his blue eyes contrasting a mane of white hair that was combed back off his forehead, each strand plastered into place. His face was so clean-shaven it looked as if it were made of clay.

"Wait'll you see him, honey. He's a born winner."

Her father owned 40 percent of Higgins. He'd bought his way into the fighter's syndicate with a thousand dollars—more than twice what Aunt Ellen made teaching third grade all year in Baltimore.

"Let's hope this leads to the big paydays," her father said. He squeezed her hand and she fought the urge to yank it back.

He couldn't possibly be nervous, could he? Dorothy knew little of what her father was up to, but the round-robin must have been weighted in Higgins's favor. The only reason Ernie was given a chance to take on a white fighter was that he had the finesse of a wild boar.

The last time Dorothy had seen Ernie he was standing on the scale at the weigh-in. She'd looked him in the eye and wished him luck. He'd nodded back while inflating his muscles and lifting both arms over his head as his trainer, Willie Brooks, wrapped a cloth tape measure around his chest. Now she prayed that all his hard work would give him a fighting chance.

Her father leaned toward her ear. "Once our boy plows through Leo, he'll take on Tommy Burns," he said, smiling.

He and his cronies had been coveting the world heavyweight title ever since Burns had taken it from Marvin Hart in February. Burns, they felt, was beatable. Even Dorothy had to admit that her father's timing was impeccable. He'd bought into Higgins on a Monday, and by Friday, Burns was champ.

Ernie windmilled his arms in looping circles from his shoulders. A group of five men sitting ringside—two rows in front of Dorothy—hurled insults at him. They all wore grubby pants and yellowed white shirts; they couldn't have been more than a year older than Dorothy.

"Here comes the whupping," the youngest one yelled, his hands cupped around his hairless lips like a ten-fingered megaphone.

"Kiss the canvas, boy!" another shouted, his dark brown eyes bulging with every syllable. Then he turned to his friend and laughed as if he had come up with a line worthy of Vaudeville.

Ernie's brown shoulders gleamed like wet stones under the glare of the torpedo lamps. Dorothy had never been attracted to a dark-skinned man before Ernie, but she couldn't help fantasizing about running into the ring and sucking him on the mouth under the glaring lights. Her corset, already biting into her bust, seemed to squeeze her lungs even more tightly whenever she looked at him.

Her father nudged his elbow into Dorothy's arm and motioned with his chin to the back of the aisle. There strutted Higgins, a tall, sinewy specimen with long arms and sweaty blond hair that dangled like string onto his forehead. He didn't have Ernie's muscles; he was lean and towered over most everybody in the crowd. He swaggered down the steps of the aisle, twisting his lanky body to avoid the outstretched arms of boxing fans hoping to shake the hand of their favorite thoroughbred.

"There's our future, honey," her father said. "I can feel it."

Dorothy excused herself, quickly making her way back up the aisle to get some air. She knew that Ernie had refused a bribe from her father's friends to fall in the seventh round. Now she wished he had taken the money, at least he would have walked away with something in his pocket.

When the bell rang, the two fighters left the safety of their corners and approached the center of the mat with their gloves raised. Dorothy watched from the cheap seats, barely able to see over the standing crowd. Every so often, between the padded shoulders of the cheering fans, she glimpsed Higgins pelting Ernie's right eye with lightning-quick left jabs. Ernie shook them off, but she'd been tagging along with her father long enough to know how quickly those kinds of punches could wear on a fighter.

The bell clanged and Ernie trudged back to his stool. Dorothy returned to her seat, knowing the fight would soon be over.

"Dorothy, get over here," her father said, smiling. "You're missing the action."

She sat down just in time to see the fighters start up again. Higgins stalked Ernie, pummeling his forehead. After a stiff right from Higgins, Ernie leaned back on the ropes and took a barrage of blows to his meaty trunk. But instead of crumbling to the floor, he pushed Higgins back, surged forward off the ropes, and lit into Higgins with a left hook that seemed to start at his knees. The blow bashed Higgins's ribcage and sent the tall man's right leg into a spasm. Higgins pinned his elbow to his midsection and took a couple of shaky sidesteps. Dorothy leaned forward, her heart racing at the thought of Ernie knocking Higgins out. But any hope she had of Higgins's demise was yanked away when the Irishman fired three rapid blows to the bridge of Ernie's flat, broad nose. Ernie's head snapped back, spraying sweat with each shot. Dorothy prayed he would fall without enduring any more punishment, but he bounced off the ropes, banged his gloves together, and went back for more. When Higgins threw a jab, Ernie ducked and unleashed another whistling left. This one landed squarely on Higgins's right temple and the lanky Irishman crumpled to the canvas, his head coming to rest on the bottom turnbuckle.

The referee shoved Ernie toward a neutral corner and started counting over Higgins. Dorothy eyed her father, who was squeezing the brim of his once perfectly formed charcoal gray homburg hat in his fists as his thousand-dollar investment lay helplessly on the mat.

Ernie was still standing, wobbly but on his feet, as the ringsiders showered him in a hail of insults, popcorn, and half-eaten frankfurters.

The referee, stooped over Higgins, kept counting but it was clear that Higgins had swung his last punch. "Seven! Eight!"

When the count reached ten, the ref walked across the ring and hoisted Ernie's gloved fist into the air. A white man in a fitted gray suit, pencil-thin mustache, and shiny black shoes climbed through the ropes and tied the *Evening-Star*'s championship belt around Ernie's waist. Crunched programs and balled-up napkins rained into the ring as Ernie held his head high, a gob of mustard on his neck and specks of popcorn in his hair. He nodded at the smattering of Negro vendors who stood ringside staring up at him, spellbound. Once he had faced all four sides of the arena, Ernie climbed through the ropes and headed to his dressing room, his round face now puffed up and bloated, the swollen bridge of his nose the color of an eggplant.

Halfway up the side aisle, as Ernie turned to shake the hand of a

Negro popcorn vendor, a wooden folding chair flew out of the crowd and smacked against his forehead. He dropped to the cement floor, wincing and pressing his gloved hands over his right eye.

Dorothy shot out of her seat.

"Where do you think you're going?" her father said.

"I'll just be a minute."

She knew she wouldn't get near Ernie—the crowd around him was as impenetrable as granite. But she got close enough to watch in horror.

Her father caught up with her, grabbed her hand, and glared at her the way he did crooked employees.

"We're going," he said. "Now."

He pulled Dorothy away from the scene and led her toward the lobby. Trudging behind him as he yanked on her arm, Dorothy cursed herself for needing his money. Once she graduated from Wellesley, she would start teaching and slam the door on her father—and his crooked associates—for good.

When they reached the main aisle, Dorothy peeked back at Ernie. He was sitting up; blood was smeared across his forehead and trickled down his right eye. He shook his head as if he'd just come out of a cold shower, and then stared straight ahead, blinking. He was no doubt trying to clear his vision, but Dorothy told herself he was looking her way.

⚎

Dorothy stood alongside her father and his two cronies as the ring doctor examined Higgins, methodically poking his fingers into the fighter's shoulder blades, then his stomach, and finally, his rib cage. It didn't take a physician to see that Higgins was in bad shape. He was doubled over, clutching the right side of his midsection, and moaning every time he took a breath. Worse than his physical condition was his mental state. The almighty Higgins didn't even remember getting hit.

"The only real problem is the ribcage," the doctor said to her father, as if he were delivering good news. "One rib is cracked. I suspect another is fractured. He'll fight again, but he'll need a couple of months."

Dorothy knew better: Higgins was done, not because of his injuries, but because he'd lost to a no-name Negro oaf. Her father would finagle a way to get his money back, assuming Higgins hadn't already spent it on equipment, meals, lodging, whiskey, and women.

Dorothy wagged a finger to catch her father's eye. She wanted to tell him she'd meet him in the lobby, but it was useless. He was too wrapped up in the doctor's medical gibberish, which seemed to be just getting started.

She eased out the door and walked to the mouth of the corridor, where three reporters stood laughing about the fight, taking turns imitating the way Higgins had fallen to the canvas. Each had a press card dangling from his neck. The shortest one—he had a square jaw and wore a brown derby—stepped in front of her to block her path. He must have seen her coming out of Higgins's dressing room.

"Hey, Sister. How bad is he?"

His press card identified him as Walter Wilkins of the *Newark Evening-Star*. His eyes were darting down the hallway with a spark that could only come from a rookie. The fellow wanted a scoop, but he wasn't going to get one from Dorothy.

"He'll be out soon, ask him yourself," she said.

"You can't tell me anything?"

"I barely know the fighters' names," she said.

Wilkins smirked and walked toward Higgins's room. The other two lingered, scanning Dorothy's body with nearly the same level of scrutiny the doc had given Higgins.

Dorothy ignored them and made her way across the back aisle of the armory. A young guard with red hair and blue eyes policed the corridor leading to Ernie's dressing room. Dorothy flashed him a smile and he let her pass. As she did, he straightened his back and puffed out his chest, apparently so eager to look like a competent guard that he forgot to actually be one.

With a few more steps Dorothy found herself in front of Ernie's dressing room, where a wrinkled Negro man with a balding pate sat guard, his large round potbelly fitting snugly between the arms of his folding chair. Dorothy recognized him as Ernie's trainer, Willie Brooks. She'd seen him at the weigh-in, and again tonight in Ernie's corner, holding the boxer's water bucket, nursing his cuts, and screaming into his ear between rounds. Apparently, Willie also worked Ernie's door. He didn't need any help manning his post—there wasn't a fan or reporter in sight.

"Excuse me, is this Ernie Leo's dressing room?" Dorothy asked, knowing full well it was.

"Who's asking, Miss?"

Dorothy figured she had a few minutes before the press arrived, if they came at all.

"I'm Dorothy Albright," she said.

Willie raised his eyebrows. He was no stranger to the surname.

"Edward Albright's daughter," Dorothy said to close the deal.

Willie nodded and got up. Then he pulled a ring of keys from his pocket and opened the dressing room door.

⚜

Ernie Leo rested his battered body on a bench in the converted storage room. Dust covered the base of the floor moldings. Four chairs, taken from the auditorium and still assembled into a single row of seats, were stacked against the brick wall. A makeup table peeked out from behind a pyramid of torn cardboard boxes but Ernie didn't go near the mirror—he couldn't breathe through his right nostril and could only imagine how bad his face looked.

He should have gone after Higgins harder and lower. The lowlife had butted heads with him three times, punched him in the kidneys twice, and hit him squarely below the belt right after the bell rang to end the first round. Ernie had kept it clean—he knew the ref wouldn't look away if a Negro broke the rules, regardless of how badly he'd been taunted. It didn't matter now, though, because lying on the bench to his right was a green leather belt with a shiny gold placard and gleaming red jewels. Ernie couldn't read the words, but he knew the fancy script on the belt proclaimed him the New Jersey boxing champion. And with that honor came twenty dollars.

Ernie's hands throbbed, his neck ached, and he could barely lift his arms to his chest. He'd slumped under the showerhead for ten minutes, hoping the heat would loosen his battered muscles, but hot water and steam could only do so much. He leaned back and held an ice-filled rubber bag to the bridge of his nose, careful not to upset the cotton bandage covering the stitches Willie had put in his forehead.

Still damp from the shower, he had a thin towel wrapped around his waist. His mitts, cut, ragged, and sweaty, lay on the floor next to his bare feet. He'd hung his street clothes—a well-worn navy blue jacket, matching vest, and creased, cuffed white pants—on a hanger in the second of three wooden lockers. He'd put his polished brown leather shoes, which would get fresh soles once he picked up his prize money, below them. On the shoes, he'd placed his straw hat, careful not to dirty the red ribbon circling its crown.

Willie swung open the door and told him he had a visitor. When Ernie saw it was Dorothy, he moved the ice bag to cover his swollen right eye.

"You were here?" he said, wishing he'd had a chance to change into his suit. "I thought you don't go for this stuff."

"Don't you need a doctor?" Dorothy said, wincing as she took a closer look at the dressing taped to his forehead. She seemed nervous and Ernie knew it wasn't because of his wound. He was antsy for the same reason: Edward Albright had no idea she was here.

"Willie patched it up," Ernie said. "It's not as bad as it looks."

"It looked awful from where I was sitting."

Dorothy ran her finger over the white gauze, touching it delicately, as if it were wet paint. The feel of her finger lightly crossing his stitched-up bruise made Ernie's ears go hot.

"What are we doing?" he asked, afraid he already knew the answer.

"What we've wanted to do for a long time now." She slipped her left hand under the towel and looked into his eyes as her cool fingers met his hot flesh.

He didn't want to give in, but his reaction was as automatic as shifting his weight when throwing a jab.

"This is trouble," he said, wanting her to stop as badly as he wanted her not to.

"So?" Dorothy said.

"I'm not lookin' to . . ."

Before Ernie could finish, Dorothy leaned forward and kissed him on the mouth. He pulled his head away.

"Dorothy, I'm afraid of what we're doin.'"

Dorothy slid her hand up his leg until it reached the knot in his towel. With one quick tug she opened his towel and continued to toy with the only part of him that wasn't resisting. She stared into his eyes and called him a champion; then she hiked her skirt ruffles up to her waist and climbed onto the table. With one knee on either side of him, she untied her undergarments and eased herself down upon him. Her weight burned his sore thighs, but the pain melted when his hardness reached deep inside her. He planted his hand on the back of her head, his fingers raking her soft black hair, and he kissed her, his passion coursing from his belly into his tongue. She responded, hungrily licking his lips and his neck. Then, in a hoarse, husky, voice, she let out a string of words he'd heard in locker rooms but never from the mouth of a woman.

Ernie gave in to his desire to swallow Dorothy's wholesome whiteness, and as she bounced on his aching thighs and bit into the top of his shoulder, he pushed himself even farther into her. And shut Edward Albright from his mind.

CHAPTER 5
1930

*I*t's eight o'clock at night and the wind is whipping so hard I hear it inside Mona's Diner. Everything in the place—the booths, the counter, even the soda jerk and the wait staff—is covered by a thin coat of grease. My father doesn't care. He loves the place because it's only three blocks from the site where he and thousands of other hardhats are putting up the Empire State Building. And because it serves colored folk any time of day.

I found him on the job a few hours ago, working on Sunday, lugging bricks from the front of the building to masons stationed throughout the site. Tracking him down hadn't been easy. I figured he'd be there but workers blanketed the grounds; some were even walking along the skeletal steel bones of the building, so high up in the sky they looked like ants on ice-cream sticks. I sifted through hundreds of ground workers—all dressed in grimy duds and bathed in sweat despite the frigid December wind—before spotting my father in beat-up dungarees and black work boots stacking bricks onto a railroad car. I've rarely seen him in anything but a suit, so I wasn't surprised when, after punching out, he stopped in his boss's trailer to sponge the sweat from his body and throw on a brown pinstriped three-piece. Its lapels were so wide, I couldn't help but realize he hadn't seen a men's shop since well before the market crashed last year.

"I gotta look professional," he said as he threw on his vest. I guess nobody told him that he's a professional brick carrier.

Now, he's munching away at a drumstick, his plump lower lip dancing as he chews. He's heavy, but he doesn't have the paunch you'd expect on a retired boxer. His is a fleshy blanket of dark brown skin, still sculpted by the sledgehammer of muscle that slammed its way to the New Jersey title twenty-four years ago.

He told me he was glad I showed up and I believe him, even though we haven't been as tight as we once were. We used to see each other every day, watching movies at the Victoria or taking the train up to the Polo Grounds. He was proud to be my father, but he sure wasn't happy when I left school to work for Jimmy McCullough.

The last time I saw him was on his birthday back in September, when Pearl and I had gone by his place on 128th Street. I'd bought him a necktie—red, with little white dots—and even had it gift-wrapped. He thanked us, but slipped the box back to me after dinner, saying he didn't want anything that was bought with dirty money. I left the tie on the table before I left but I'm sure he's never worn it.

"So how's Pearl?" he asks me, spearing four string beans with his fork.

I've got a bowl of chicken soup sitting in front of me but I'm not hungry. "Why do you ask?"

He chomps on the beans, his right cheek bulging. "She seems like a nice gal."

I notice he didn't say she was a beauty, but it doesn't matter because she's not mine to defend. Besides, the truth is that Pearl's not a looker. She's too heavy, has a doughy neck and her ears are too small for her head. But hearing her say my name was always enough for me.

"She's swell," I say, which isn't a lie as much as a distortion of the truth. "But I'm here for something else, Champ. I need your help."

I'm not sure what he can do for me, but he's strong as a bullwhip and has a list of friends as long as the Manhattan phone book. It's like he's an albino in reverse—everybody loves him the minute they meet him. When we lived in Hoboken, strangers used to stop him on Washington Street just to shake his hand and talk about the night he beat Higgins. Years later, when we moved to Harlem, our neighbors boycotted the local white businesses, even their favorite stores, because he spent a few nights handing out flyers for the Colored Merchants Association. I've been pretty popular myself at times—I pour drinks in a speakeasy—but I'd have to flash my brass knuckles to get people to follow me around town like I was the pied piper.

My father knows where I work, so I don't pull any punches. I spill the whole story, including the part about Jimmy being ready to drop the hammer on me.

He listens to every word; he even stops chewing. When I finish he tells me, "You don't got one problem. You got two problems." He holds up one finger and says, "Gazzara." Then he holds up a second finger and says, "Hector."

"Yeah, I thought of that," I say, shaking it off. "But I'm not buying it, Champ. Gazzara set me up. It all leads back to him."

"Maybe so," he says. "But I never heard of no boss sending a bone collector to do his dirty work. A hood like Gazzara, from what you say, he'd send one guy. Not with a cleaver. With a roscoe." He pushes his plate toward the center of the table. He's done eating.

The waitress is short, skinny, and about ten years older than my father. She drops the check on the table, eyeing my chapped skin as she does so. My father reaches for the tab and slides it next to his plate. Money is hard to come by lately and I know he's proud he can spring for dinner. I don't tell him that I could take him out for two-inch steaks every night of the week.

"Thanks," I say and nod toward the check.

He waves it off with a brush of his hand before reaching into his jacket pocket, the edge of which is frayed. He puts a couple of bucks on the table and leaves some change for the waitress.

"So can you help me out with Gazzara?"

"I won't help you with the sugar pop stuff. That'd be like workin' for McCullough." He shakes his head in disgust. "But yeah, I'll help you with Hector. I'll do some diggin'."

I was hoping for more, but what can I expect? He isn't about to run down to Philly and beat Gazzara to a pulp—although I'd pay to see it.

"You think you can find something out about Hector? Here in New York?"

"I'm tight with loads of guys at work. Johalis, Florencio, they're both from Philly. Somebody's gotta know two Spanish kids out to chop up an albino."

"You think they wanted to chop me up because of the way I look?"

"Everything happens because of the way people look," he says. I sense the anger inside of him—it doesn't crackle often, but once it's lit it blazes like a crumbling tenement. I'm glad I never had to get in the ring with him.

"In your case," he says, "you're an albino."

"What if you're wrong and Gazzara's pulling Hector's strings?" I understand he doesn't want to help Jimmy, but I'd love to hear him say he'd help me.

"Then we got a different situation," he says. "For now, let's see what I can dig up on this Hector. If he's on his own, he's gonna be sorry he ran into us."

He gets up to leave and I follow behind him, a smile forcing its way across my colorless cheeks.

⊰⊱

I've been back at the Pour House for ten minutes. The bogus booze sitting in the ratacombs has got me feeling like Denny Gazzara's patsy. Still, there's not much I can do tonight except watch over the place and make sure nothing else goes wrong. Diego did an okay job running the joint over the weekend—no fights, no raids, no major purchases of counterfeit moon. That's a hell of a lot better than I did, and he had no support other than a hodgepodge staff of busboys. I taught him well.

Tonight, Diego is working the door. He isn't big enough to play the heavy—he's barely Santi's height and can't weigh more than a buck-forty soaking wet. But Diego's beady black eyes don't miss much, and he makes up for that slight frame with the Colt he keeps strapped to his ankle.

Santi is tending bar and I'm sitting on a barstool across from him. I'm keeping an eye on the door but I'm not afraid of getting raided; we're only serving eleven customers and they're all locals. Street cops rarely bust a speakeasy unless they think they're going to land a big fish.

Santi is filling a shaker for two newlyweds sharing a single barstool. The room looks good, but I still want to add some bottles on the shelf behind the bar to mimic the mirrored setup at that drugstore down in Philly.

"But Not For Me" comes on the radio and I think of how easily Pearl was able to walk out of my life. I shake myself loose of her memory and ask Santi to fill me in on what I missed since this morning. He joins me at the end of the bar.

"It's a good thing I got back," he says. "Diego nearly ran out of moon. I brought up ten cases, but the rest is skunk. It's a dwindling situation."

"Seventy cases," I say, shaking my head.

"Of pure piss," Santi says.

I can't help but wonder if I could pawn the cases off on some other unsuspecting sucker. "How hard would they be to sell?" I ask, keeping my voice low.

"Are you nuts?" he whispers. "Things are bad enough now. You want somebody coming back here, chasing you the way you're chasing Gazzara? What'll you tell Jimmy then?"

I'm only half-listening. "I won't have to tell him anything, because I could replace the money. Or we can use it to buy some decent liquor. Either way, it'd straighten things out."

"And where do you think you can unload all of this bad booze?"

I see Larch at the bar sipping a Rob Roy. I like him, but I don't feel the same way about all of his comrades. Maybe the precinct would buy seventy cases of shine? Doubtful. Cops expect their drinks for free, and if I tried to charge them they'd simply raid us and make off with the booze. Still, the thought of selling Gazzara's cow piss is worming its way through my brain like a double-shot of bathtub gin.

Santi sees that I'm looking at Larch.

"Absolutely not," he says. "I know what you're thinking, and it would be sweet, but it would turn bitter once the sugar is gone."

Once again, Santi didn't make any sense, but I got the general idea.

"Okay, but we've got to think of something to do with that turpentine," I tell him. "I've only got seventy-two hours."

"Maybe we should just dump it," Santi says. "We could replace it with money from the till and tell Jimmy we had a slow week."

"We couldn't skim enough to cover seventy cases," I tell Santi. "We need forty-eight hundred bucks. I'd have to leave the register empty."

"You're right. But we can't pawn that stuff off on somebody else. That's just asking for trouble."

"Fine. Just help me figure something out."

The door opens and in walks a tall character with a thick black woolen overcoat and dark brown fedora. He's got a long face with a hooked nose and his eyebrows are bushy, like hairy slugs. He could be trouble, so I walk over as Diego pats him down.

"Welcome to the Pour House," I say.

"You Snowball?"

"Depends on who's asking," I say, as if anybody else in the room is pale enough to carry that nickname.

"Denny Gazzara," he says.

I wanted this but I'm shocked as shit that I'm getting it. I nod to Diego to let him pass. Diego shoots me a concerned look, but it doesn't matter because the hood isn't waiting for an invitation. He walks into the dining room, well beyond earshot of Diego.

"I hear you made a bit of noise in Philly," he says.

"What can I say? It's a quiet town."

"We want to keep it that way," he says.

He's not smiling, but neither am I.

"I've got a problem with Gazzara," I say.

"That's obvious. You've also got a big mouth."

"Let me guess. A bartender with nuts the size of cranberries went running to Gazzara screaming, 'Daddy, a weird-looking man was bothering me.'"

"Something like that, yeah."

I try steering him toward the bar, closer to Santi and Larch, but he doesn't budge.

"That bartender was right," I say. "I really rode him. You want to know why? Because I knew a thug like you would show up and start asking questions. So now I've got some questions of my own."

Before I can spit them out, Larch walks over, a full Rob Roy in his hand. I've never been happier that we pour the guy for free.

"Things okay here, Snowball?" Larch asks.

"Yep," I say. "This gentleman and I were just coming to get a drink."

"Oh, good," Larch says. He takes a hard look at the hood before heading back to the bar. "I'll be waiting for you."

The hood doesn't say anything. He walks past the empty tables and stands beside the pocket doors, next to the fireplace. I wonder if Larch will notice we never made it to the barroom.

"What's your problem exactly?" the hood says. He's smiling and nodding at me, trying his best to make us look like two old buddies reminiscing about the joys of grade school.

"Why don't I piss into a bottle of shine and show you?"

The smile leaves his face. "I'll ask again," he says. He's agitated, but I'm starting not to give a shit. "What's your problem—"

I cut him off. "Save your energy. Gazzara sold me eighty cases of sugar pop moon. You ever hear of it?"

"Keep going," he says.

"Seventy are as drinkable as furniture oil."

"You got your facts wrong," he tells me. "Gazzara doesn't sell his sugar pop moon by the case. His regular moon? Yeah. His sugar pop moon? Never. You want it, you gotta buy it by the glass, like one of those Rob Roys that tin badge was drinking before. Sugar pop moon is his, his alone, and he ain't selling it to the likes of you."

"If that's the story, why don't you buy back the seventy cases of sugar pop piss *he already sold me.*"

"You don't get it, pal. If Gazzara wanted to take you, you'd know it."

"He did take me and I do know it. What are you trying to say here? I should just drink his swill and thank him?"

Santi walks over from the bar. He's carrying two drinks on a metal tray. The hood stops talking.

"Sidecars," Santi announces, smiling. I can tell Santi's up to something but I'm not sure if Denny's boy realizes it. Maybe he's like Larch and thinks drinks are free at the Pour House.

Santi takes two more steps and trips over a dining room chair. He regains his balance, but he's not able to stop the two cocktails from flying off of his tray and crashing to the floor at the thug's feet. The scent of cognac wraps itself around my nose as Santi takes a bar rag from his apron and gets on his knees to wipe the floor.

"You sprayed my cuffs," the hood says.

"Many apologetics."

The hood bends down to wipe the side of his shoe.

"Sorry, I dampened your wool, too," Santi says, wiping the side of the hood's overcoat.

Santi's going to pick the guy's pocket, I'm sure of it. He doesn't need my help, he's the best dip in Harlem, but I focus my eyes on the shining light fixture until they start shaking—and then use them to distract the thug.

"What's your point?" I ask him, staring him down.

"Simple," he says, a confused look on his face. "Stop shooting off that mouth of yours. Next time I won't be this nice."

He doesn't wait for a response. He walks to the door as Santi wipes the last traces of cognac off the fireplace hearth. I trail the hood to the front of the room.

"Be sure to give my regards to Gazzara," I tell him, not sure why I can't keep my mouth shut.

"Don't worry about it, I will," he says without turning around. He walks out into the blustery cold, leaving the door open for Diego to close.

"I don't like the look of that guy," Diego says as he shuts the door. "I'm sure he was packing heat but I let him slide like you told me to."

"It's okay, he's gone now."

Diego nods, but I can see he's still worried. I scoot to the back room because I don't want him to see that my hands are shaking.

Santi's back behind the bar, spiking steins of beer for three out-of-work locals who are cursing Hoover for ruining the country. I walk over and tell them that the next round is on the house. We're in the red, but I won't take anybody's last pennies.

My nerves are still hopping from the run-in with Gazzara's messenger so I grab an open bottle of bourbon and walk to the end of the bar. Taking the corner stool, I pour myself a double shot and down it. Then I put my empty glass on the bar and wait for my throat to cool.

Santi walks over and joins me. "I don't know what that guy wanted, but he likes the holidays."

He hands me a business card that he lifted from the hood's pocket. It reads *Christmas Tree Farm at Princeton* and has a drawing of a tree next to a slogan: *Holiday Cheer Year 'Round*. It's missing a name and phone number.

I pocket the card with a fairly good idea of where I'll be going in the morning.

⚔

It's not quite eleven o'clock and I've already been in the Auburn with Santi for hours. We're on Route 27, almost in Princeton, and he's behind the wheel. It's always tough for me to be inconspicuous, but it's even harder today. Gales of icy wind whipped across 125th Street as if they needed to be back at the North Pole by noon. The cold stung like the dickens and I'm sure my cheeks look as though I tried warming them on a clothes iron.

I put on my fedora and wrap my scarf around my face.

"Santi, can you tell I'm albino?"

"You're something alright, but I have no idea what the hell it is." He pulls a blade out of his boot and hands it to me. "Take this, you might need it."

I toss it on the seat. "I'm fine without it." I've already got my revolver tucked into my waistband and my knucks in the pocket of my overcoat. I'm out of hands.

"You sure you don't want me to go in?" he says. "You're going to stick out like a sore thumb."

"You can't go in," I tell him for the third time. "You don't know what Gazzara looks like."

"You told me he's got a scar on his ear and two different colored eyes. Not exactly a tree in a forest."

He's right, but I can't let him do my dirty work. As far as I know, Hector is sitting in there, waiting by the door, licking his chops.

I've got a plan and it's not all that elaborate. I'm going into the farm to see if I can spot Gazzara. If I do, I'll push him to buy back the moon. If he gives me a hard time, I'll tell him the message is coming from Jimmy McCullough. I just don't want his boys to spot me first because if he finds out I'm here he'll slip out the back. At least that's what I'd do if I had double-crossed a walking blister and he showed up looking for me.

Santi guides the car around a bend and we cruise alongside a tree farm to our right. A voice on the radio says that athletes keep fit by smoking Lucky Strikes and I wish I'd been indulging more often.

A store looms ahead, about fifty yards off the right shoulder of the road, and Santi slows down. The place isn't nearly as scary as I'd pictured it. It's a boxy cedar shack with a pair of sliding garage doors serving as an entrance. Two steps lead to a square wooden landing in front of the doors. On either side is a window that lets out a soft glow from inside. The parking area in front is nothing more than hard, frozen dirt that's been cleared for cars. A burly man in a black ski cap and woolen dock jacket is helping a young kid lift a Christmas tree onto the roof of a Plymouth parked in front of the landing. He's probably the boy's father. If he is, he's giving the kid something I haven't had since I started at the Pour House: a family on Christmas.

Santi steers the Auburn off the highway, between two utility poles, and onto the unpaved parking lot. The car jostles from side to side as it rolls into the spot next to the Plymouth; the sound of crunching gravel and dirt comes from under our tires as we pull to a stop.

"I'm going in," Santi says, yanking the brake handle. "Two bucks says I find Gazzara."

The little bullshitter is out the door in a flash. He takes the two wooden steps onto the rickety landing in a single jump and disappears into the place, sliding the doors shut behind him.

I get out of the car, light up a smoke, and take a deep drag. My heavy gray flannel pants and chesterfield are keeping me warm, but the cold air is biting into the exposed skin on my face and hands as if it's got teeth. The guy in the ski cap has the tree hoisted onto the Plymouth and he's tying it to the car with fat twine. The boy looks up at me; he's got some frozen crust under his nose but doesn't care.

He smiles at me and says, "Merry Christmas."

I grin and say the same, wondering if his father knows how good they've got it right now.

The bright sunshine makes my eyes feel as though the Feds are holding a lamp to them, so I tug my fedora down to the middle of my forehead. The doc keeps telling me to wear sunglasses, but the damned things make it even harder to see.

I throw down my cigarette, crush it under my oxford, and head inside. I walk into an open, rectangular space that has a cashier's counter in the back right corner and roped trees displayed in bunches throughout the store. Three lights hang from overhead and I'm grateful that they're not especially bright. There's a half-dozen customers in the place; each will surely leave with a tree being that it's already the fifteenth of December. They're buzzing about—looking at trees, wreaths, and bushels of holly—and are providing me with a small measure of cover. I spot Santi at the back of the store; he seems to be asking a worker about a tree that can't be more than four feet tall. Above him, a smiling cardboard Santa holds up a White Rock ginger ale. It's starting to curl at the edges.

I walk over to a rack of wreaths and stand behind Santi. I keep my fire engine of a face turned toward the wall as I listen to his conversation.

"Nice place you've got here," he's saying.

"It ain't mine, but thanks."

"Ain't yours? Who owns it?"

"My boss," the worker says.

Santi's doing okay without me so I do some investigating of my own, lobster-face and all. There are only two staffers in the place. I head to the one manning the till. Between me and Santi, we've got the place covered.

"Excuse me," I say.

The cashier looks up from the till but doesn't seem concerned that my face is the color of the cardboard Santa's leggings. He's wearing a nametag that says his name is Frank. His look is easy to forget—medium height, not too heavy, brown hair—but his long, yellowing teeth seem one size too big for his lips.

"What can I do for you?" he says.

"I could use a Christmas tree," I tell him. "But I also need to see the owner. Is he around?"

"I run the place," he says.

I don't want to rile him like I did the tender in Philly so I make a point of using my friendliest tone. "Actually, Frank, I'm more interested in a stiff drink than I am in a Christmas tree."

"Thirsty, are you?" His unshaven face breaks into a smile and he flashes those king-sized ivories at me.

"More than thirsty," I say. "I'm parched."

My eyes start shimmying again and Frank avoids them, choosing instead to look over my shoulder.

I lean toward him and lower my voice to a whisper. "I'd love to get my hands on some sugar pop moon, if that's possible."

His smile evaporates. "Who told you to come here?"

"A gentleman in New York gave me this card," I say, showing it to him as if it's some kind of free pass. I hope he doesn't ask for the guy's name.

"Yeah, well, we sell Christmas trees," Frank says. "I don't know anything about any sugar pop moon."

I can't say I expected a different answer. I feel like everybody has a sugar pop membership but me—and it's really getting my goat.

Santi walks up next to me. "Find anything?"

"Frank here was just helping me pick something out," I tell him.

Frank looks at me and then at Santi. He's gotten that we don't want a tree, but he can't seem to figure out why we're so desperate for a shot of moon.

He makes a show of examining some trussed trees marked *Blue Spruce*. Then he asks me, "Do you like these?" He says it loud enough for those around us to hear.

He keeps talking, so we must be getting somewhere, but I'm too jittery to waste more time. If I weren't so afraid the store was crawling with hoods, I'd drive my fist into his kidney and force him to tell us where we can find Gazzara.

"I'm looking for a tree that's away from these people," I say.

I can tell he's as jumpy as I am but he's seasoned enough to keep it under wraps. In his world I could mean big business.

Santi points his chin toward a pair of double doors behind the till.

"Maybe back there," he says, letting his coat drape open to show Frank he's not armed. If Frank knew the kid, he wouldn't be surprised. Santi rarely carries a gun—just holding one turns his knees to jelly.

Frank shakes his head; he's not bringing us by the till. He motions toward the front door, probably figuring it's safer to talk outside. He'll soon wish he could rethink that decision.

He walks out of the shop and we trail him into the blustery out-doors. My face feels like a corn fritter sizzling in a frying pan, but I'm too caught up in finding Gazzara to care.

The parking area is clear, the cars are gone, and our breath is turning to smoke in the frigid air. The father and son must be at home, setting up their tree, having a swell Christmas. I, on the other hand, am standing on the side of a highway trying to get a yellow-toothed tree salesman to finger the bootlegger who sold me a truckload of bogus sugar pop moon. From where I stand, the father and the son have got it made.

"What's your deal?" Frank asks me.

"What's yours?" Santi asks.

"I work here, remember?" Frank says, taking a step toward Santi.

I put my hand against Frank's chest. "Lay off."

When he stops dead in his tracks I wonder just how scary I look.

"My deal is I want to find some sugar pop moon," I say.

"That's a pretty specific drink."

"I've got a pretty specific thirst."

We're not that far from the highway, and cars are whipping past us. Each time one passes a gust of dirt sandblasts my face.

"Like I already told you," Frank says. "You're in the wrong place."

"And like I told you, I don't believe you," I say. I reach into my coat pocket and slip on my brass knuckles. I don't want to use them but I will, especially now that we're standing outside the shop, alone.

"But you know what sugar pop moon is, don't you?" Santi says.

"Never heard of it."

"So how do I get a drink?" I ask him.

"You get in your car and drive somewhere that'll serve you. And good luck. They don't serve your kind around here."

"And what is my kind?" I ask him, feeling my anger race from my gut to my fists.

"Fuck if I know," Frank says. "You ain't normal, that's for damned sure."

I reach out, grab him by his lapels with both hands—the right one wrapped in raw brass—and push him into a telephone pole. I press my hands against his throat and he claws at them to get some air. His eyes are bulging, so I back off his neck and slide my hands down against his chest, keeping him pinned against the pole.

He's croaking as he sucks for air. "Do you know what you're doing?" he chokes out. "Or who you're doing it to?"

I'm too riled to think about the answer. "Santi, open the door," I say.

Santi heads for the store.

"The car door," I tell him. I can feel myself coming unhinged.

Santi rushes over to the Auburn and opens the passenger door and

I shove Frank away from the pole. I can't move him more than a few yards because his feet are pressed against the ground and his knees are locked.

"Where are you taking me?" he asks me, still coughing.

It's an excellent question and I have no answer. I throw him back up against the pole.

"Sing," I tell him.

"About what?" he asks.

"Denny Gazzara."

"Never heard of him," he says.

I need answers and my only hope is that Frank has them. I pin him to the post by pressing my left forearm against his chest. Then I hold my right fist to his face so he can get a close look at the dull, molded brass decorating the base of my fingers.

"You're gonna miss those choppers," I tell him, my jaw tight.

Santi comes up beside me. He's got his hands in his pockets and he's nervously rocking back and forth on the balls of his feet.

"Jersey, this is irreparable," he says, his voice charged with panic. "You've done some messed-up things, but this is unforeseen and irreparable."

Frank's not saying anything—he's clutching my left forearm, which is pushing against his Adam's apple. He can't move my arm because I've got the leverage and I'm leaning all my weight into him. His eyes are fixated on the brass wrapping my right fist, which is poised in the air next to his left temple.

"Santi, lay a towel down and cover the back seat."

Frank's eyes widen even more.

"Where's Gazzara?" I ask again.

"You're that albino freak," he says, his words clipped by the pressure of my arm. "The one from Philly. They said you were white, not red."

"It's the wind," I tell him, as if he cares about my condition.

"We don't have a towel," Santi says.

"Then find one," I yell, surprised at the manic sound of my own voice. Desperation is driving me and, at this point, even I don't know how far I'll go.

"Where the hell am I going to find a towel?" Santi asks me. "Look where we are."

"Go into the shop and get one of the blankets from under the trees," I say. "I'll be damned if this cat-got-my-tongue peon is going to bloody up my seats."

Santi runs off and Frank is still gasping for air. He's turning red and I get some satisfaction seeing that his face looks no better than mine.

His eyes bulge like golf balls and this time I don't back off.

"He's out back," he manages to choke out through his gritted donkey teeth.

"What?" I ask, even though I'm pretty sure I heard correctly. I pull back just enough to give him some air.

"Gazzara, he's out back in the woodshed," he says. "He's making moon. But you're a dead man if you go back there. And I'm a deader one for telling you."

I take my hands off him and smile. Then I extend my hand—the knuckles still on it—for a shake.

"I won't say a word," I say.

Frank is staring at me like I'm Nosferatu. The poor bastard's got to be spooked for sure.

"Really, pal, you're fine," I tell him. "I'm a clam."

Santi comes running out of the shop with a blanket.

"Dump it, Santi. We're going out to the woodshed. Frank's going to get us some sugar pop moon."

Santi smiles and tosses the blanket onto the landing in front of the store. I'm sure he's relieved that we're not going to lay into Frank, but he probably hasn't considered what we'll have to do to Gazzara if he doesn't cough up our cash.

I'm on Frank as he leads us around a stack of bundled trees to the back of the store then takes us down a frozen dirt path that winds between two rows of Christmas trees. We walk the green corridor, which is covered with pine needles. The stiff iced branches scratch at our arms and faces. We don't go more than thirty feet before I start feeling lost, so I slip the brass back into my overcoat and pull out my revolver. I press its short barrel between Frank's shoulder blades.

"I know you're packing, you don't have to jab me with it," he says. I pull it an inch away but keep it trained on his back.

After we've gone about a hundred yards, Frank points to a cabin partially hidden among a random collection of lush ten-foot tall Christmas trees. The place looks like it's made of logs; it's the type of cabin I imagine Abe Lincoln grew up in, except this one is bigger. It's two stories high and seems deep enough to house a few small rooms— or one large still—in the back. The front door is painted black and there's a plume of smoke coming from a brick chimney on the roof. I can't help but give Gazzara credit. It's a nice cover.

I motion for Santi to check behind the cabin. I'm not the smoothest operator, but even I know that distilleries have escape hatches.

As Santi heads around the place his footsteps fade out of earshot.

"Knock," I tell Frank.

Frank walks to the door but it swings open before he raises his knuckles. A bald guy jumps out—he must weigh two hundred and fifty pounds, and he's got a machine gun pointed right at me. He's wearing a suit and a dark red bowtie; his head doesn't have a hair on it and his neatly trimmed Vandyke is waxed into place. He's got the type of face you'd expect to see on a tin of shaving soap.

"You don't have to kn-knock, Snowball, we've been expecting y-y-you," he says.

I don't know if I'm more thrown by his stutter or by the fact that he knew I was coming.

Frank sees that I'm confused and laughs out loud, his yellowed teeth looking as if they're about to leap off his gums.

"Surprise," he says.

I'd love to send a bullet into the bridge of his nose, but I'd be dead before he starting bleeding.

"Frank, grab his h-heater," Baldie says.

Frank takes the gun from my hand and then reaches into my overcoat pocket and snatches my knuckles, too. "He's got a buddy going around back," he says as he points the pistol at my forehead.

Baldie seems unconcerned. "I'm d-d-delighted you took the trip," he tells me. "I've heard such interesting things."

There are times that sarcasm is hard to swallow; standing in the woods at the mercy of a stuttering bald goon definitely qualifies.

"How'd you know I was coming?" I ask.

"You better teach that boy of yours how to p-pick someone's p-p-pocket," he says, walking into the cabin. "Freddy says your boy's hand is as g-graceful as a horse with five d-d-dongs."

He heads into the cabin but stops in the doorway to kick off his shiny black leather shoes and slip his stockinged feet into a pair of red velvet slippers. They look ridiculous with his brown herringbone suit, but I keep my opinion to myself.

I follow him into the cottage and my eyes are so cooked from the sun that I can't make out many details. We're in a front room—I know that because there's a door on the back wall. I'm guessing the door leads to the still where the moon is fermented. A wooden table with thick legs sits in front of me; it looks like a slab of tree resting on four chopped telephone poles. The walls of the cabin are made of rough, unsanded wood, just like the outside of the place. If I didn't have a machine gun in my face, I'd find it a decent place to grab a shot or two.

Baldie rests his gun on the table but doesn't stray more than a step away. My only hope is that Santi is coming up with some kind of plan.

"That's a lot of metal," I say, pointing my chin at the Tommy gun.

Baldie nods. "Thanks," he says, as if I meant it as a compliment. Then he adds, "I see you've met Frank."

My eyes are still smarting. I'm staring at two Franks and two Baldies. "Yeah, he's brighter than he looks."

"Yes, he is," Baldie says, wiping the top of his dome with a handkerchief.

Frank smiles behind my revolver, which he still has trained on my head.

"Where's Gazzara?" I ask Baldie.

Frank laughs.

"Is that funny?" I ask.

"It is to me," Frank says.

"You're looking at h-him," Baldie tells me.

Something's not adding up. "I mean Denny Gazzara."

"That's me," Baldie says. "Denny Gazzara." He holds his palms in the air as if he were Harry Houdini.

The door to the back room opens and in walks Santi. He's got his hands over his head. Behind him, pointing a gun at his neck, is the hood from the Pour House. I now know that guy's name is Freddy.

"Sorry, Jersey," Santi says to me.

I'm boxed, but I'd like to get that thug off Santi.

"If you're Denny Gazzara," I ask Baldie, "then who the hell sold me the bogus moon?"

"You're Denny Gazzara?" Santi asks. He shoots me a look that says I should have given him a better description, as if I would have left out that Gazzara's as bald as a cue ball, wears a Vandyke, and stutters.

"There seems to be a misunderstanding about some b-bootleg moon," Gazzara says to me. "I don't make bad moon. And I don't like f-fucking nigger albino gutter freaks like you, no offense, going around telling people I do. It m-makes me uncomfortable." He leans his elbows on the table and lightly bounces the tips of his fingers together. "Although I do give you credit for balls. You've got a pair."

"I bought eighty cases of piss off a Joe who said he was you."

"And that's why you're not dead yet. You're going to sing, and I'm going to listen. Frank, p-pour some sugar."

Two benches run the length of the table. Gazzara points at one and tells me to sit. I do, and Santi takes a seat on the bench opposite me.

"If you're telling the truth, whoever the f-fuck is using my name is a dead man," he says. "But if I find out you're full of shit, the first thing I'm going to do is k-k-kill your boy here." He points at Santi.

"Fuck you," Santi says, spit flying out of his mouth.

"He's got nothing to do with this," I say.

Gazzara shrugs, he's obviously not concerned about nailing the wrong man.

Frank grabs four shot glasses from the assortment sitting on the table and fills them with sugar pop moon. We each down one, and as far as I can tell, it's the same stuff the guy gave me on the train. And I'll say the same thing now that I said then. It really is good moon.

I just hope Santi lives to drink another shot of it.

CHAPTER 6
1906

*A*n icy sweat dampened Dorothy's spine as she stepped off the trolley at Hartford's Consolidated Railway Station. It was already the fifteenth of October. She'd had no choice but to leave Wellesley—her belly would be blooming by the first of November and she wasn't about to be grist for the school's gossip mill.

She made her way into the station, the tail of her bell skirt dragging behind her. To avoid being spotted, she hid behind three elderly, silver-haired ladies clustered at the ticket window. But once the women had bought their tickets and left for the train platform—all three hunching over canes and shuffling their feet—Dorothy had to step up to the brass bars of the black granite booth and face the ticket seller. Alone.

"Where to?" the seller said, slumped on a stool and looking up just long enough for Dorothy to smell the liquor on his breath. His face wasn't familiar, but Dorothy didn't want to push her luck. If the man gambled—as did half of Hartford—he surely knew her father, and possibly knew her. She pretended to scrutinize the small printed schedule taped next to the window as she slid three dollars across the counter.

"Baltimore," she said. "One way."

As the seller flipped through a stack of tickets, Dorothy said goodbye to her dreams of becoming a teacher.

"Here you go," the seller said, pulling out a greenie, stamping it with a rubber design-maker and sliding it under the brass bars. Dorothy picked it up, hoping her fingers wouldn't tremble.

She'd spent the night in a tizzy, her nightdress stained under her arms and damp across her back. For hours, she'd stared at the dancing shadows cast by the flickering candle in her dormitory sconce. In them, she saw her father screaming at her for destroying her future and then beating Ernie to death for violating his only daughter.

She jumped out of bed at dawn, ate her eggs, and took the first train to Hartford to see Father Jennings. He only confirmed what she had already suspected: there was no undoing the sin she had committed. She couldn't cleanse herself of the child. Nor could she raise it on her own and remain in God's good graces. It was against the law for whites and Negroes to marry and a sin to live with Ernie out of wedlock.

Bowing to Father Jennings's urging, Dorothy had agreed to have the child and give it to the Sisters of Charity. That's why she found herself back at the station running to Aunt Ellen's. She didn't want to see her aunt any more than she wanted to quit school, but she knew she could have the baby, quietly and shamefully, in the narrow brick row house where she'd played marbles on holiday weekends during grade school.

Aunt Ellen could be trusted to keep Dorothy's secret. The woman despised her brother-in-law. She'd been calling Dorothy's father a gangster since Dorothy could remember, blaming him for the death of Dorothy's mother even though he'd had nothing to do with it. Everybody knew the story of Harriet Albright: she'd been trampled by a police horse while throwing rocks at Hartford's City Hall during a protest for women's suffrage.

"He's the one who made Harriet angry in the first place," Aunt Ellen once told her, nodding at Dorothy with her thin lips pressed together, her tightly curled brownish-red hair capping her bony face, a stack of ungraded English assignments waiting in her lap.

Dorothy thanked the ticket seller with her face to the floor, her mumbled words surely lost in the hubbub of the railway station.

"Good day," he said, looking only at the series of blue train passes he was marking.

Dorothy reached into her suitcase, pulled out a Bible, and tucked the green ticket into her bookmarked page—Psalms, chapter 82, verse 3—where she'd underlined the words, "Give ear to the cause of the poor and the children without fathers; let those who are troubled and in need have their rights."

Her timepiece read half past noon, which meant she had a few minutes to kill. She walked over to a newsstand where a tiny man with enormous bug eyes was hawking papers. She picked up a copy of the *Evening-Star* and handed him a nickel. As he reached into his canvas apron to make change, the bottom of the paper's front page caught her eye. There, next to a photograph of White Sox pitcher Doc White, was the unmistakable face of Ernie Leo, his bare fists held up to his chin, the New Jersey belt draped over his shoulder. Dorothy recognized the wad of gauze on his forehead, just as she did the tiled corridor over his shoulder. Ernie was standing next to his dressing room door at the Third Regiment Armory—the same door she'd slipped out of that night in July, her new skirt rumpled, stained, and wet.

The large type above the photos announced that the White Sox had beaten their crosstown rivals, the Cubs, to win the World Series. The headline about Ernie was barely the length of a hatpin and contained all of five words: *Dalliance to Cost Leo Title?*

Dorothy felt the color drain from her cheeks as she slumped onto a hard wooden bench and riffled through the pages of the paper to find the rest of the article. As she read on, she felt as if she'd been socked in the gut by one of Ernie's body blows. *The commission, appointed by this newspaper, is considering stripping Ernie Leo of the New Jersey Heavyweight Boxing Championship after learning that he may have engaged in a postfight dalliance with an unidentified white female.*

The article claimed that while the commission couldn't prove that Leo had broken New Jersey's antimiscegenation law, it retained the right to revoke the title because, according to the commission, *the mere act of being alone with a white woman is behavior unbecoming a Negro champion, and therefore a violation of the conduct clause in Leo's contract.*

Dorothy remembered bumping into the reporter at the armory. She thought she'd left him behind at Higgins's dressing room, but the little nuisance must have tailed her. Luckily, she hadn't given him her name.

She buried her face in her palms as her immorality gushed out of her eyes in large salty teardrops. She'd ruined her life and that of her unborn child. And only God knew what she had done to Ernie.

Her tongue turned bitter when she thought of her father. He'd gotten what he wanted again. He and his shady friends had been scheming for months, trying to find a way to give Higgins the title he hadn't been able to earn for himself. They'd all just been handed another opportunity, gift wrapped in Dorothy's sin.

Wiping her face with a tissue, Dorothy went back to the window to exchange her ticket. Baltimore would have to wait; she had a stop to make in Newark. She swept her hair up to the top of her head, tying it into a knot over a horsehair rat. Then she took her new ticket, pulled her flowered maroon and black shawl around her shoulders, and carried her suitcase through the heavy doors of the station and onto the platform. Wilkins hadn't known who she was when they'd bumped into each other at the armory, but he would find out soon enough.

⊰⊱

The sun was still shining when Dorothy's train pulled into Newark. She hoped she could find Wilkins quickly because she had told Aunt Ellen she would be arriving at dusk and she was already hours behind schedule.

The *Evening-Star* occupied a five-story red brick building on Clinton Street. The stately structure's massive arched windows towered over downtown Newark. Dorothy strode through the lobby and walked up the marble stairway at the far end of the hall. On the second floor she spotted a door of brass with dimpled green glass and gold leaf letters that identified it as the *Evening-Star* headquarters. The sign wasn't necessary; the sound of clacking typewriter keys would have been indication enough. She knocked on the door, but when no one greeted her, she walked in unannounced.

The *Evening-Star* operated out of a large open room with a single office door in the far left corner. Everything in the place—the walls, the round pillars, and the vaulted ceiling—was painted white. Along the right wall loomed two large black printing presses, each one reaching halfway to the ceiling. The smell of ink was so strong it tickled the lining of Dorothy's nostrils.

Four large windows stretched across the back wall. In front of them, six jacketless men wearing suspenders sat at heavy wooden desks, typing, as the fading orange sun lit their backs.

A lady with strawberry blonde hair, a large nose, and pimply cheeks hunched over a small table to Dorothy's left, scratching a pencil across a sheet of paper, apparently crossing out an entire page of notes. She seemed to be a secretary, so Dorothy started with her.

"Excuse me, I'm here to see Walter Wilkins."

"Who are you?" the woman asked. When she looked up, Dorothy could see that the long hours at the *Evening-Star* had begun etching themselves under the woman's eyes.

"My name is Dorothy Albright." It came out a bit terser than she'd intended.

Her sharp tone sent the woman scampering to the far side of the room, where she huddled with one of the reporters. When he looked up from his typewriter, Dorothy recognized his face even though he wasn't wearing the brown derby he'd had on at the armory.

He left his desk and smiled at her as he approached. "I'm Wilkins," he said. "Do I know you?"

He didn't act at all like the heel Dorothy pictured. In fact, he came across as quite the opposite. His face had the same square shape she remembered—he looked as though he was grinding his molars even when his mouth was open. He seemed young and eager. His wide eyes had the excited look of a young boy about to put on his first pair of roller skates.

Dorothy waited for a wave of realization to pass over his face, but it never came. "We met the night Ernie Leo fought Barry Higgins."

Wilkins wagged his finger at her. "Yeah, yeah."

He may have recalled her face, but it was clear he didn't see her duck into Ernie's dressing room.

"I read your article in today's paper," she said.

He had the nerve to smile. "Thanks."

"I hope you're satisfied," she said, not even trying to mask her disdain.

He looked startled, as if he'd just found out the cute puppy he'd taken into his home had fangs. Then his eyes narrowed. "What's it got to do with you?"

"Everything," Dorothy said, nearly shouting. Then she hesitated, not sure how far she should go, but there was no point in dancing around the truth now that she was standing in the *Evening-Star's* office. "I'm the unidentified white woman who had the so-called dalliance with Ernie Leo."

Walter started to speak but Dorothy cut him off.

"You've got it all wrong," she said, her cheeks reddening. "You made it sound sordid, like a backroom fling. You've ruined lives with that smut." Then she added, "I hope you sold a lot of papers." Her words dripped with disgust.

She stopped there because she was afraid she'd betray herself. Wilkins had run with the truth, but was he really that far off the mark? He'd accused her of the very thing that Father Jennings had pegged her for: unholy urges of the darkest kind.

One of the presses started to roar—it was loud enough to rattle every piece of furniture in the room.

"Look, Sister, I'm sorry if you're not happy with the story, but the facts are the facts."

A reporter wearing brown suspenders over a yellowed shirt ripped a sheet from his typewriter. "Copy!" he shouted over the din.

A hoarse voice barked from the back of the room. "Wilkins!" A balding, gray-haired man standing by Wilkins's desk was holding up a sheaf of papers. "This is no time to be socializing," he said. Then he shook his head so hard his wireframe spectacles came loose.

Wilkins shouted back to the man but didn't take his eyes off

Dorothy. "Coming, Mr. Glenny." Then, to Dorothy, he said, "That's my editor. If you'll excuse me, Sister, I've got a deadline."

"Good. Maybe you can print a story that matters. Like the fact that some hooligan threw a chair that hit Ernie Leo in the head and nearly killed him."

She felt her voice waver and her eyes well up; she wasn't sure if her tears came out of love for Ernie or anger at Wilkins.

"Ernie's a sweet, kind soul," she went on, "and he never broke a contract with anybody, especially over a conduct clause. He'd handle himself just fine at a dinner with President Roosevelt if he had to, *Brother*."

Wilkins took a step back. "I did mention the chair," he said, weakly.

Dorothy's anger rose like a blast inside a coalmine. "If you want a story, I suggest you look into the crooks who handle Barry Higgins. That's the story you should've written."

Wilkins smirked. "Really? What do you know that everybody else doesn't?"

"I know plenty," she said, poking her index finger toward Wilkins. "My father is Edward Albright. And I guarantee he'll figure out a way to get Higgins the title even though Ernie won that fight, fair and square."

A buzz of enthusiasm lit up Wilkins's face. "Is that so?" he said, the corner of his lip rising as he tapped his chin with his forefinger. "And exactly how is he going to do that?"

"I don't know," Dorothy said. "But I'm sure it will be sleazy and underhanded, which makes you the perfect person to write about it— assuming you want to write about something that matters."

She started for the door but then turned back around when she realized her father would maim Wilkins if he disparaged her in print. "And if you're smart, you'll keep my name out of it."

"Goddammit, Wilkins!" the editor called over the rumbling engines, this time holding his spectacles as he shouted. "Now!"

In a different place, Dorothy would have told that editor what she thought of his use of the Lord's name, but she skipped the lecture and focused on Wilkins, who stood with his mouth slightly open and his eyes sparkling like a fireworks show. He said nothing but his mind was clearly alive with possibilities.

Dorothy walked to the door. "I hope you do what's right and stop smearing good people."

"I may be a rookie but I'm no dummy," he said. "If your story's on the level, I'll be on it. The name Walter Wilkins comes with a seal of honesty. That's my pledge to my readers."

"Given your age, I hardly think such a pronouncement is justified," Dorothy said, tossing the end of her shawl over her shoulder and walking out.

Dorothy had no idea what to expect from a kid like Wilkins, but he certainly had plenty of zeal. If he had half the mettle he claimed, he would go after the crooks and wind up keeping her father off Ernie's back—which was more than she'd be able to do. It wouldn't be easy, though. Wilkins would have to figure out a way to get close to her father. And one thing was for sure: Edward Albright didn't take kindly to snoops.

CHAPTER 7
1930

I take another belt of sugar pop moon and Denny Gazzara waits for my reaction.

"It's the same stuff," I tell him.

I'm at the table in Gazzara's cabin. Santi is across from me, nervously glancing to his left at Freddy, who's got a pistol trained on his ear. Gazzara is sitting in an armchair at the head of the table, pointing a machine gun at me as I recount the events of the last week. Frank is standing behind me; I can't see him but I don't have to. A cold steel muzzle is pressing against the back of my head.

"I've got eighty cases of it," I tell Gazzara. Then I think about it. "Actually, I've got ten cases. And seventy cases of coffin varnish."

Gazzara stares up at the ceiling as if my story is chiseled into the raw wooden beams overhead. "So you're t-t-telling me some crazy goon with a scar on his ear says he's m-m-me, lets you taste some moon—this moon—and then pulls the b-bait and switch."

"That's exactly what I'm telling you."

Gazzara looks at Freddy and smirks.

"Why would I lie?" I add.

"Because we've got a gun p-p-pointing at your boy's thick skull."

"And I've got one aimed between your ears," Frank adds.

Gazzara looks at me and waits to hear more.

"What I mean is why would I mess with you if I didn't think you double-crossed me? I wouldn't have a lot to gain, would I?"

A gun goes off behind my head and I nearly jump out of my bleached skin. My ears ring as a few splinters flutter down from the ceiling and I realize Frank has sent a bullet into the roof. He's so damned close to my head that had he shot me I'd have been dead before I heard the blast.

Santi is staring at Frank, his eyes wide.

"Put that away," Gazzara tells Frank. "You scared the b-bejesus out of me."

"And me," I add. I still hear a tinny whine from the gunshot and I shake my head, as if a whistle might dislodge and come flying out of my ear.

"Sorry, Whitey," Frank says, chuckling.

I think of Pearl sitting at my funeral—not that she'd show up—dressed in black and weeping. If I live through this standoff with Gazzara I've got to see the doc and find out the odds that my kid would be a bleached Oreo like me. It won't matter to Pearl, but the thought of telling her that our children would be normal, garden-variety Negroes makes it worth walking out of here alive.

"Here's a question," I say to Gazzara. "Do you know a Spanish Joe named Hector? He likes to swing a cleaver and he pals around with a little guy with a mustache."

"Hector with a c-cleaver?" he asks, laughing.

To me, it doesn't sound any nuttier than a stuttering bootlegger holed up at a Christmas tree farm, but that would be lost on him.

I try a different route. "And you're sure you don't know the grifter with one green eye and a scar on his ear?"

"I didn't say that," Gazzara says. "I know who s-sold you the moon. At least, I think I do."

At this, Santi perks up. "Well, who the hell is he? Jersey needs to get his money."

"His money is the least of the p-p-problems, as far as I'm concerned."

"What's your beef?" I ask him. "So you lost a few bottles of moon."

He slams his palms on the tabletop. "My beef, you red-faced jigaboo freak, is that I don't like people ripping m-m-me off."

He's in a lather and every time he gets caught on a word, his eyes bulge.

"I don't like them selling my m-m-moon. I don't like being asked questions. And I d-don't like having to d-d-defend myself to McCullough. He's an honest businessman, like me. Now I've got to t-t-tell him that even though his bony, b-b-bug-eyed, zebra-nigger-lackey-coon got ripped off buying a truckload of bogus hooch, it wasn't m-m-me who did it."

I'm so angry, I don't even think. I whirl around and grab the revolver in Frank's hand. It goes off as I wrestle for it, shooting across the room and popping two bottles of shine. I'm trying to stand up but Frank is beating on my head with his free fist. I yank his wrist and take back my gun, then keep him at arm's length by training the pistol at his chest.

I'm ready to shoot Freddy before he plugs Santi, but the kid is already grappling with him. He's clutching Freddy's wrists, trying to get at the gun, but he slips and lands with his back on the bench. Freddy puts one hand around Santi's throat and, with the other, aims his pistol at Santi's forehead.

I get out from behind the table and look over at Gazzara, who is aiming his machine gun at me.

"You really are a f-f-fucking idiot," he says.

"No, I'm really not," I say.

I pull Frank closer and shove the revolver up under his jaw so hard he must feel its barrel pushing against his tongue.

Gazzara shrugs. "So what are you gonna do now? Do you ever use that thing or do you just w-w-wave it around?"

I guess that's the difference between me and a gangster. Gangsters pull triggers.

"I won't use it as long as I can walk out of here with Santi and know I'm square with you."

"We're f-f-fine," Gazzara says.

"I'll take you at your word, even though you've got that Tommy gun on me."

He chuckles and rests the machine gun on the table. When he pulls his hands away and shows me his palms, Frank's eyes dart to me.

"Relax, F-Frank," Gazzara says. "The man just said he's not going to kill you."

Now he's calling me a man. A second ago, I was a zebra-nigger-lackey-coon. Amazing how effective a pistol to the jawbone can be, even when you admit you're not going to use it.

"Now, back your boy off Santi," I say.

"Freddy," he says to the hood. "Let the kid get up but stay on him."

"Take the gun off of him," I say. Frank's wriggling under my arm, but I've got his neck pinned under my elbow.

Gazzara shakes his head. "The rod stays. You plug Frank and the k-kid goes down."

Santi gets up and wipes his shirt clean, as if he's got an appointment later on and needs to be presentable.

"I want the name of the grifter who sold us the piss," I say.

Gazzara shrugs. "Fine. His name's Joseph Gazzara," he says. "But if you go after him, I'll kill you."

"His name's Gazzara?"

"He's my pain in the n-n-nuts brother. Last I heard he was jacking sugar from Cuba, but I guess he's back. I mean it, though. You press too hard, I'll k-k-kill you. He's a troublemaker, but he's still my b-brother."

"I'm going after him," I say, "but only to get my money back, no more, no less. Fair enough?"

Gazzara nods. "You're still alive," he says, "so it must be fair." He's got nerve, considering I'm the one with the weapon.

Frank pulls on my elbow, he needs more air. I loosen my grip a bit, but not enough for him to get any leverage. I've already learned not to trust the little prick.

"Another thing," I say. "Get Hector off my back."

"You mean the guy with the c-cleaver? That's some funny shit. I wouldn't help you if I could, but as it t-turns out, I can't. I've got no idea who the f-f-fuck that is." He palms his bald head and then rubs the back of his left ear.

"You're sure he's not another relative?" I ask.

"Why would I lie? You think I'm sc-scared because you've got a rod on my boy? I'll rub you out right now. I just don't w-want to make these guys d-dig your grave in this weather. The dirt is f-f-frozen solid."

I know he's telling the truth and I think about putting the gun on the table. I don't—I keep it clutched in my right hand. Part of me is itching to put a bullet into Frank's sinuses, but if I did, Santi would be leaving in a trashcan.

"I have to ask one favor," I say. "Keep this quiet. I've got to settle up with your brother before Jimmy gets back. I fucked up and I need to straighten things out."

"Too late for th-that," Gazzara says. "McCullough already knows. His boys are asking around about me. And he's looking for you, too, I hear. Now drop the metal or you'll b-be eating it for dinner."

"Baloney. Jimmy's not due back until the day after tomorrow."

"I said p-put the rod down."

I hate to do what he tells me. The gun is all the leverage I've got, but I'm a dead man if I don't drop it. He may not take me now, but he'll find me eventually, and I've got enough to worry about. I let go of Frank and put the pistol on the table. Frank takes a couple of steps away, clearing his throat.

Gazzara nods his approval. "I don't know when he was d-due back, but I assure you, he's in Hell's Kitchen right now. And he's not happy. Of course, I'll straighten out my part." Then he smiles at me, his round face beaming above his stiff bowtie, and gives me a look that says, *but you're a goner.*

"C'mon, Santi," I say.

Santi walks up behind me and we head for the door.

I stop and tell Gazzara, "Sorry if I fucked you over with Jimmy."

"I'm not s-scared of Jimmy f-f-fucking McCullough," he says. "And if he p-presses my brother too hard, I'll prove it. You can t-tell him I said that."

"He's not going after your brother and you know it. He's coming after me. When he does, I'll give him your message." I don't bother mentioning that Jimmy may not give me a chance to speak before he guns me down.

Santi and I step outside, but I pop back into the cabin, walk over to the wooden table and grab the half-filled bottle of moon.

If I'm going to be ducking Jimmy while I hunt for Joseph Gazzara and Hector Cleaver, I'll need something to make my balls bigger.

⊰⊱

Doc Anders leans in and shines his tiny flashlight at my cheeks, which are still smarting from yesterday's bout with the Princeton wind. I'm leaning back on the black leather couch in his private office, avoiding the glare of the overhead light by staring over his shoulder at the gold striped curtains. The doc has made it clear he'd rather look me over in the exam room across the hall, but we've been friends since I started hosting his late-night poker games at the Pour House, and as far as I'm concerned, that gives me the right to be examined in his office.

I feel more civilized here. The smell of musty old textbooks reminds me he's smart. Five diplomas hang in polished frames on the wall behind his mahogany desk—the large one is from Long Island College Hospital and proclaims him a *Medicinae Doctor*. When we're in the exam room, the odor of rubbing alcohol makes me feel like a specimen—a freak of nature—especially when one of his young clear-skinned nurses is standing next to me, taking notes as the doc ticks off his various diagnoses. He's not calling out any terminology now, he's just looking, but by the time we wrap it up, he'll have spouted a few doozies that are nothing but fancy medical terms for zebra-nigger-lackey-coon.

If you met the doc at the Pour House, you probably wouldn't trust him to find his house keys. He's got kinky white hair that's greased on the sides but sticks up on the top, a long face with a narrow nose that holds a pair of brown horn-rimmed eyeglasses, and he mutters to himself when he's deep in thought. But he knows his stuff.

He pulls down the lower lid of my right eye and tilts my head toward the light.

"You haven't answered my question, Doc."

I'm not here for a checkup; I know I'm an albino. I'm here to get the lowdown on my genetic future. I need something new to tell Pearl.

"Hold on, Snowball," he says.

I've told him to call me Jersey, but I let it slide. He's heard me called Snowball too many times to think of me by any other name.

He clucks his tongue twice, mutters something under his breath, and scampers out of the room. I'm not sure what he's found, but my money says it's got something to do with a lack of pigment.

He comes back in and hands me a tube of cream. "Twice a day on your face until the redness goes away."

"Swell," I say. Then I get back to the reason I came. "Doc, if Pearl and I had kids, what are the odds they'd look like me?"

He straightens up and looks me in the eye, taking inventory of what he finds there: a nagging love for Pearl, along with a pressing need for a clean bill of sperm-health.

"I thought you two finished before you got started," he says.

I'm not sure if he's answering my question or asking me another. It doesn't matter because there's no point in bullshitting him. The doc knows everything about Pearl, as does anybody who sits in front of me at the bar for longer than fifteen minutes.

"Just answer my question," I say.

"Albinism takes on many forms. Even if you were to have an albino child, he or she may have very few symptoms." He stops for a moment; he's looking for a way to explain a scientific mystery in plain language. "There's no knowing," he finally says, and leaves it at that.

"I need something better than that, Doc," I tell him. "I need something new."

"It's not likely that your child would be an albino. In order for that to happen, both parents would need to be carriers."

I think of my own parents, the two random carriers that created me. The champ doesn't like to talk about my mother, but he's told me enough to fill in the blanks. She broke off from her family when she met my father, then cut out on him right after I was born. She didn't leave anything behind, not even a clue to my bloodline. The champ knows his own grandmother was an albino, but he's never laid eyes on my mother's parents. He doesn't even know their names.

I think of Pearl and a smile cracks my chapped lips. "But Pearl's not a carrier, right?"

"Probably not," he says. "But she could be. Anybody could. Albinism is recessive. If Pearl's great-great-great-grandmother was albino, then it's possible your child would inherit the condition. Not from you, but from you and Pearl."

He looks at me and I think I spot pity in his eyes, but maybe I'm as oversensitive as my skin.

"It's unlikely, Snowball," he says. "I'd bet the house that Pearl's not a carrier."

It's hard for me to feel good with that answer because I've seen the doc bet the house—and lose—about three times a week for the past two years.

My eyes start shimmying again.

"Your eyes are still giving you trouble," he says. It wasn't a question, so I don't give an answer. "I'll give you drops, but they won't help unless you stay out of the sun and away from bright lights. Have you been wearing your sunglasses?"

"All the time," I tell him, even though he probably knows I'm lying. Then I get back to Pearl. "So I should just walk away?"

He sighs and leans against the side of his desk. "Snowball, uh, Jersey, this isn't a medical issue. Do you want me to answer as your doctor or your friend?"

"Both."

"As your doctor, I'm telling you that in all likelihood your children will be fine. But as a friend, I think you're beating a dead horse. There's nothing you can say that will win Pearl over. Walk away."

But I'm not ready to move on. "Can you change the way I look?" I ask. Rumor has it the doc helped a few of his friends run from the law by altering their faces. And I happen to know the rumor is true.

"I can put you in touch with someone," he says. "But there's only so much he can do. Change your hair, maybe. Fix in here." He drags his finger along a tender patch in front of my earlobe. "But it won't rid you of the albinism."

I walk to his bookcase and look into the mirror he keeps next to a photo of his infant son. My cheeks are a random pattern of pink and red blotches. I spent one day in the wind and came out of it a chapped checkerboard.

"We're keeping up with it, Snowball." Then he mutters, "Almost."

I want to pound my face with his desk lamp until he tells me I'm normal, but I know he won't lie to me. I gather up my jacket and hat and leave his office feeling the way I did when I got here: alone.

⚜

Walking home from the subway, I pass the tailor shops, delicatessens, and pawnshops on 125th Street. They're all empty; nobody in Harlem has a nickel. Usually I make my way down Seventh Avenue but today I turn on Lenox. I'm happy to avoid the Salvation Army Santas—those ringing bells do nothing but remind me that I'll be spending the holiday on my own. Besides, if Denny's right and Jimmy got back on Monday, then Jimmy's triggermen are already out looking for me. I'll approach my place from Lenox and, if anything smells fishy, I'll spin around and duck back inside the subway station. I won't be able to live like this for long, though. I've been in hiding for two days and it's already getting to me. I'm going to have to take a permanent vacation or sit down with Jimmy.

Walking down Lenox, I spot my father on the corner of 123rd Street. He's only five blocks from his place—he moved us to Harlem from Hoboken ten years ago. But he's not heading home; he's pacing in a small circle. He's wearing a tan overcoat with wide shoulder pads and a dark brown fedora. He runs over to head me off at the corner of 124th.

"Ya got trouble, son," he says, nervously looking over each shoulder as if he'd just robbed a bank.

He grabs my elbow and pulls me under the awning of Pete's Shoe

Repair. He steers me into the vestibule and stands between me and the road. I can't see past his broad shoulders. He's hiding me.

"What's going on?" I say, tugging my elbow out of his hand.

"I just went by your place to tell you about Hector. Some thug was there, started questionin' me, askin' where you were."

"One of Jimmy's boys," I say.

"I knew this would happen." His voice has a sharp edge to it; he wants to yell but he's controlling himself. He's got a right to be ruffled. He's witnessing his worst nightmare.

"I can straighten this out," I say, hoping to calm him down, but my pulse is quickening and the back of my neck is getting hot.

A car rolls up to the curb and I pull my fedora down over my forehead. My father reaches around me, opens the wooden and glass door to Pete's and pushes me into the shop. As the door swings open, a sleigh bell attached to the jamb jingles overhead.

Pete's shop is painted the color of pea soup and it smells of dust and cowhide. Two heavyset cobblers are working in a room behind the counter. I only see their heads but can tell they're both swinging small rubber mallets. I take a good look at each of them, just to be sure I've never seen their round faces in Jimmy's company.

The counter is in front of us. There are shoe supplies—brushes, bootblack, laces, and horns—displayed on the right wall, and a row of four shoeshine chairs along the left wall. We settle into the two chairs at the front of the store, away from the counter. I keep my eyes trained out the window.

An old white man with large ears and sloped shoulders rushes over with a rag to buff our shoes. Normally, I'd feel for him, hoping he hadn't been reduced to shining shoes because he lost a million when the market crashed. Now I'm worried that I may soon be joining him on the bread line. I've got a bundle of cash socked away inside the hollow leg of my brass bed at home but I'll never be able to get at it, not with Jimmy's boys hovering. I can't go back to the Pour House, either, so I'll have to live off what I've got in my locker at the Hy-Hat.

"This is a tough one to straighten out without talkin' to Jimmy," my father snaps in a hoarse whisper. "The thug at your place meant business."

"What'd he say?"

"Not much, 'cause he didn't know I was your father. Before I buzzed you, he asked if I was a friend of yours. I said no, but he pushed me against the railin' and asked if I was sure—he even had a picture of you, the one from the *Herald-Tribune* when your club was raided."

That was almost a year ago now. I was hoping my father hadn't seen it, but I guess that was too much to ask. The story was everywhere. *McCullough Locked Up.* It made the cover of every daily paper in town and it had my picture front and center. Jimmy McCullough may make the headlines, but I've got the mug to sell papers.

"I'm sorry you got dragged into this, Champ," I say.

When the shoeshiner hears the word "champ," he looks up at my father, but seems disappointed when he doesn't recognize him. Then he takes out a brush and goes back to working on his heels.

"I'm in it now, too," my father says. He's leaning over and talking so low I can barely hear him. "He pulled a roscoe, so I rabbit-punched him. I didn't want to beat on the guy, it just happened."

I can't help but smile. "I thought you weren't going to get involved."

"I'm glad you're enjoyin' this," he says, shaking his head. "Because I'm not. We're knee-deep in horseshit."

As he talks, I feel the grin drain from my lips.

"I'd fight for you if I thought you was right," he says. "But you're tryin' to pull me into the gutter. I'm not gonna help you pour your speakeasy booze."

We both quiet down as the shoeshiner finishes my father's oxfords and slides his bench a few inches to work on mine. I keep my eye on the street, but the only two people who have passed the shop were elderly women.

"What were you going to tell me about Hector?" I say.

"My friend Johalis knows people in Philly. There's a gang down there, some kind of occult group. These people think albino bones are lucky."

"They should try living in them."

"Are you listenin' to me? This ain't a joke. They collect albino bones. You know how they get 'em?"

I think back to the Excelsior and my throat closes when I remember the front page of Baines's newspaper.

"With a cleaver," I croak out.

"Damn right, with a cleaver. I was gonna try to help you set that straight but this is evil," he says. "Listen to me. Stay away from your place and stay the hell away from Philadelphia."

Joe Shinebox barely touches my shoes and holds out his hand to be paid. I can't blame him for not wanting to stick around for this conversation. He waits for his money and I hand him a dime. Shoving it in his pocket, he thanks me and scampers back behind the counter.

"Okay, there's some good news here," I say, trying to calm my nerves.

"How do you figure that?"

"First, Hector isn't a concern," I say, "at least not right now."

"Not a concern? These people are dangerous."

"But we're in New York and Hector's in Philly," I say. "Right now, I've gotta worry about Jimmy McCullough, and I'm a step ahead of him."

"Son, you're ahead of nobody. If anything, he's a step ahead of you."

"Fine," I say. "But at least we can figure out what he's thinking."

"How the hell can you do that?" He punctuates his question by slamming the chair's armrest.

The two cobblers behind the counter stop their hammering and look over at us. I've never been thrown out of a shoemaker's shop and I don't intend to start now.

I lower my voice to a whisper. "Jimmy's gotta be expecting me to show up at the bar and explain what happened with Gazzara."

The champ nods. "It's your only move."

"It's also a bad one. If I show my face, I'm a dead man. But if somebody went there for me, Jimmy would have to listen because I'd be nowhere in sight."

My father glares at me because he knows he's the only person that could pull it off. I can't look him in the eye, so I focus on the scar on his forehead.

"If that's the case," he says, his jaw tight, "you're gonna have to find somebody who's willin' to fight your battles for you."

"Alright, I'll just go in myself," I say. Then I get up and walk out of Pete's, leaving the door open. I stand on the sidewalk hoping my father will join me. I check every auto that passes Pete's corner, afraid I'll spot a triggerman leaning out of a car window and pointing a machine gun at me. Four cars roll by before I hear my father leave the shop.

"If I talk to McCullough," he says, "I'm gonna tell him what I think of him."

As if Jimmy could care.

He shuts the door behind him and the bell rings. This time, it sounds less like the jingle of Santa's sleigh and more like the clang of a fight bell.

⚞⚟

Darkness fell over an hour ago, my father has gone home, and the streets are white from a flurry of snow that's been falling since sundown. The sidewalks have emptied; those who are lucky enough to have families are with them, eating dinner. Now that the champ and I have broken the ice, I'd love to be sitting with him at his place sharing a bowl of hot beef stew, but I can't risk running into one of Jimmy's hatchet men.

The smartest place to hide out is the Hy-Hat. Santi will fix me up with a mattress and a pillow in the back room until I hash out a plan. I'm skulking to the club with my scarf pulled high. I'm thankful for the snow because winter clothes keep me well hidden.

I can't stop myself from taking a short detour and walking past Pearl's place, a basement pad she shares with her mother in a four-story townhouse on 124th Street.

The streetlight on Pearl's stretch of sidewalk hasn't been lit and the path leading to her apartment is pitch black. I hide under a tree and scan the block as best I can. My guess is that one of Jimmy's boys is nearby, and he either killed the light himself or he greased the lamplighter's palm to do it for him. I don't see anybody, but I'm no sucker. Just as I'm about to turn around and head to the Hy-Hat I spot Pearl standing in front of her gate.

Even in the dark, she's hard to miss. The lamp from across the street puts her in silhouette and I recognize her broad hips and round chest. My blood warms and I head toward her, careful to walk only in the darkest stretches of sidewalk. I'm not sure what I'll say. Maybe I'll let her know that Doc Anders gave me a green light on having kids—like that matters—or maybe I'll just break down and beg her to give me another shot.

I'm halfway down the block away when I see she's not alone. A guy about my age is with her; he's holding his hat in his hand and chunky snowflakes are landing in his slicked hair. I can tell he's tall and thin—he's built better than I am—and his light brown skin is as smooth as a freshly blended malted. He leans over and kisses Pearl. My insides tumble so violently that my throat tastes like acid. I stand there like a fool, watching as he puts his fingers in the hair of the only woman I've ever loved. I stay in the shadows, clinging to the one glorious night she almost loved me back.

There's a rustling by a tree across the street and I recognize the sound of feet crunching the frost on the sidewalk. That's my cue. I turn away just as Pearl wraps her arms around her lover's shoulders and pulls him closer.

Tugging my hat down low, I slink along the snow-covered sidewalk and head back toward the avenue. The snow's coming down harder. It hits my face and covers the tears that are turning to ice on my zebra-nigger-lackey-coon cheeks.

CHAPTER 8
1906

*W*alter Wilkins tried to shake off his meeting with Dorothy Albright as he shouldered his way along State Street, zigzagging through the maze of suited men hustling in and out of their offices. He couldn't get over Dorothy's nerve. She'd stood in front of him, pointing her finger at him as if he'd written nothing but lies. What did she expect him to do after she'd ducked into Ernie Leo's dressing room?

One good thing came from Dorothy's rant, though, and that was her tip on Edward Albright. Walter could just imagine how fed up Dorothy must have been to sic a newspaperman on her own father, but that wasn't Walter's problem. His only concern was whether the story was newsworthy—everybody in the Northeast already knew that Albright was a crook, and the truth was that nobody cared. But if Dorothy was right and Walter could nail Albright screwing with the *Evening-Star*'s prizefighting competition before the *Daily Press* got wind of it, Walter would be on the front page in as little time as it took the pressmen to pour the ink.

Walter hadn't wasted a second. He'd picked up the phone as soon as Dorothy left his office, nearly dropping the receiver when Albright suggested they meet at a local pub. Now, turning onto Prospect Street, Walter ran through the list of questions he had tucked inside his breast pocket. Every one boiled down to the same thing: What the hell was Albright up to?

Halfway down Prospect, Walter passed the Hartford Club, a

swanky place that had stemmed glasses, silk napkins, the works. He'd had a chance to work at a place like that, H. Grant's of Newark, after high school. But unlike almost every other boy in his class, he'd passed on the opportunity and gone to work shuttling copy at the *Evening-Star*. Now that choice was leading him past the shiny brass entrance of the Hartford Club and down a sloping dirt road to the humble, boxy architecture of the Iron Horse Tavern.

The front doors of the tavern were made out of crudely sawn wood. Walter pushed through them and found himself in a room that had about as much light as it did elegance—and it was stingy on both.

It didn't take but a second to spot Albright, who was marking time at a round wooden table. His dark blue suit and cream-colored vest were practically a uniform at the Hartford Club, but they were out of place in the Iron Horse. The tavern regulars, judging by their dirty overalls and stained sweatshirts, worked at Luna Park, the amusement center on the other side of town.

"Hello!" Albright said, standing up and patting Walter on the back. He had the hands of a banker: clean, tanned, and manicured. His knuckles looked as if they'd never been exposed to snow, rain, sleet, or for that matter, the Iron Horse.

The two sat down. The table was empty, except for Albright's hat and two mugs of beer.

"I like it here," Albright said, looking around as if he were evaluating the marble interior of the Hartford Club. "I'm thinking of buying it. What do you think?"

Walter's first reaction was that Albright already had too much money but he kept his opinion to himself. "It's comfortable," he said. "I just wouldn't expect you to like it."

"Just because I buy a business doesn't mean I'd patronize it." Albright flashed a grin and exposed a row a spotless white teeth.

Walter would have returned the smile but he couldn't live with being that phony.

Albright pointed at the mug of beer on Walter's side of the table. "That one's yours."

"Swell," Walter said, but slid the beer aside. He hadn't forgotten Glenny's warning that the easiest way to blow an opportunity was by getting liquored up.

"That was a heck of a story you wrote," Albright said. "Leo and the dame. Beauty and the beast. Fantastic." He smiled as he spoke and then swigged his brew. "You're on your way," he said, looking at Walter with admiration.

"Thanks," Walter said, even though he knew Albright valued him about as highly as a wet cigarette. "I'm thinking of doing a follow-up piece on Higgins."

"Smart move. Higgins is training hard, you should see him go at it." Albright leaned forward and feigned a combination of punches in front of his chest. "What heart. He's going to be a heckuva champion someday."

"That's why I'm here," Walter said, pulling out his notebook. "Tell me about his plans. Does he want a rematch with Leo right away? When will he be ready?"

"Leo won't be a problem," Albright said, dismissing the notion with a quick shake of his head.

"You're not worried?" Walter said. "Higgins took a beating. What'll he do this time that he didn't do last time?"

"He won't have to do anything. He doesn't have to fight Leo. Don't you read your own articles?"

There was no way Albright could imagine just how much reading Walter had done. Walter had sat in Glenny's office for hours, ransacking the *Evening-Star* files. Nothing seemed suspicious about the Higgins–Leo fight, but a story on how Albright had run a lottery without paying out a penny made it clear he had a sweet tooth for rigged games.

Walter wondered what kind of con Albright was trying to pull now. "The commission only said it was reviewing the situation," he said. "They're not about to take Leo's title just because he got a little too close to a white woman."

Albright took a long slurp of beer and studied Walter over the rim of his mug. Then he put down the mug, picked up a napkin, and patted the foam on his lip.

"Here's your story," he said. "Higgins is on his way to becoming champion, and I don't mean New Jersey. I'm talking about the world."

"Higgins will never get a fight with Tommy Burns. He can't even get past Ernie Leo."

"Sooner or later, Higgins will be the world heavyweight champion. You'll see."

Albright polished off the rest of his beer and, judging by the expression on his face, had finished the conversation along with it.

Walter was desperate to keep Albright talking. "Higgins had trouble defending his right side," he said. "Any boxer with a decent left will give him trouble."

Albright shrugged. "Just keep your eye on my guy," he said, getting up and putting on his hat. "He'll be the champ, it's a fact." Then he told Walter it had been a pleasure and walked out of the bar.

Walter looked over Albright's quotes and replayed the conversation in his head. *Higgins will be the world heavyweight champion. Leo won't be a problem.* How could he be so certain? Dorothy was right: Albright was up to his ears in something, and whatever it was stunk like hell.

That's when it struck Walter. He popped his derby on his head and left the bar like a hunting dog who'd picked up the scent of rabbit. There was only one way that crook could be so sure Higgins would get past Leo. He must be bribing the commission. Which meant he was bribing the *Evening-Star*.

⊰⊱

The newspaper's boxing commission was due to meet at the home of Foster Werts, a local wannabe politician who'd lost four races for mayor of Newark. Everything Walter had dug up on Werts was fishy, particularly that his mayoral campaign had been paid for by Richard Canfield, the financier who'd been exposed as an underground casino lord two years ago. Canfield was the law's worst nightmare: he was rich, powerful, and as crooked as a rusty screw. Nobody who claimed to have any integrity wanted to deal with him. Nobody except Foster Werts.

Walter stood on the carved steps that led to Werts's front door and looked up at the Victorian mansion. The three-story jewel sat behind four massive oak trees whose leaves were already turning orange and red. It looked like a castle, complete with stained glass windows, turned wood trim, and rooftop tower. Walter had no insight into Werts's finances, but this seemed like an awful lot of house for a four-time loser who made a living by sitting on state commissions every now and then. He pounded the knocker and waited, not sure what to expect. Werts had agreed to let him sit in on the meeting, but the double-dealer would probably be a lot less hospitable if he figured out that Walter wasn't interested in what the commission was doing—only why it was doing it.

After a short wait, Werts opened the door. He was shorter and squatter than Walter had expected; he had a sloping forehead, a chin that disappeared into his neck, and bulging eyes that gave him the look of a reptile in a suit. He shook Walter's hand and walked him into the dining room to meet the other members of the commission: Robert Walker, John William Dobbs, and Patrick Bagley. The charlatan and his three puppets sat on the far end of a long, polished mahogany table. Walter took a seat on the opposite end. That was close enough for him.

"We're ready when you are," Werts said.

Walter took out his notebook as Dobbs, a chunky man with muttonchop sideburns, poured glasses of Chianti. He didn't offer one to Walter, and Walter didn't care.

"I'm sure you're expecting my first question," Walter said.

Werts shrugged his rounded shoulders, as if the commission had countless decisions other than ruling on Leo's title.

Walter spelled it out for him. "What's your decision regarding Ernie Leo?"

"It's an interesting case," Werts said. "We've reviewed the particulars, spoken with various parties, conducted an investigation, and, sadly, after much consideration, we've decided to take away his title."

"And his prize money," Dobbs added as he swirled the Chianti in his glass.

"His conduct has not been what we'd expect from the New Jersey champion," Werts added. "Not to mention that miscegenation is against the law." Then he folded his arms across his chest, almost defying Walter to follow up with more questions. "We're perfectly justified in our actions."

It was an odd comment, being that nobody had suggested they weren't.

"It's disgusting," Dobbs said, shaking his head.

Robert Walker, the puppet across from Dobbs, added, "We can't let that nigger keep the title."

Bagley nodded in agreement, his brown beard bouncing on his chest.

Walter looked for a trace of compassion in any of the four men, but found none.

"How do you know he broke the law? You don't have any idea what went on in that room," Walter said. "Besides, when did a fighter's conduct outside the ring become grounds for losing a championship?"

"Since it was put in his contract," Werts said.

"I'd like to see that contract," Walter said. He had already checked the file at the *Evening-Star* and found nothing but photos of Ernie and Higgins.

"I don't have it here," Werts said. "And even if I did, it's confidential."

Walter wondered if there had ever been a contract. He jotted down a note to call on Ernie Leo.

"Have any of you spoken with Leo?" Walter asked. "Did you get his side of the story?"

"We didn't have to," Werts said. "We spoke to Higgins."

"Why speak to him? What does he know about how Leo conducts himself?"

"Doesn't matter, really," Werts said. Then he smiled and added, "All the details were in your article."

"Nice piece of work," Dobbs agreed, tipping his glass toward Walter before downing it.

"I didn't write it so you could screw Ernie Leo out of his title."

The lines on Werts's forehead arched at the accusation. "First of all, we're not screwing anybody. Second, there were other witnesses, too. You're not the only person who saw what went on."

Werts was spewing pure bullshit. The only others who'd been outside Ernie's dressing room that night were his trainer, Willie Brooks, and the guy who'd given Walter the story—the young, red-haired security guard patrolling the corridor.

"Really? Give me some names," Walter said, picking up his pencil.

"We can't divulge names," Werts said. "They're confidential."

"All of them?" Walter asked.

The four commission members nodded.

Walter shook his head, amazed that Werts and his pals weren't even dressing up their lies. "So what's going to happen to the title?"

"We haven't ruled on that yet," Werts said.

Walter knew that Werts had already come to a decision, or more accurately, that a decision had come to him. "Is the belt going to Higgins? Without a rematch?"

Werts nodded as if Walter had just given him an idea that hadn't yet crossed his mind. "That Higgins is some fighter, isn't he?"

"If he isn't, I'm sure you'll make him one," Walter said, shutting his notebook, unable to continue the farce any longer.

But as much as Walter wanted to write a story that ripped the cover off these four imposters, he knew he'd need some proof they were on the take—especially since his own paper had handpicked them. He had to find someone who wasn't on Albright's payroll and wasn't too scared to talk.

He would start tomorrow, and his first stop would be the very man who had stood up under the pressure of body blows and head butts, succumbing to nothing other than his love of a white woman.

CHAPTER 9
1930

*I*t's a week before Christmas and instead of wrapping gifts for Pearl, I'm hiding out in Old Man Santiago's office at the Hy-Hat, afraid I'll catch a bullet if I venture outside. The office is a tiny room; it used to be a pantry before Old Man Santiago redid the place. It's opposite the kitchen in the back of the club, so if Jimmy's boys were to walk through the front door, I'd see them straight away and be out the fire exit before they made it through the game room.

It's dinnertime and Old Man Santiago brought me a plateful of roast turkey and mashed potatoes. The meal is sitting on the desk in front of me, half-eaten. I can't relax, not only because I'm ready to leave for the Pour House—which would be reason enough to be anxious—but because I've got my father talking to Jimmy McCullough for me.

It seems crazy, but the champ was the only person I could send to the Pour House. I thought about sending Santi, but I'm already upset with myself for letting the kid finagle his way to Philadelphia. Besides, Jimmy won't touch my father. They know each other from the old days in Harlem; Jimmy surely realizes the champ wasn't involved in any bootleg deal.

Still, I'm not sending my father to the wolves alone. I figure I'll enter the row house next door, crawl through the ratacombs, and listen in from the stairway outside the underground entrance to Jimmy's office. If things get ugly, I'll enter shooting.

Santi walks in with a bowl of stuffing and slides it next to my turkey.

"Your dad's a saint," I say.

"He says he owes you," Santi tells me, leaning on a metal file cabinet.

"Not lately. This place has been running without my help." I don't mention the cash I've been leaving for Old Man Santiago on the first of every month. I drop it right here next to the telephone in an unmarked envelope. We never discuss it, but the old man must know it's from me—nobody else around here can come up with that kind of cash on a regular basis.

"So does your father have a plan?" Santi asks. "He can't just tell Jimmy to get off your back. The odds of that working are negligible."

"I'm not expecting Jimmy to get off my back. I just want him to hear my story. Then I'll sit down with him."

"You're expecting me to believe you're not going to the Pour House to back your father up?"

"No, I don't expect you to believe it. I just don't want you coming with me."

I can see Santi's disappointed. And scared.

"Be careful," he says. "If it occurred to me that you're going to be there, it must have occurred to Jimmy, too."

The clock on Old Man Santiago's safe reads eleven.

"It's time," I say.

Santi tells me to avoid Fifty-Third Street, but I ignore him. I slip my revolver into the waistband of my pants and throw on my overcoat. Then I walk through the game room and pass the teens playing ping-pong. All four tables are manned with fresh faces; the regulars are next to them, shooting pool. "I Got Rhythm" is coming from the phonograph and I wish I could join the gang. Instead, I wrap my scarf around my chafed jaw and step outside for the first time since I got here last night.

When I reach Fifty-Third Street and Ninth Avenue—the block of the Pour House—I slow down. I want to know if I'm up against the regular staff or if Jimmy has hired extra triggermen to throw me a homecoming. The easiest way to tell would be to see who's manning the door, but I can't make out the entrance of the joint. I'm not surprised. Jimmy pays off the lamplighters to keep the street dark. He figures there's no better cover than evening shadows during a nighttime raid, because we all know the block better than any cop or Fed.

I creep along the sidewalk opposite the Pour House, my breath turning to smoke and drifting off in the icy wind. When I'm halfway down the block, I position myself behind a tree for a closer look. Despite what Santi thinks, I'm relatively safe because nobody at the Pour House is expecting me to show my face. In fact, I'd rather be here than home, since Jimmy's boys are probably still camping out there.

A couple of boozers stagger across the street and walk the short path that leads to the Pour House steps. They hike the stoop and knock on the front door. It feels strange that they can walk into the Pour House while I've got to creep around outside simply because Owney Madden's boys wouldn't sell their precious liquor to the likes of me.

The drunkards are at the door and I can't make out their faces—but I do spot a head of plastered-down, spiky black hair, and I know it belongs to Diego. He's working the door, which means it's business as usual.

I cross the street quickly, hoping my black chesterfield helps me disappear into the shadows around me. The block is quiet except for the soft sound of snow crunching under my feet and the faint music coming from the Pour House. For a second I make a mental note to tell Jimmy about the leaking music until I realize it's no longer my concern.

When I arrive at 321 West Fifty-third, I inch my way up the path. I'm trying to act like I belong here but a cab pulls up and leaves me no choice but to crouch down behind the row of shrubs that separates the property from the Pour House walkway.

A man and woman get out and are standing only feet away from me; they're talking as they make their way to the door. I reach into my pocket and slip on my brass knuckles but these two customers sound harmless. He's got his date on his arm and he's telling her that he won't keep her long. It's a familiar tune.

Then he adds, "Just until Jimmy has a chance to meet you" and I realize the voice belongs to Antonio, an up-and-comer that Diego brought by the bar a few months ago. He's got one of those long, horse-like faces—closely set eyes, slender nostrils, sunken cheeks—and he's as skinny as a streetlamp. I don't remember much about him, other than he likes his martinis with a splash of olive juice. My hunch is he's brought a looker so he can impress the boss.

The woman is speaking now. "I don't even know Jimmy McCullough. Let me go home."

I know that voice. It's Pearl's.

I want to jump up and tell her I saw her kissing that guy in front of her place. I want to ask her what she's doing at the Pour House. I want to cover my face with my hands. I want to apologize, again, for being so stuck on her.

But I don't move because the pieces fall into place as quickly as my heart kicks into gear. Jimmy told Antonio to bring Pearl to the Pour House because he's trying to bait me. This is what I get for telling everybody at the bar my business. Jimmy knows how much she hurt me, and he's counting on the fact that I won't let her get dragged into my muck. He's right. I don't owe Pearl a thing, but she deserves more than being treated like a stolen toy. Antonio will bring her straight to Jimmy, so now I've got another reason to get my cold, pink ass to that underground entrance in the ratacombs. The minute Jimmy leaves his office I'll spring her.

A branch snaps behind me. I wheel around and spot two figures in black. The short one has a piece of metal over his nose—it's covering a wad of gauze and is held in place by two strips of white tape that reach his cheekbones. The tall one has sweaty skin and sunken eyes. And he's holding a cleaver.

"It's him, Hector," the little guy says. He sounds strange, as if he's stuffed up from a bad cold. His eyes have the look of a miner who just struck gold.

I've yet to unlock the door to 321, so I'd never beat them inside. If I try for the shrubs, I'll run smack into Diego.

Hector and his pal are walking slowly toward me, giving me a bit more respect than they did when we met in Philly. I don't have time to reach under my coat and grab my gun, but my right knuckles are wrapped in brass.

The little one is smiling, the tape on his face bending upward as his mouth curls. A thin mustache peeks out from below the bandage. "I was afraid we wouldn't find him," he says.

"How's your nose?" I ask him. I sound calm but my heart is doing a Gene Krupa solo.

His expression changes under the wad of gauze. "Fuck you," he says. "You broke it in two places. It hurts so bad I can't even chew." He turns to Hector. "Get it right this time." Then he looks around and adds, "And keep it quiet."

Keep it quiet? Even Hector looks at him like he's nuts.

That moment's hesitation is my opportunity. I run right at the little guy and slam a fistful of brass between his eyes.

"Oh fuck, my nose!" He's doubled over, holding his face with both hands.

Hector rushes at me, but I lunge at him and grab his wrist before he can swing his cleaver. I've got his right forearm in my hands and he's punching my head with his left fist. My right eye is taking a beating.

"Goddammit, his femurs, Hector," the little one yells with a pathetic whine, still pressing his hands against his twice-broken nose.

My arms are going weak. I can't hold the cleaver forever, so I break the cardinal rule of the Harlem streets: I knee Hector square in the balls. He crumbles to the ground so fast that his arm yanks itself out of my grip. When he lands, he pins his knees against his shoulders and wraps his arms around his ankles—but his right hand still grips the cleaver. He vomits a bucket of spew that looks like corn chowder. On his third heave, the cleaver finally falls free. I grab it and turn just in time to see Diego inching toward me. He's got a pistol pointed at my chest and his black eyes are darting left and right, taking in the scene around us. I must look like a one-man army.

"Sorry, Snowball," he says, "But I gotta bring you in."

He steps toward me, slowly, keeping his eyes trained on me as if I could pull a gun out of thin air. I wish he were right. Instead, I'm wheezing, trying to catch my breath.

He keeps the pistol on me. "Jimmy's out for you," he says.

"Tell him to get in line," I say between gulps of air. My voice is so shaky I barely recognize it.

Diego's not laughing. It can't be easy for the kid to take me down. He's barely Santi's age and I'm the one who put him on the door. If it weren't for me, he'd still be rolling kegs. My guess is that he'd want to help me out, but he's not brave enough—or stupid enough—to go against Jimmy.

He sees I'm still sucking for air so he gives me some space. "He's got your girl," he says.

"She's not my girl anymore, remember?"

"C'mon, let's go," he says, nodding toward the Pour House with his chin. "You have no choice."

"Not really," I say, my breath coming back to me. "I've still got a cleaver and nothing to lose."

I brandish the blade but Diego doesn't back off—he raises the pistol so that it's pointing squarely between my eyes.

Hector gets to his feet and lets out a long, slow moan. He's got a trail of vomit hanging from his lower lip and I feel like apologizing, but it's not like he didn't come at me with a fucking butcher's knife.

I back away from Diego, waving Hector's steel in front of me as I step toward the street. With any luck, I've got enough chips with Diego that he'll hesitate before pulling the trigger.

"Hey, Snowball," I hear behind me.

Diego brings the pistol down to his side and hides it behind his hip.

I turn around to a beautiful sight: Larch and his Clara Bow wannabe in a police car. And Larch is in uniform, which makes him untouchable to all but the craziest. Diego's close enough to the shrubs that he's out of Larch's line of sight. He's got an easy path back to the Pour House and he'd be an idiot not to take it.

"Good evening, Officer," I say, loud enough for Diego, Hector, and the little guy to hear me. Larch is no Einstein but he's got to know something's up.

He leans out the window. "What in God's name is going on here?"

I realize he's talking about the cleaver, which I'm still holding in front of my chest the way Douglas Fairbanks wielded his sword in *The Iron Mask*.

"Oh, this? It's not mine."

"Who are they?" Clara Bow asks, pointing over my shoulder.

I turn to see Hector on his feet. He's no longer vomiting, but he's still clutching his groin. The little one is yelling at him, the gauze around his nose now soaked in blood.

"Long story," I say, trotting around to Clara's door and squeezing into the back of the car. I toss the blade into the street and shut the door as it clangs on the pavement.

"Go, Larch. Now. Nail it."

Larch takes off and we pull away from Hector and Diego—and my father and Pearl.

"Start talking, Snowball," Larch says over his shoulder.

My hands are shaking and I can't stop them. I spot a flask sticking out from under Larch's seat, so I grab it and take a hearty slug straight from the canister. The rye burns my chest and my throat closes. I cough in mid-swallow, spraying the back of Clara's seat with hooch. I wipe it with my coat sleeve and then lay the whole story out for Larch. The bogus moon. Joseph Gazzara. Hector. Jimmy.

"Now Jimmy's got Pearl," I say. "And my father is on his way over there, if he's not there already."

Clara's face twists with confusion. She's having a tough time following and I don't blame her.

"It's complicated," I say.

I'm so rattled I almost tell her I hate myself—and that I'm only in this predicament because I look like a blanched freak. But I don't open up to many people and I'm not about to start yapping to Larch's mistress.

"I've got an idea, Snowball," Larch says, "but I'm not sure you're going to like it."

I have no idea what he's got up his sleeve, but I can't imagine that he'd go too far out of bounds for me. Then again, I've been good to him so maybe it's time for some payback.

"If it gets me out of this mess, I'm all for it," I say.

"Alright, then trust me."

He grabs the flask, swigs from it, and wipes his lips with the back of his wrist. Then he turns down Broadway and heads back toward Fifty-Third Street, toward the Pour House.

On the way, he picks up the handle of his police radio and calls for backup.

⁂

I watch the raid from the safety of the police car, which is a far different viewpoint than the ones I've had in the past. It's helpful to see the game from this side of the table—the experience can only help me if I'm ever pouring moon in a speakeasy again.

West Fifty-Third is crawling with police. Eight squad cars and four paddy wagons line the street and a cluster of patrolmen block the intersection. A half-dozen blue jackets are positioned on the Pour House steps, ready to charge. They're expecting to find Tony Accardo, one of Capone's triggermen, sitting at the bar, and they've got good reason: Larch told them a local snitch fingered him sipping a martini behind the pocket doors.

A stocky, barrel-chested patrolman with broad shoulders knocks on the door and Diego opens it. The cop pulls Diego out by his lapels and drags him to the first of the paddy wagons. The wagons are big, boxy, and black—they look like penitentiaries on wheels. Diego's eyes are crazed with fear, the poor kid seems as close to crying for his mommy as he is to pulling out a machine gun and taking down the cops. Six more blue jackets rush into the Pour House, drawing their guns and barking commands; a dozen others wait in silence by the windows and basement exit. They've even got two marksmen stationed on the roof.

Within minutes the police are pulling Jimmy's men out of the Pour House, snapping handcuffs on them, and loading them into the paddy wagon. Larch has the last of the wagons reserved for his own use, though, and when my father and Pearl finally come out of the place, also in handcuffs, Larch personally escorts them to it. The champ has his head high and his jaw tight—but Pearl is begging Larch to let her go. Neither one realizes that this is all a show. They'll sit in the wagon for a few minutes and then be on their way.

Jimmy's next. Two cops take him out of the Pour House and walk him over to one of the wagons. He's as done up as ever—a dark chesterfield draped over a pinstriped suit, white tie, matching hat, and two-tone dress shoes. Underneath the hat, I can see that the sides of his hair and his side-burns are neatly waxed, as always. His hands are cuffed behind his back.

Strange as this may sound, I feel like a heel for pulling the police into the deal—it's as dirty a move as kneeing Hector in the nuts. Even my father would understand that calling a cop into a personal war is off-limits.

Jimmy's no idiot, though. He knows I'm here. He directs his sagging brown eyes into the police car and nods with an expression that says, "nice move." I nod back and, for a brief moment, all is the way it used to be: Jimmy, proud of his best student, and me, flattered by the acknowledgment. Of course, my satisfaction will be fleeting, because I can only imagine Jimmy's next move now that I've changed the rules.

Larch orders two patrolmen to load Antonio and the rest of the Pour House busboys into the third wagon before he walks over to me.

"We'll let your father and Pearl go once the others are brought to the precinct. You can join them in a couple of minutes."

"Swell," I say, and step out of the car onto the iced street.

"One more thing," he says. "Where's the liquor? The sugar pop moon? There's not much behind the bar."

Larch doesn't want the sugar pop moon, he knows it's bogus. He's looking for a free score—his payment for saving my bony ass. Still, I can't give it to him. I owe him one, that's for sure, but I'm still hoping I can live the rest of my life without looking over my shoulder. If I tell Larch about the ratacombs and spill Jimmy's double-dealings, Jimmy would have every right to come after me. There are some moves that can't be undone, and for now, those are the ones I'm refusing to make. I may have pulled the cops into my shenanigans, but I won't become one of them. I won't sing.

My father and Santi are all ears as I tell them about Hector and Diego. We're sitting in my booth at the Hy-Hat, the one without the reading lamp, the tall one in the back that Pearl and I sat in, six nights a week, for years. Pearl's here now but she's itching to leave.

"So when do I get to go home?" she asks me. I can hear in her voice that she's done with me. Any hope I had of winning her over is dead now that she sees me as a refugee of Jimmy's sleaze joint and not a volunteer helping out at the Hy-Hat.

My eyes are twitching like crazy and I wish I had my dark glasses to cover them. Instead, I look down at the wooden table between us.

"I don't know," I tell her.

It's embarrassing to admit that I'm flummoxed but it's the truth. Jimmy won't be in jail for more than a few hours and I've used up favors with just about everybody I know, even Larch.

Pearl drums her fingers on the table and has me wishing I'd taken a bullet from Denny Gazzara's machine gun. We've convinced her she'll be safer at her grandmother's place on the Lower East Side, assuming she can stay clear of Jimmy's thugs—no strolling, no shopping, no breadlines. I'm also laying low, so Old Man Santiago will take the Auburn and drive her downtown after he closes up for the night.

"You better come up with somethin'," my father says. "I told McCullough that Joseph Gazzara's got his money but he don't care. He wants it from you."

Santi shakes his head. "I was hoping he'd be soundly copacetic."

Santi's gibberish is lost on my father.

"Ya know that thug at your place?" my father asks me. "I musta rammed him pretty hard. He was at the Pour House, moanin' that he couldn't piss right. He almost came at me but McCullough stopped him."

My father should be proud, but instead he's upset that he hurt one of Jimmy's hired guns.

"I wouldn't lose any sleep," I say. "I'm sure that thug has done plenty worse."

My father nods, but I can tell he's not buying it. "I almost gave McCullough more of the same," he says.

He's got his head down, as if the image of Jimmy getting his head ripped off might be unnerving to anybody in the room. Had he gone ahead and done it, my only concern would have been the aftermath. The last person any sane man would jump is Jimmy McCullough. Of course, my father doesn't see him as a captain of organized crime, he sees him as a local thug who took his boy out of college.

"You did the smart thing," I say. "You swung when there was no other choice."

"I did what I hadda do," my father says, obviously trying to convince himself that slamming the triggerman square in the kidney was the result of some kind of moral code.

He's probably hoping I'll do more to alleviate his guilt, but I'm peeking over at Pearl. Maybe it's me, but it sure seems like she's been stepping it up since pushing me out of her life. She's got a stripe of eyeliner running across each lid and a smear of rouge on her cheeks. She's also wearing a pair of red rhinestone earrings that I can only assume somebody gave to her. I want to rip them off her ears, toss them down a sewer, and watch as they splash in the sludge. Then I'd like to throw my arms around her shoulders and kiss the soft, back part of her neck that bulges over her collar.

"Forget Jimmy McCullough," Santi says. "Here's a more important inquisition. How did Hector find Jersey? What is he doing now—working for Jimmy at the Pour House?"

"No," my father says, nodding. "It ain't hard to find Jersey. Everybody knows where he works."

I don't look my father in the eye, because I know it kills him to admit I break the law for a living. Staring at the floor, I pretend to clean the heel of my oxford.

"Let's face it, Jersey," Pearl says to me, "you're not hard to spot."

She's getting close to my nerve but I let it pass.

"Hector probably figured he'd find you behind the bar," my father says. "But he caught you outside."

His theory fits. But it's hard to accept anything as fact since I shelled out Jimmy's money for sugar pop moon and wound up in a standoff with a stuttering gangster at a Christmas tree farm.

"If that's the case," I say, "I don't have to worry about Hector, unless I'm in Philly or at the Pour House. So what's my next move?"

Santi answers before my father can speak. "We've got to find Joseph Gazzara. We know he takes the train back and forth from Philly, so we should start there."

"Didn't I just say Hector's in Philly? What's Plan B?"

Santi, my father, and Pearl stare back at me in silence. I really wanted to handle this without leaving Harlem, but I can see that's not in the cards.

I shrug my shoulders in agreement. "Okay, if it's my only option, I'll go down there, and I'll stay clear of Hector."

"Just disguise yourself," Pearl says, chuckling.

It's a wisecrack. I'm ready to bite back with a remark about that guy outside her house when her eyes twinkle. She's teasing, just like she did in the old days. It stings more now knowing those times might as well be a previous life altogether.

She looks at her watch—the small, gold Gruen I'd given her after Jimmy dumped a crate of the hot timepieces onto the Pour House floor. I'm glad things haven't gotten so bad that she had to sell it—seeing that watch around her soft brown wrist makes me feel as though she still thinks about me.

But then she looks toward the door for Old Man Santiago. "Where the hell is he?" she says, which answers any question I might have as to where she wants to be right now.

<hr />

I down a double shot of bourbon and chase it with a spiked beer. I'm in the Ink Well, a speakeasy in a brownstone at the corner of Juniper and Vine, a few blocks from Philadelphia City Hall. Driving down this morning wasn't easy—the Auburn's wipers were barely able to keep up with the blizzard of snow pelting the windshield. I'm here to meet my father's buddy, Johalis Cervera. The champ says Johalis could fill in some of the blanks on Hector, but I'm also going to hammer him with questions about the crevices of Philadelphia—especially those that might lead me to Joseph Gazzara.

The Ink Well is nothing like the Pour House. First of all, it's a colored joint. It's also in a basement. The ceilings are so low I can practically jump up and touch them. There's a Christmas tree decorated with sparkling red lights near the entrance and a coatroom about as roomy as a phone booth hidden behind it. Three black iron tables fill the space up front and a shiny oak bar runs along the left brick wall in the back. A short Negro bartender with round dark eyes, a high forehead, and gray hair is working the bar. He looks close to sixty but still has a solid physique. The countertop behind him is stocked with all sorts of hooch and there's a radio playing Bessie Smith's "Empty Bed Blues." The back room is nice and dark; the only lights worth mentioning are the small Christmas bulbs that twinkle from the cash register alongside the radio. If I were ever forced to move to Philly, I just might be a regular here.

Unfortunately for the owners, the place is empty. I'm not sure how much business this joint needs to do, but if Jimmy owned it he'd be screaming his butt off. He wouldn't care that Christmas is six days away and everybody in town is penniless. Lunchtime on a Friday has to bring in a few bucks.

I'm leaning on the end of the polished oak bar. The doe-eyed brunette running the coatroom walks over and takes the stool to my right. I'm not sure why she's saddling up next to me, but then again, there's not exactly a rush of customers with overcoats looking for her.

"Still waiting?" she asks me. We chatted when I first walked into the place—she knows I'm hanging on a friend, but that's about it. Her name is Angela and she seems like a straight shooter, but I haven't forgotten what happened the last time I trusted a woman in Philly. I'm being more careful now.

Angela's a chatterbox. She's already told me she flunked out of high school six years ago; she's working here because the tender is her uncle and he runs the place. I think about what it would be like to work at a colored joint instead of the Pour House. At least I wouldn't be running for my life over a shipment of counterfeit moon.

"I heard you tell Uncle Doolie you were from New York. I'm thinking of moving there."

I now know that the tender's name is Doolie and that Angela has superhuman hearing.

"Don't," I tell her. "Nobody's working." Including me, now that Jimmy's put the screws to me.

"Damn," she says, shaking her head. "I guess I'm lucky."

"You have no idea," I tell her.

She's not a peach but she's no mutt either. She's got a decent chassis, a load of energy, caramel skin, and a pair of dark brown eyes that seem as big and round as the buttons on her maroon jacket. The right side of her head is missing a patch of hair about the size of a silver dollar; the exposed skin is patterned with a web of pink and white lines that look like they've been lifted off a road map. My guess is that she was burned some time ago.

"What's your name?" she asks me.

"Jersey."

"Jersey from New York," she says. "That's funny."

She's laughing at my name, not my skin, and that feels nice. The warm glow of the whiskey doesn't hurt, either.

"Names don't matter, people do," I say, trying to sound philosophical but making about as much sense as Santi.

She nods to say she knows what I mean.

Over her shoulder I spot a tall Spanish guy walking through the door. He has a long chin and the tip of his nose is shaped like a teardrop. When he takes off his overcoat and leaves it on the counter at the coatroom, I see that he's skinny all over except for a basketball-sized belly that pops out over his belt. That must be Johalis—my father described him to a tee.

"I've been to New York once," she says, lighting up a cigarette between her lean, tan fingers, apparently in no rush to hang Johalis's coat.

I'm not sure where her conversation is heading but I don't have time to find out.

"Here's my friend," I say, motioning to Johalis. My eyes shimmy so I turn away from Angela, hoping she'll miss the show. I stare instead at a small pile of cardboard coasters that Doolie's got sitting next to a bowl of lime wedges on his side of the bar.

"We'll have to pick this up another time," I say, still looking away.

"Okay, Jersey York Delaware," she says, laughing, as she heads back to the coatroom.

My eyes calm a bit and I wave Johalis to a seat in one of four booths across from the bar. I join him, but not before telling Doolie to send a couple of bourbons to our table and a whiskey sour to the coatroom.

"So you're here about some guy named Hector," Johalis says. His voice belongs on radio; it's as warm and rich as hot cocoa.

"I'm here about a couple of people," I say, shifting in my seat as his brown eyes size me up from behind their wrinkled lids.

"Fire away. I'll tell you whatever I know." His bourbon arrives and he takes a hearty sip. "Assuming what you want to know is public knowledge."

His comment gives me the feeling he's not quite as straight an arrow as my father, but in this situation that could be a good thing.

"I know my father told you about Hector," I say. "He carries a cleaver and he's not afraid to use it. He's also got a buddy—a little guy with a busted nose. Crazy as it sounds, I think they want my bones."

I'm holding out hope that he'll disagree with me, but he doesn't. "Like I told your old man, my guess is that Hector is connected to that occult ring that's been dropping bodies all over Philly. Those people are nuts."

"You're telling me I'm dealing with the devil?" Suddenly, Denny Gazzara seems like a teddy bear.

"In a way," he says, dragging out the last word with his husky voice. "There have been a few killings down here. Mostly albinos. Word is they're using the blood and the bones for some kind of crazy-shit voodoo medicine." Then he ponders what he's said and adds, "Hector's got a prescription to fill." He lets out a husky laugh, but he's not the one with the albino bones.

"I'll straighten this out," I tell him. "Thanks for your help." I'm about to leave but his expression turns serious.

"Hold on," he says. He downs the rest of his bourbon and motions for Doolie to bring us another round. "I told your old man I'd help you out and I meant it. If it weren't for him, I'd be missing a few bones of my own."

I'm confused and I don't bother hiding it.

"I don't know how much your father told you, but he used to work with me here in Philly. He saved me from a couple of overenthusiastic bagmen. Took them on himself. They would have killed me, just like Hector would've dropped you, except they didn't need a cleaver."

Doolie refills our glasses and Johalis and I both take a belt. I'm hoping the bourbon will wash the blood off my mind. Judging by the look on his face, Johalis is doing the same.

I change the subject.

"I'm also looking for a counterfeiter," I say. "His line is booze. Joseph Gazzara. Scar across his ear, two different colored eyes."

Johalis is nodding. "I know him, he's a small-time grifter who'd cheat his own mother at craps to turn a buck. One minute he's selling Cuban sugar cane, the next he's running card games. I didn't know he was jacking booze, but it fits. I'll tell you one thing. You're lucky you're not dealing with his brother, Denny."

"I've met Denny. Spent a little time with him in Princeton."

"Then you know he's trouble. Joseph is another story."

Johalis sips his bourbon, moistening his golden vocal cords. He winces after he swallows, his eyes turning even farther downward as his face crinkles.

"Joseph Gazzara's name pops up everywhere around here," he says. "He's burned a lot of bridges. If that worries him, he doesn't show it. He just keeps pulling his two-bit scams and his brother keeps bailing him out."

"He pulled one of those scams on me," I say, my voice losing its strength, "And it worked."

Johalis lets out another hearty laugh. "I'm sure he gets a lot of people, don't let it bother you. How'd he take you?"

I tell him about the sugar pop moon and he doesn't interrupt. When I finish, he leans back and rubs his chin.

"So you've got to find Joseph and get your dough back."

"Impossible?" I ask.

"Nothing's impossible," he says. "But guys like Joseph Gazzara tend to move around a lot. I'll put some feelers out and see what comes back. I'll also do some more digging on Hector, not that I'm eager to find out much more about him."

With that, Johalis clinks my glass with his and downs the rest of his bourbon. I pay Doolie and we go to the coatroom, which is barely visible behind the Christmas tree. Angela's waiting for us inside the room; she hands Johalis his overcoat and gives me my chesterfield. Her whiskey sour sits untouched next to a rack of empty hangers on the counter behind her. On the doorjamb above her head, a lone piece of mistletoe dangles.

I give her a half-dollar even though I'm trying to hold on to whatever I've got in my pocket. She smiles as she palms the coin.

"Have a nice night," she says and gives me a kiss on my right cheek. My blood courses to my face as if it wants to rush out of me and pour onto her.

"Merry Christmas," I say, wondering whether she, too, will be spending the holidays alone.

I stand there for a moment but then follow Johalis out the door. When we hit the frosty winter air, he pulls up the lapels of his overcoat and shakes my hand.

"I'll be in touch," he says before walking down Juniper toward city hall.

I think about going back inside to chat with Angela, but I don't. The last thing she needs is to get caught up with a walking blister who spends the better part of his days on the lam from Jimmy McCullough.

I wrap my scarf around my neck, tug on the brim of my hat, and thrust my hands into my pockets. My black leather gloves are in my left pocket—which is where I left them—but in my right pocket I find a matchbook cover for Emilio's Trattoria on the south side of town. Angela's name is scrawled on the torn cardboard. At first, I'm excited because I think she wants to see me again, but I soon see the message is about Joseph Gazzara. She's got a line on him and she's passing the info on to me. I owe her one.

I stuff the note back into my pocket and put on my gloves. Then I turn into the wind and head back to the Auburn as the raw wind blows my cheeks to smithereens.

CHAPTER 10
1906

*E*rnie knew that sooner or later a newspaperman would come knocking. It only made sense; his face had been on the front page of the *Evening-Star* two days in a row. He was sorry he'd opened the door.

"Ernie Leo, right?"

The reporter smiled, which only made Ernie trust him less.

"Yeah, I'm him."

If winning the title had taught Ernie anything, it was that reporters didn't care a lick about a Negro champion. They'd never even bothered to interview him after the fight. Instead, they'd flocked to Higgins's dressing room and gave the Irishman the ink for losing. Now this reporter appears at his door, no doubt following up on the story that painted him out to be nothing but an uppity nigger lusting after white women.

"I'm Walter Wilkins, *Evening-Star*," the reporter said as he stood outside Ernie's doorway, his raincoat damp and his brown derby dripping water onto the floor. This was the newspaperman who'd written the article, the man who'd tossed a stick of dynamite into Ernie's life. He couldn't have been a day over eighteen.

Wilkins peeked into the room, probably looking for something racy like a corset or a pair of leggings that would make for a good headline. Ernie let him look; there was nothing to see.

"Mind if I come in?" Wilkins asked. He tapped a folded *Evening-Star* against the side of his leg, not seeming to notice the rainwater spilling down his arm or the smell of burning tobacco wafting up from the cigar store downstairs. "If you've got a second, I'd like to talk to you about the Jersey championship."

"What about it?" Ernie said, ready to shut the door at the first mention of the so-called mystery woman.

Wilkins glanced at Ernie's hand on the knob. "I'm not here about the sister in the trainer's room," he said. "I promise."

Ernie wanted to believe him. Life would be a hell of a lot easier if Wilkins asked him a couple of questions about the fight and went back on his way. But if Wilkins wanted to bring him down, especially with another story about Dorothy, things could get worse than they already were. Ernie knew he should shut the door, but he couldn't close it in the guy's face.

"In here," he said, promising himself he wouldn't give Wilkins any information that could come back to haunt him.

The room fit just enough furniture to make Ernie comfortable— a daybed, a side table, and an armchair left by the previous tenant. The autumn rain pattered against the room's only window, which looked out onto Grand Avenue.

"My friends call me Walter," the reporter said as he took a seat on the daybed.

"Okay," Ernie said, far from convinced that Walter was a friend, or even friendly. He sank into the armchair and waited for the first question.

"Ernie," Walter started, shifting his weight, "I, umm, I owe you an apology."

"Why's that?" Ernie said, certain that the *Evening-Star* was about to thump on him again.

"I know the piece I wrote got you in hot water with the commission. I needed a story, and it never occurred to me that they'd take it out on you."

The guy had no idea of the trouble he'd caused. Ernie couldn't even buy a cigar without being pestered.

"It's done now," Ernie said.

Walter shook his head. "Not as far as Dorothy Albright is concerned. She really let me have it. It's not as if everything she said is true, but she got me thinking."

Ernie's stomach flipped. He'd done everything he could to keep Dorothy's name a secret. "Why was she talkin' to you?"

"She showed up at my office," Walter said. "Told me she was the woman in your dressing room and that I botched the story."

Ernie panicked, but Walter shot his hand out to stop him from speaking. "Don't worry," he said. "I'm not going to print it, I promise."

Afraid he'd say the wrong thing and make things worse for Dorothy, Ernie tried to keep his mouth shut. But he deserved some answers.

"She say where she was stayin'?" he asked. He knew she'd disappeared a couple of weeks ago because Willie Brooks had heard as much from Edward Albright, but he figured she'd be running from the newspapers, not to them.

"I have no idea, I only saw her that once," Walter said. Then a smile crossed his face and he offered Ernie the newspaper he'd been clutching. "But she'll like this. You will, too."

Ernie took the paper and flipped it in his hands. Then he tossed it onto the floor next to his armchair.

"Don't you want to see it?" Walter asked, the lines on his forehead rising in surprise.

Ernie wasn't about to admit that he couldn't read. "I seen enough."

"Well, all I can tell you is that the commission won't take your title now, not after that," Walter said, nodding his chin toward the paper.

Ernie fought the urge to kick Walter into the street and run down to the basement to find Mrs. Reilly, the cleaning woman, so she could read it to him.

"What's it say?" Ernie said, hating that he had to ask but unable to stop himself.

Walter looked at the paper lying by Ernie's feet and his facial expression went from bewilderment to realization. He didn't comment on Ernie's ignorance and Ernie was grateful. Instead, he leaned forward, put an elbow on his knee, and pointed at the paper.

"It says you were assaulted with a folding chair on your way out of the ring. It says you conducted yourself like a champion. It says that my prior article had gotten it wrong, and that I was to blame. It's the kind of piece that will help you keep your title."

Ernie hated to disappoint Walter—he seemed like a nice guy, but he was no match for a crook like Werts.

"Don't matter what it says," Ernie said. "If they want to take back the title, they'll take it." Then he muttered, "Same goes for my money."

"But don't you care? Don't you want to know why the commission wants it back so badly?" A mischievous grin stretched across Walter's lips. "I do."

Walter sure was full of hope, but there was stuff he didn't know, including how far things had gone with Dorothy the night of the Higgins fight. Eventually, Werts would find out and nail Ernie—and he wouldn't need Walter's article to do it.

"It's in my contract," Ernie said. "Conduct unbecomin' a champion."

"Are you sure you read it carefully?" Walter glanced toward the untouched newspaper on the floor and then looked back at Ernie. "Let me take a look at it. Maybe you missed something."

Ernie's secret was out, so he had nothing to lose by showing Walter the contract. It was on the side table, wedged under the base of his reading lamp. Normally he'd have thrown it away but this time he'd decided to hold onto it until he got paid. He pulled it out and gave it to the reporter.

Walter skimmed through the two sheets, the dry parchment crinkling in his hand. Then he looked them over again, more carefully the second time.

"The handwriting is really loopy, hard to read," he said. "But I can tell you there's nothing in here about conduct unbecoming a champion."

"Nothin'?" Ernie said. He knew the commission was crooked, but he never expected they'd lie about something like a contract.

Walter shook his head, an apologetic look on his face.

"Look, Ernie, I'm trying to do what's right, but I need help unraveling this mess." He reached into his jacket pocket and pulled out his notebook. "You know the people involved. You've got to give me some names. I need something to go on."

Ernie wanted nothing more than to see Walter bring down the commission. He needed that twenty dollars—he was low on food and a month behind on his rent. But the greenhorn was in over his head.

"Can't you tell me anything?" Walter asked again, practically begging for help.

Ernie's thoughts returned to Dorothy. He'd fallen for her somewhere along the way—he realized that now—and he wanted to help her any way he could. She must believe in this kid; she was the one who'd sent him here.

He nodded toward the notebook. "I got some names," he said.

A grin crossed Walter's square jaws.

"One condition," Ernie said, holding up his index finger. "Ya gotta keep Dorothy out of it."

"Fair enough," Walter said. Then he opened his notebook and started scribbling.

⚜

Glenny ground his cigarette into an ashtray. It took a lot to sell him on a story, especially one with New York's most connected gambler in it. He and Walter were in the *Evening-Star*'s bullpen: Walter was in his usual seat; Glenny had a foot up on Crager's chair. Crager had spent the day out of the office—he was trying to drum up a story about a rash of sick elms in Elizabeth Park. Here was Walter handing his boss a bona fide scoop, far ahead of the *Daily Press*, and Glenny wasn't sure he wanted it.

"You're telling me that Richard Canfield runs the Higgins syndicate? He owns Higgins?" Glenny asked. He cleaned his spectacles with the cuff of his shirt and then put them on, wrapping the loops of the wire frames around his ears.

"It's a great story, sir," Walter said, exasperated.

"I guess that means I should run a story saying Canfield bribed the commission in big, fat, juicy type on page one?" With that, Glenny moved his outstretched palm through the air as if the headline were right in front of him. Then he whacked his fist against his knee. "That's asking for trouble, dammit."

Walter barely let him finish. "You told me that nobody messes with the *Evening-Star*," he said, his words getting louder and faster as his frustration rose.

"And I still believe it. But we better be damned sure we're right when we print that our own paper is playing dirty."

"We're not saying that," Walter said. "We're saying that Richard Canfield has the commission in his pocket."

"*The* commission is *our* commission," Glenny shouted. "And you want to print that they're taking away Ernie Leo's belt for no good reason."

"That's right," Walter said with a stiff nod. "And that they lied about it." If his boss okayed the article, he'd nail that Foster Werts but good.

Glenny pulled on his lower lip and stared at the ceiling.

Walter egged him on. "You're the one who always told me to dig until we have all the bones."

"And I meant it," Glenny said. "But this could make us look really bad." He sighed and tapped his thumb against his chin. "How many sources do you have on this?"

Walter had been waiting for that question. He knew Glenny wouldn't trust him, especially after he'd sourced the first story with nobody other than that young guard who wouldn't give his name.

"This is different than the last story," Walter said. "No guesswork. No innuendo. I have it thoroughly sourced. I just can't tell you where I got it."

"It's Leo, isn't it?" Glenny said.

Walter's jaw dropped. If Glenny had any doubt, Walter's reaction just squashed it.

"And you think he's trustworthy?" Glenny asked, smirking. He paced in a small circle and shook his head. "Wilkins, you can't source a story like this by talking with Leo, he's got too much riding on it."

"Ernie Leo isn't lying." Walter was surprised by how much conviction spilled into the tone of his voice. "His story makes perfect sense. We already know that Canfield paid for Werts's political campaigns."

"It doesn't matter, you gotta get it somewhere else," he shouted. "Find somebody else who says the commission is out to help Canfield or Albright or Higgins—*anybody*! And make it somebody who's not involved, for Chrissakes. If it's legit, I'll go with it." Then he smacked the desk in front of him as if the sound of flesh on wood somehow made his decision irreversible.

Walter knew he'd never get anyone other than Dorothy or Ernie to rat out a bigwig like Canfield. He had only one shot. He had to shadow Albright. Or Canfield. Or both.

CHAPTER 11
1930

I'm sitting in the Auburn with my eyes trained on the red doors of Saint Mark's church. Angela had written few words on the matchbook, but they said plenty. *Joseph Gazzara runs Saint Mark's on Locust Street.* I have no idea how she knows Gazzara, or what he could be running at an Episcopalian church, but I don't question the details. In one sentence, she'd managed to give me the lowdown on the grifter, which beat anything Johalis had to offer. Once I settle up with Gazzara, I'll make it up to her, somehow.

The brick steeple and stained glass arches of the church loom over Locust. About a dozen locals are milling around the front door but I can't make out their faces from where I'm sitting. I get out of the car and Philly's icy air makes my eyes feel like they've been doused in bathtub gin. I wonder if my burning eyes and blistering cheeks are payback for having my boss hauled away in a bogus raid.

I'm on South Seventeenth Street—only about a hundred yards from the church—but the men and women climbing the steps are hidden under wide-brimmed fedoras and coquettes. I make my way to the church grounds and spot a young priest with curly black hair. He's about my age and I think about chatting him up, but he's got a group of grade-schoolers circling him. He could probably clue me in on Gazzara, but I'd rather avoid the attention. Instead, I fall in step with a white-haired priest who is shuffling toward the entrance. He's got a cane in his right hand, and judging by the way he's leaning on it, he shouldn't try walking without it.

He stops and introduces himself to me as if I'd asked. "Father O'Neill," he says.

"Jersey Leo," I tell him, avoiding the name Snowball as if I've got any kind of cover.

The padre's skin is a rosy pink. Time has beaten up his body and rotted his teeth. He's got a brown mole in the center of his left cheek that's tough to ignore. His eyes, though, are still young—they're as blue and lively as those of an adolescent boy's—and they're staring at my ravaged, blotchy face from behind a pair of heavy black glasses.

"Yellow hair," he says to me, his breath turning to smoke in the late December air. "An albino."

"I was, but I converted."

"A funny albino," he says, correcting himself. "And you're here for our evening services."

"Good guess," I say and he smiles. I'm trying to figure out if he wants to be a detective or a mind reader. Either way, he won't impress me unless he guesses that I'm here to find a grifter with two different colored eyes and a warehouse full of counterfeit booze. He resumes his walk and I tag along on his right. I keep my left arm poised to catch him in case he teeters over.

"I'm hoping to meet a friend of mine," I say. "Maybe you know him. Joseph Gazzara."

The bridge of his nose wrinkles like a prune as he scrunches his eyes to think.

I try spurring his memory. "He's got one brown eye and one green eye. And a scar on his ear."

"Sounds like the fella who runs bingo in the basement. He's not here tonight, though."

"No problem, I'll catch up with him soon enough." I take a step and put out my hand to help him. He grabs my palm and hoists himself onto the stone landing and into the church.

The place smells of holiness and money, and I wonder how much of the latter is being poured into Gazzara's pockets. Six soaring stone arches run alongside the right and left aisles, and a stained glass depiction of Christ centers the brick wall behind the altar, towering over us. A row of brass organ pipes spans the wall under the glass. Parishioners are lined shoulder-to-shoulder in the pews; most seem to be about sixty years old and all look like they're dressed in their holy best. Many are holding missalettes, ready to read along with the mass. I step into the rear pew in case I need to slip out quickly, but that plan goes down the toilet when Father O'Neill shuffles in next to me and blocks the aisle. I sit down and keep my fedora low, hoping the lighting isn't strong enough to reveal my yellowy-green eyes to anybody on the lookout for a rogue albino. I'm the only one in the place with a hat on his head, but considering the circumstances, I'm leaving it where it is.

A priest steps to the altar—it's the young, curly-haired one—and I scan the crowd for Gazzara, even though O'Neill just told me he only shows up for bingo. A baby starts wailing and the noise scratches at my raw nerves. I dry my palms on my pants and check the faces in each pew, one at a time. If Gazzara's here, I'll wait for him outside. If not, I'll keep snooping.

The mass begins and the priest recites a verse about Jesus and salvation. As he reads a passage in Latin, I case the joint. I try to memorize the four passageways that lead to and from the basement because the day may come I stop in for a surprise round of bingo. Father O'Neill is standing close to me, his sharp eyes tracking my gaze.

I whisper to him. "It's my first time here. Beautiful church."

He smiles and waves his hand in the air, blessing me. A funny bird, the padre.

The priest on the altar sits in a high-back chair as the organist plays one of those holy dirges. Meanwhile, two ushers parade up and down the aisles with wicker baskets attached to six-foot poles; they extend the baskets into the pews and make it easy for the parishioners to fork over their last nickels. So many folks have lost their jobs over the past few months I'm surprised these people can cough up anything at all. I know it doesn't say much for me, but I can't help thinking that Saint Mark's would be a profitable place to pour moon.

One of the ushers is walking down the right aisle. It's not until he's a

few rows in front of me that I recognize him. He looks different now—
he's in a suit and his hair is slicked back—but I know that clammy skin and
the sagging flesh under his jaw, I see them in my sleep. He doesn't have his
cleaver, but that's Hector, plain as day, and he's heading directly toward me.

I turn away from him. My heart is pounding so ferociously I can
feel a vein on the side of my neck pulsating with it. I face the back wall
as I scramble out of the pew, tripping over Father O'Neill's cane and
stepping on his toes in the process. I put my hand over the side of my
face and duck out the side exit. When I reach the far side of the parking
lot, I take big gulps of frosty air and pace in a tight circle. I light up
a Lucky Strike but have trouble putting it between my lips. My teeth
are chattering, either from the biting chill of winter or the fear that's
rushing out of my body. Probably both. I button the top of my overcoat
and take a deep pull on the cigarette.

Either Joseph Gazzara and Hector are working out of the same
church, which seems highly unlikely, or Angela set me up for no good
reason. I could pull Hector into a side hall, whip out my gun, and pelt
him with questions, but for some reason—and I'll admit that reason
might be his cleaver—I feel safer grilling Angela. I cross the street, hop
in the Auburn, and spin back to the Ink Well to find out why she sent
me to a church that has its collection basket in the hands of the devil.

◦❧◦

The Ink Well is the same as it was when I left it: cozy, dark, and inviting.
There are two locals at the bar, sitting on stools and nursing spiked
beers. Doolie's got Ruth Etting on the radio—"Ten Cents A Dance"—
and he's pouring a round of smooth sipping scotch.

Angela spills whatever she's got on Gazzara, and it's next to
nothing. She ran into him playing bingo in Saint Mark's basement
about two years ago and never noticed him volunteering for any other
activities at the church. When she overheard me describing him to
Johalis she figured she'd help me out, so she slipped me the matchbook
cover. She says she doesn't know Hector and has never seen his pal with

the busted nose. I believe her. It's clear she didn't intend to put me in danger, which is more than I can say for any other woman around me. I look over at Johalis—he met me here after I filled him in on how popular Saint Mark's had become with underworld scum—and I can tell that he's buying Angela's story, too.

"Joseph Gazzara and Hector are in this together," I say. It's not a question, but I wait for Johalis to respond.

"No doubt," he says, his voice as smooth as the scotch in our glasses. "And they're doing a lot more than playing bingo. Gazzara must be out for albino bones, too. So there are three of them at the very least." He holds up his fingers to count them off. "Gazzara. Hector. And the pip-squeak with the busted nose."

I don't want to admit it, but it hits me that Gazzara duped me right from the get-go. He's not a bootlegger at all.

"The bastard only sold me the moon 'cause he knew I'd come looking for him in Philly," I say. "He couldn't kill one of Jimmy's boys right outside the Pour House."

Angela's eyes shift from me to Johalis. She looks scared and I can't say I blame her. Johalis doesn't seem to notice her—he's too busy figuring things out.

"You're right," he says. "When you showed up in Philly, you made things easy for him. But Hector messed up, so they came after you in New York. Had they killed you then, the only response they'd have gotten from Jimmy would've been a thank-you note."

I've got no choice but to find Joseph Gazzara before Hector finds me. Otherwise, I'll be spending the rest of my living days running from him—and from Jimmy. "I'm going back to Saint Mark's," I say. "I've got to tail Hector."

"Why go near him?" Angela says. "Why not wait until bingo night when you can get Gazzara?" It feels good to have a woman showing some concern for me.

"I can't go at Gazzara on bingo night," I tell her. "Too many people will be there. I need to get him alone. Following Hector will lead me to him."

"Makes sense," Johalis says. "And tonight's as good a night as any, assuming Hector's still there. I'm coming with you."

I want to tell Johalis to stay put, that I don't need my father's friends to help me clean up my messes, but even I can see that I'm in over my head on this one.

"Okay, right after this round," I say. Nobody could get on me for wanting a shot or two to steady my nerves before tailing a cleaver-swinging lunatic.

Johalis must agree because he's motioning for Doolie to pour two more.

I take a look at the Ink Well and hope it's not my last time here. Big Bill Broonzy's singing the blues and Angela's sipping her scotch; the tips of her fingers caress her shot glass and her lips sparkle from the fresh coat of whiskey. She lights up a Lucky, leans back, and blows a plume of smoke up toward the ceiling beams. And in that fog, hanging directly over us, is my hope that simplicity will return to my life.

I down my drink and tell Doolie to hit me again. After a couple of shots, my memories of the Pour House begin to fade, along with my love of Pearl and my fear of Hector's cleaver.

⊰⊱

The effects of Doolie's whiskey are long gone as I stand next to Johalis outside Saint Mark's, shivering. My eyes are so beaten up by the cold that tears are frosting my bottom lids. The church doors are locked, so I'm peering through the stained glass windows to see if I can spot anything peculiar. It's hopeless. The sky is an inky black and the inside of the church is dark as hell.

Johalis trots to the back of the building, so I do the same, the patter of our leather soles echoing across the parking lot. He gets down on his right knee and presses his forehead against the basement window. The glass has been painted on the inside, so he can't see anything, but he swears to me that he hears movement in the cellar.

"Jersey," he whispers. "Listen here."

I take my scarf away from my left ear and lean in against the chilled glass. I'm pretty sure something's going on down there, but it could be anything, maybe even a dog. We certainly have no reason to believe it's Hector.

"I'll jimmy the window," he says.

"Are you kidding?" I say, my teeth chattering. "We don't even know who's down there. And they'll definitely hear us."

"It's better than breaking the glass."

He pulls out a blade and slips the steel between the window and the frame, trying to trip the catch. It hits me again that he's Joe Criminal, maybe even a pro. I'd been kicking myself for not bringing Santi with me, but now I realize my father cashed in his chips with Johalis for a reason: this guy can cover my ass.

Johalis slides the catch, but it doesn't move enough to free the window, so he tries again, this time shimmying the blade. The catch doesn't give and Johalis grimaces. Then he pushes the knife so hard that the window rattles as if it's battling a windstorm. The catch slides, but not quietly.

We stay there in silence, shaking from the cold, waiting to see if anybody comes to check on the ruckus. I'm not sure what we'll say if we're caught. I'm wise enough to know that any explanation involving an usher who wants to chop off my femurs would seem a bit far-fetched.

Johalis gets tired of waiting and pries the window open with the tip of his blade. As he does it, I hear a sound coming from the basement. It's a human voice—it sounds wild and desperate. Somebody is gagged and pleading for help. It's sickening. My stomach rolls like it's on a fun-house ride and my mouth tastes of vomit.

I'm about to wriggle through the window when Johalis taps my shoulder and wags his hand at me. Slow down, he's saying. I take a deep breath but it doesn't do much good. Adrenaline is flooding my brain like gin on a martini olive.

Instead of racing down there—which is what every cell in my body is itching to do—I poke my head through the window to see what awaits me. The heat from the radiators is doubly strong against my freezer-burned face; my skin feels like chilled steel that's being torched by a welder's gun. My eyes are too sore to see anything but blackness, but I can hear that the voice is coming from the far end of the room. I can't keep listening to this without doing something.

I pop my head back out and tell Johalis, "I'm going inside."

I don't wait for a response. I slide into the room, feet first, landing on a table and kicking something metal that bounces and clangs onto the hard stone floor. It sounds like an empty metal coffee pot.

Johalis whispers through the window. "Jesus Christ, watch where the hell you're going," he says, as if I planned on making as much noise as a marching band.

My eyes adjust to the darkness as I try to shake the feeling that I'm a burglar who's stealing air every time I inhale. I already can't wait to be back outside on the Philly streets, where it isn't a crime to breathe.

The cries have turned to whimpers. As I approach, I see a boy tied up and gagged on the floor, face down. I can barely see his face under the handkerchief that covers his mouth, but I can tell by his bony frame that he can't be more than twelve years old. His arms are bound behind his back, his legs are tied at the ankles, and the two knots are tied to each other by a short section of rope. There are chalk marks and candles on the floor around him. I'm no expert on the occult, but I've been to enough Catholic masses to know that this has nothing to do with Saint Mark's.

"I'm putting an end to this," I whisper to him, hoping that's the truth and wishing I could give my words the same thunder they'd have coming from a tough guy like Jimmy.

There are two ways to get down here from the church and I check both doors. They're locked, so if Gazzara and Hector show up, I'll hear them futz with the lock before they're on me. I unholster my gun, tuck it into the waistband of my pants and leave my chesterfield hanging open. Then I go to the window and tell Johalis that I'm not coming out alone. I take his blade and return to the kid, desperate to do the right thing for the first time since this whole episode started. I've never been a hero, at least not the kind that would make my father proud, but for a split second I feel like Wallace Beery springing Robert Montgomery in *The Big House*.

After I cut the rope and free the boy's wrists, I roll him onto his back and the Wallace Beery in me crumbles. The handkerchief is distorting the kid's mouth and he's bleeding from a gash about four inches long under his jawbone. He's weakened and scared. And albino.

I slice the ropes around his ankles and untie the gag from his mouth.

"Let's go," I whisper.

He's scared of me, and for once in my life, it's not because of the way I look.

"I'm not one of them," I say. When I see his stringy white hair and translucent green eyes, I add, "I'm one of you."

He nods but can't move quickly. He's rotating his wrists and kicking his legs to restore movement to his limbs. Grime covers his round cheeks and spindly nose, and I wonder how long he's been lying on the cold floor, hog-tied, waiting to be butchered.

We move toward the window and I help him onto the table. He wrestles his head and arms out the window and Johalis pulls him the rest of the way.

As I'm about to climb on the table, I spot a stack of the church's weekly announcements next to a dusty water pitcher. I want to check the schedules, but I'm afraid a key will slip into one of the door locks at any second. I grab a handful of papers and flip through them as quickly as my shaking hands will allow. I can barely read the small, mimeographed print but one of the sheets is for the bingo club. I jam it into my coat pocket, climb through the window, and join Johalis and the boy outside. The poor kid is blotting the cut on his neck with the same handkerchief that had been used to gag him.

We hustle back to the Auburn, staying off the church's main walkway and away from the streetlamps. I've got my right hand on the butt of my gun the whole way. The wind whips across Locust Street, but it's never felt so crisp and clean. The boy's blood is obviously circulating again. He's got some spring in his step as he ducks next to trees and scampers behind parked cars. His straight white hair is blowing in the wind and he raises his arms over his head while sprinting to the Auburn. He reminds me of myself at his age. He's young, he's alive, and he's free. Above us, the bells of Saint Mark's ring—it's midnight—and for the first time all season, it feels like Christmas.

CHAPTER 12
1906

*W*alter couldn't shake his own body odor as he crouched behind the Soldiers and Sailors Arch in Spring Grove cemetery and watched Edward Albright meander between tombstones. He tried to tell himself that he smelled of dedication and the pursuit of justice, but the truth was he reeked of anxiety. And failure. He hadn't yet found a single shred of evidence that connected Richard Canfield to Edward Albright and he was running out of time. Glenny hated waiting on stories, but Walter had convinced him to part with ten days of expenses so Walter could follow Albright and come back with a "humdinger of a headline." Six of those ten days were already chewed up and Albright had yet to meet with Canfield, Higgins, or the commission. No sir, until this morning, Edward Albright hadn't even left his house.

When the front door of 1116 Weatherbee Road had finally swung open at ten o'clock and Albright, dressed in a dark suit, white vest, and dotted necktie, stepped down the gray slate steps of the brick-and-stucco Tudor, Walter had been sitting next to a streetlamp with his derby on his head and two bites of a ham sandwich in his mouth. He jammed the rest of his lunch into his pocket and took off after Albright, shadowing the gray homburg hat across town, ducking behind horses, trolley cars, and at one point, a rolling ice wagon, to avoid being noticed.

When Albright had gotten to Main Street, he'd turned down Cemetery Lane and walked into the graveyard. Walter wasn't a trained gumshoe, not even close, but he could tell that something stunk, and it wasn't just the damp yellow sweat stains under his arms.

But Albright had been full of surprises since he'd stepped into Walter's life, and today was no different. Just as Walter leaned against the arch expecting to spot a meeting of underworld kingpins, Albright paused in front of a tombstone, knelt down on the moist morning grass, and prayed.

Walter didn't get it. Was Albright really here to grieve over his lost wife? If that were the case, not only was Walter following the wrong lead, he felt guilty for doing so. He knew how Harriet Albright had died; he'd found a reference to her in a 1903 *Evening-Star* article on suffragettes demonstrating outside City Hall. He turned away and hid behind the arch, letting Albright share a private moment with his wife's spirit. The next time he peeked, Albright's face was red, the skin around his eyes wet and shiny.

Then Albright stood, straightened his jacket, and followed the winding dirt path out of the cemetery. Walter shadowed him but stayed a safe distance behind—making sure to pass the marker that brought the crook to tears. When he reached the gravesite, he checked the name chiseled into the granite and then fumbled for the notebook in his pocket. The name on the stone was not Harriet Albright.

⌗

The window in the garden of the Hartford Club gave Walter a clear view of the fancy food being served inside the restaurant—raw oysters, champagne, roasts, asparagus, liqueurs. The world had its share of haves and have-nots, and it was obvious to which category Walter belonged.

Walter's deadline was fast approaching and he couldn't afford to waste time. After tailing Albright to the cemetery, he'd raced back to the inn, jotted down his notes, bathed, changed his suit, and arrived back at Weatherbee Road just in time to catch Albright leaving his house. Albright looked remarkably unlike the man Walter had followed to Spring Grove earlier that morning. He'd replaced the tears on his cheeks with an arrogant smirk and had donned a dark tailcoat, cream-colored vest, crisp winged-collared shirt, and white bow tie. Right now, Edward Albright looked less like a crook than a man of high society.

Walter stood outside the club, his feet planted against the base of a maple tree and his forehead resting against a windowpane, watching Albright hand his top hat to the maître d'. It was six o'clock, so Albright was most likely meeting somebody for dinner. The maître d' led him past the piano player, who was working on a slow rag. Albright and the maître d' went up the main stairway and into the large dining area, out of Walter's sight. Unless Walter scrambled up the drainpipe, crawled along the gutter, and peered through one of the dormers, he would lose his man. He ran around to the back of the restaurant, mud splashing onto his leather boots. Bolting through the delivery doors, he looked around the kitchen for a waiter. A cook with a dark, stubbly beard came over to him. His apron was bright white, except for the greased and bloodstained section that stretched across his bulbous stomach.

"What do you want?" the cook asked, shouting to be heard over a cacophony of clanging pots, pans, and dishes. The look on his face made it clear his time was precious.

Walter tried to sound seasoned. "I'm looking for a waiter who wants to make a couple of bucks and knows how to keep his mouth shut."

The door leading to the restaurant swung open and two waiters, both in the club's signature white jackets, rushed into the kitchen. The first walked to the stove and ladled soup from a tall pot into small white bowls. Behind him, a heavyset waiter with pigeon toes and a barrel chest barked out, "Table four is breaking my ass."

"There's your boy," the cook said, pointing at the bigmouth. With that, he went back to his station and manned a large, smoking kettle.

Walter scurried to the waiter, who was leaning over a counter, rear-ranging greens on a flat dish. Walter put out his hand.

"Walter Wilkins, *Newark Evening-Star*."

The waiter didn't look up. He kept shuffling the lettuce leaves, turning the salad into a blooming flower.

"Louis Hoenig," he finally said, still working his creation.

"You out of the Pub?" Walter asked, figuring if Hoenig had graduated from Hartford Public High, he would appreciate the neighborhood slang.

"Me and everybody else in the place," Hoenig said. "You?"

"My cousin."

Hoenig smirked and turned his attention back to that damned
bowl of greens.

Walter pictured Albright chatting it up at his table as the clock
ticked away. He reached into his pocket and pulled out two dollars,
which amounted to two days' worth of expenses.

He palmed one of the coins and flashed the other, rolling it over his
thumb. The silver worked. Hoenig focused on the face of Lady Liberty,
suddenly losing interest in the hearts of romaine.

"I'm looking for somebody who knows how to keep his lips glued
as tight as one of your overpriced oysters."

Hoenig raised his chin as if he were posing for a portrait. "The Pub
is a bond," he said.

Walter took inventory of Hoenig—arrogant, hypocritical, and
money-hungry. And worth a gamble. Walter flipped one of the two
coins to Hoenig, who caught it in midair.

"I'm tailing a guy sitting somewhere upstairs, his name's Edward
Albright." Walter figured Hoenig would know Albright, everybody did.

Hoenig nodded. "Table sixteen," he said as he put the coin in his pocket.

"I need the full scoop," Walter said. "Who he's with. What they're
talking about. Who says what."

Hoenig nodded as he ticked off his assignment. "Albright, his
friends, and the topic du jour."

"That's it," Walter said. Then he added a white lie to keep Hoenig
honest. "And, Hoenig, you're not the only one I've got on his tail, so
don't try selling me horseshit."

"Of course not," Hoenig said, as if he were of the highest character
even though he was about to spy on a steady customer for a dollar.

Walter held up the second coin. "I'll be back at closing time."

He put the money in his pocket and walked back out through the delivery entrance. With a little luck, Hoenig would come back with something useful, Walter would grab the front page away from Crager, and Canfield would find out that the only way to buy the *Newark Evening-Star* was off a newsboy on a street corner.

⊱⋈⊰

Ernie Leo didn't recognize the tall, thin man leaning against the front door of his rooming house. He had wide shoulders, the kind you get from spending your life hauling ice or digging roads. His nostrils appeared pinched closed and his eyes seemed too close to the bridge of his nose. He was leaning on the door, so nobody would be able to get in or out of the place without plowing over him.

Since the man was white, Ernie assumed that he'd shown up to dish out the usual "how dare you touch one of our women" crap. Walter's story on the commission came out two days ago. It had shaken Foster Werts off of Ernie's back—the commission had decided to let Ernie keep his title—but that didn't stop every white person on the street from making life doubly hard on him.

"'Scuse me," Ernie said, thinking this wouldn't go well but hoping he was wrong.

"Ernie Leo," the man said. His speech was thick and he swayed from side to side as he jabbed his left index finger at Ernie. "You're the Jersey champ."

The word "champ" was soaked in scorn. Ernie didn't bother with the empty chitchat he gave to fight fans or to the Negro folk who saw him as a crusader against white bosses.

"I need to get inside," Ernie said.

"I'm not done talking." The boozer leaned forward and put his face inches from Ernie's. His breath reeked; the putrid odor smelled of one part liquor and one part rotting stomach.

"My people don't like you," he said. The look in his eyes said he wanted to settle the score right then and there.

"Your people?" Ernie said, keeping his voice calm to avoid riling the drunkard any further.

The man raised his right hand and aimed a gun at Ernie's gut. "Let's take a walk," he said.

Ernie took a single step backward but stopped. He'd be better off staying on Grand Street than disappearing into a side alley.

"Talk here, I'm listenin'," Ernie said, slowly putting his left foot a few inches in front of his right, positioning himself to throw a mustard-packed left.

"You're going to fight Higgins," the man said, raising the gun a few inches so it pointed at Ernie's head.

"I just fought 'im."

"Again," the man said angrily, a wad of spit now hanging from the corner of his lower lip. "You're going to fight him again. And you're going to lose." His eyes twinkled as he listened to himself speak. "You're going to take a beating and your bloody face is gonna bang the canvas. And this time they won't take no for an answer."

The guy had a wild look about him, like he was thrilling at the idea of putting a bullet in a nigger's forehead and watching his blood spill onto the grimy cobblestones of Grand Street. The creep started laughing, a raspy chuckle from deep behind his stained teeth. His gun drooped and was aiming at Ernie's shin.

If Ernie was going to live, he had to make his move before the guy's trigger finger got an itch it couldn't control. He didn't hesitate. He uncorked a left that was rivaled only by the one he'd used to drop Higgins.

⌐⌐⌐

Walter snuck behind the Hartford Club to the delivery entrance. The air was moist and the sky foggy, unnaturally warm for so late in the year. He found Louis Hoenig pacing behind the restaurant, his black necktie pulled away from his collar, a cigarette dangling from his lower lip.

"Get anything?" Walter asked. He could tell by the way Hoenig kept looking toward the window that the shifty waiter had gotten plenty.

Hoenig nodded. "I set myself up at the table next to them and refilled all the salt shakers we had in the kitchen. Then I did the pepper."

"What did you hear?" Walter asked.

Hoenig leaned forward and talked in a low whisper. "Your man Albright's in the fight game, owns a piece of a fighter."

"And?"

"And table sixteen tried to pull some strings to get their boy the title but it didn't work out. Now they want a rematch, and it doesn't sound like they care how they get it."

Sweat beaded up on the back of Walter's neck as he thought of Albright's roughnecks coming down on Ernie. He should have seen this coming. Bribing the commission didn't work, so the syndicate would put Higgins back in the ring and fix it this time.

"Who was at the table?" Walter asked.

"I didn't get names, except one. The guy running the show. He wasn't there and I was glad. It's not a name I want to tangle with."

"You won't have to," Walter said. "I will."

Hoenig sucked on his cigarette and blew a mushroom of smoke into the air. "The name Richard Canfield came up," he said. "A lot."

Bingo. That linked Albright to Canfield, and both of them to the commission. Walter had his second source. He'd flesh out the story tonight and bring it to Glenny in the morning. The cook had been right—Hoenig had wound up being a worthwhile investment.

"Anything else?" Walter asked him.

"How long do you think I had?" Hoenig said. "I was refilling shakers, not barrels."

Walter reached into his pocket. He had two dollars left and one of them belonged to Hoenig.

"Thanks," he said, handing the waiter the coin.

"Oh, one more thing you might want to know," Hoenig said.

"Yeah?"

"This might be worth an extra buck."

"We made a deal," Walter snapped, itching to get back to the paper.

Hoenig flinched, but was obviously too proud of his success as an underhanded snoop to stop talking.

"When I was serving them coffee, one guy was talking about planting a story in the *Evening-Star*, muscling a kid reporter to do it. Said he was a greenie, really young and desperate. Called him Wilkins. That's you, right?"

Hoenig knew damned well it was Walter.

"Yeah, that's me, young and green," Walter said, looking directly into the waiter's dark-ringed eyes, wondering if Hoenig had overheard the conversation, or had opened his mouth to Albright and was now delivering a message straight from the syndicate.

"But they're coming down on the wrong guy," Walter said. "I'm not going to cave." Then he reached into his pocket and flipped the last of Glenny's coins to Hoenig.

"Thanks," the waiter said, smiling.

As Walter made his way to the front of the Hartford Club, he kept thinking about Hoenig's final comments. Young and desperate? He would show them. He would go back to the *Evening-Star* and expose Canfield, Albright, and the rest of the commission, regardless of the consequences.

He skulked his way onto State Street, wondering how the tables had spun so quickly. He'd been following Albright all week and somehow wound up looking over his own shoulder.

CHAPTER 13
1930

I'm sitting at the Ink Well with Johalis, listening to Blind Willie McTell on Doolie's radio, waiting for my father to arrive from the Broad Street Station. The minute the champ heard that Joseph Gazzara was connected to Hector's albino hunt, he was all too happy to help me track the bastard down.

I called the champ late last night, right after Johalis and I had driven the albino kid, Tommy Sudnik, to his row house on Chatham Street in the Port Richmond section of Philly. It turned out that Tommy had been missing for two days and handwritten notices were tacked to every utility pole, mailbox, and store window in the neighborhood.

We'd pulled the Auburn up to Tommy's house at half past midnight. Johalis got out and rapped on the wooden door while I took out a cigarette, still shaky from my adventures at Saint Mark's. I went over to a streetlamp and lit up, wrapping my chesterfield tightly across my chest to keep warm. Tommy's mother, a chubby brown-eyed woman with dark hair that defied gravity, opened the door wearing a red flannel nightgown. Johalis must have told her how I'd slid into the church basement and rescued her son, because she vaulted the wooden steps and hugged me right there on the brick sidewalk, the streetlamp beaming down on us as she planted kisses all over my face. For the briefest of moments, I was royalty, a ray of hope for a widowed woman on the downtrodden streets of Philadelphia. I wished Pearl were there to see it.

Tommy's mother wanted to go to the newspapers with my heroism, but I didn't want to advertise that I was in town. She did insist, though, on calling the cops to blow the whistle on Gazzara after Tommy told her how Hector had dragged him into Saint Mark's with a cleaver pressed against his neck.

"I don't think the cops will do much," Johalis said. He mumbled it softly but still managed to unnerve the woman.

"But what if men come for Tommy?" she asked him in a rich Polish accent, her face taking on the panicked look of a grade-schooler who couldn't find her parents. "The police stop them, no?"

Johalis didn't answer because the truth was that the Philly cops have no way to rid themselves of Joseph Gazzara. Yeah, they might slow him down by throwing him in jail for a while, but it wouldn't take long for him to get out and start up again. To make matters worse, half the city cops are on his brother's payroll. They sit in Denny's speakeasies, pocket wads of hush money, and sip free shots of moon as their radios ring, unattended. If they ever got a call about Saint Mark's, they'd surely sit on it. Or they'd start asking questions and my cover would be blown in no time.

When Tommy's mother realized Johalis had no answers, she turned to me. Fresh tears soaked her full, round cheeks. "If cops do nothing, what can I do?"

I wanted to step up, to tell her that I'd be the hero. Me. Denny Gazzara's zebra-nigger-lackey-coon, Pearl's discarded toy, the world's punch line. I wanted to tell her that I'd keep her son safe, that Johalis would help me, and that even my father would help protect her boy. I wanted to say I'd stop at nothing, that I'd put an end to Gazzara without any regard for the consequences. But I couldn't make that promise in front of the kid without soiling his soul, without glorifying the street laws that have got me on the run from Jimmy McCullough.

The woman grabbed my shoulders, looked into my eyes, and pled for justice. Then she started bawling again. She laid her head on my chest and sobbed into the dark wool lapels of my overcoat. I put my hand on her shoulder as she wailed for somebody to fight for her son—and I nearly cried myself when she looked up and begged me to stop the crooks from snatching Tommy again.

I stood there, mute, afraid of poisoning her son with hateful promises. Buried deep in my silence, though, was a vow of retribution that didn't need a voice to be real.

I haven't forgotten that vow as I sit in the Ink Well with Johalis, nursing two fingers of bourbon, and waiting for the champ to arrive. When the front door finally swings open, my father walks in wearing a tan coat over a dark blue double-breasted suit. When he sees me, he smiles, the cleft in his chin deepening as his lips curl.

I'm as happy to see him as he is to see me. I've always thought this Gazzara mess was disproportionate to any crime I'd committed. Simply by showing up, the champ is telling me that he agrees.

My mood darkens, though, when Santi slinks in behind my father. Johalis doesn't realize I've been protecting the kid, so he throws up his arms and lets out a rich whoop when he sees that we've got extra reinforcement. He tells Doolie to bring two more glasses and leave the bottle, and within minutes the four of us are sitting around one of the Ink Well's iron tables, a fresh shine on each of our tongues. Santi's avoiding my glare—his eyes are darting all over the cramped room—but I soften after another belt of bourbon. I tip my glass to him and he does the same.

My father pours himself a second shot and I'm sure the only reason he's drinking underground whiskey is that he's grateful I'm still in one piece. He sips the hooch and swirls it in his mouth as if it's a fine wine. I don't tell him that this bottle of bourbon has all the subtlety of the market crash.

He relishes his last drop and puts his glass on the table. "So this was never 'bout moonshine," he says, his round eyes sparkling.

"Nope," I say, impressed that his moral sense is so strong that he's ready to fight a gang of albino bone hunters but wouldn't go up against a lone bootlegger.

"How does Saint Mark's fit in?" Santi asks, keeping his voice low. He's probably afraid I'll send him back to New York if he shows too much enthusiasm.

"There's some kind of occult thing going on downstairs at the church," Johalis says. "Hector works for Joseph Gazzara; so does the little guy with the busted nose."

"The devil's in the basement," Santi says, his lips tight as if he's trying to crack a crossword clue.

"It must be a ritual," I say. "Who'd run a black mass out of a church? It's like opening a speakeasy in a police precinct."

"Santeria," Johalis whispers. "It's gotta be a Santerian group. They're the only nut jobs who mix Catholicism with voodoo."

A nervous silence fills the room, so I take out the bingo schedule I palmed on the way out of the basement. Below the list of activities are the phone numbers and addresses of each of the regular players.

I read the fourth name out loud. "Joseph Gazzulo, 368 Tenth Street, first floor."

The name is too close for coincidence. The four of us clink our glasses and down our drinks. I throw a few bucks next to the bottle for Doolie.

After we don our coats, I linger by the coatroom, wishing Angela were working.

The champ sees me slow down but he doesn't know why.

"Let's go, son," he says, resting his palm on my shoulder. "We're ending this cleaver thing now."

Damn, I'm glad he's here.

⚜

The four of us—me, my father, Johalis, and Santi—are piled into the Auburn as we drive past the Excelsior Hotel. The sun went down hours ago and the darkness brought a heavy flurry of big, wet snowflakes.

I turn down Tenth Street, rolling past the locked warehouses and retail shops, and I've got a sinking feeling I've been here before. When we reach number 368, I'm sure. Gazzara's address is home to the cellar club where I first ran into Hector. It's the joint where I splintered the little Spanish guy's nose—the same hole with the squalid mattress where I shot my seed into a double-talking hooker named Margaret.

At least I know what we're up against.

I guide the Auburn into a parking space across the street from the building. It's almost Christmas and the whole country is broke, so I'm figuring the joint's regular customers will want to tuck their kids into bed before coming here to drink Santa's empty sleigh off their minds. My hunch says the club won't start filling up until about ten o'clock—and the bartenders are just readying themselves for business now.

I tell my father, Johalis, and Santi the little I know about the place, but since the champ is here I leave out the part about the hooker.

"The entrance is on the side," I say. "The club is in the back."

Johalis nods. My guess is that he's also been here before, and I wonder if it was for the drinks or the hookers.

"Santi and I will duck down the alley and go around back," Johalis says. "They must have a delivery entrance or an escape hatch. You and your father go in through the side entrance, but give us a minute or two."

He and Santi take off for the back of the building—both holding onto their hats as the snowy wind swirls around them. Johalis is about a head taller than Santi but not as quick on his feet—and the ankle-high snow can't be helping either one of them. When they enter the alley between the building and the butcher shop they're no longer covered by the glow of the streetlamp. In silhouette, their billowing overcoats make them look like they're wearing long black capes.

My father and I sit in the Auburn and the conversation turns to, of all people, Pearl.

"I liked her," my father says, "but I'm not sure she's what you want her to be."

Not sure? He should get a load of her slobbering all over lover boy in the middle of the street. That'd open his eyes.

"Let's go," I say, getting out of the car without telling him how much I hate Pearl, or how much I love her.

We trudge through the snow and enter the alley next to the butcher shop. It feels creepy—I'm standing in front of the unmarked entrance that Margaret showed me only nine days ago. I unholster my gun and slip it into the pocket of my overcoat. Then I grab the metal knob and lead my father to the cellar club. We stand outside the door, listening. There are a few soft voices inside the club, accompanied by Fats Waller on the music box. From the sound of it, the place is nearly empty.

I back up against the wall and motion for my father to open the door. We've already talked this through. He'll go in and plant himself on a stool at the bar. I'll wait a few seconds before following—as far as we know I'll start a riot just by stepping foot into the joint.

The champ walks in and shuts the door behind him. I linger in the hall, brushing the snow off my shoulders and hat.

A minute later, I step into the bar. It's underlit and nearly empty. My father is sitting on the same stool the ciggy-smoking flapper occupied the last time I was here. The place looks the same, right down to the tender—he's the one who poured Margaret and me our shine. He takes a glance in my direction but then turns away to clean a shaker. If he hasn't already begun praying that I've forgotten his face, he soon will.

The door to the back room is open and I recognize the rancid mattress on the floor. The thought of paying for pleasure in that hole nauseates me, especially now that I'm no longer intoxicated by the candied smell of a two-bit hooker's perfume. Just seeing that stained thing makes we want to apologize to the champ, who's ready to punch his fists raw at my say-so. I fight the impulse to leap across the bar and beat my brass knuckles into the tender's temples until he turns the calendar back and restores the simple life I had two weeks ago.

"Snowball," a voice calls out from one of the booths along the left wall. My eyes shimmy but I know that twinkling green eye and scarred right ear. It's Joseph Gazzara.

I cross the wooden floor as Fats Waller pours out of the music box. Most of the time Fats makes me want to dance, but right now that banging piano is scraping at my nerves. The music sounds as if it's getting louder with each chord, like Fats is pushing me to grab my revolver, shove it into Gazzara's mouth, and empty the chamber.

"Joseph Gazzara," I say, standing across from him, my breath short, hardly believing that I'm finally in front of the bastard. "Or should I call you Denny?"

He chuckles, his brown eye glimmering as brightly as his green one. He makes a move to stand up but I push him back into his seat.

"Sit down," I tell him.

Fats is still hammering away. He's relentless. And now it's not just the piano rattling me, a trumpet is screeching notes shrill enough to break glass.

"Fine," Gazzara says, shrugging his shoulders and motioning for me to take a seat opposite him.

"I'll stand," I say. My voice sounds as edgy as the ear-splitting shit coming from the music box. "And then I'll leave—right after I get the forty-eight hundred bucks you took for that sugar pop piss." That's not the whole truth. Even if I get the money, I've still got a score to settle for Tommy Sudnik.

He laughs me off. "You're funny," he says.

"Not tonight, I'm not."

"Well, you look funny, anyway."

With that, I yank out my gun push it under his chin. If I could, I'd ram it straight up into his skull.

"Listen, you two-eyed, fucked-up, devil-loving scumbag. There are people who'd pay me way more than forty-eight hundred to decorate that wall with your twisted brain."

Now Gazzara's eyes are wide—they're filled with the same panic that gushed through Tommy Sudnik's veins as he lay hog-tied in the basement of Saint Mark's bleeding from his jawbone.

The trumpet is fucking screaming and the rage seeping out of my palm is drenching the wooden handle of my revolver.

The tender calls out behind me. "Hey, pal," he shouts. "Let's calm down or I'm calling the cops."

"We're way past the cops," I say, keeping my eyes trained on Gazzara.

I know the tender doesn't have a prayer of reaching the phone. The champ grabs his striped shirt, pulls him over the bar like a sack of rusty hardware, and works him over as if he were an untethered dummy bag.

I pin Gazzara to the back of the booth with the muzzle of my gun and watch the champ pummel the tender with one left hook after another, knocking him across the room three feet at a time. It's a horrifying dance accompanied by Fats's incessant banging. Only now the record is skipping and that same trumpet note is shrieking over and over again.

I nod toward the champ and ask Gazzara if he wants a shot at the title.

"Laugh it up, wise guy," he says. I've got the gun pressed so hard under his chin, he's talking through clenched teeth. "You're a dead man if you pull that trigger."

"And if I don't? You'll only hack my legs off?"

"So go ahead and shoot, you blanched freak of nature."

This time I pull up on the gun so hard I practically lift him out of his seat. Still, I can't bring myself to squeeze the trigger.

The front door bursts open with Hector behind it. He races toward my father and grabs his left arm, pinning it behind his back. Now the tender is punching at my father with what little steam he's got left. I'm watching the champ throw haymakers with his right hand, but the punches are too limp to carry any weight.

A blinding pain suddenly shoots up my forearm. I wheel around to find Gazzara stabbing at it with the point of a blade. The sleeve of my shirt is soaked with blood and I'm losing feeling in my fingertips. My elbow feels like it's in the clenches of a rabid dog's teeth.

Hector pulls out a blackjack and pelts the champ across the back of his head, spilling him to the floor as if he were a bucket of mop water.

Johalis and Santi crash through the back entrance and head toward my father. Johalis swings at the tender and Santi jumps on Hector's back to pull him away from the champ. The music box is still blasting that one incessant chord and the horn is wailing that screechy note on top of it. Gazzara's cursing at me, calling me a stained nigger zero and sticking me in the arm with his knife. I picture Tommy Sudnik tied up, waiting to be sacrificed for God knows what. I remember Denny telling me not to touch his brother, and I hear Tommy's mother pleading for justice. My eyes are jumping and Fats is banging away on those same fucking piano keys.

I can't take it anymore. I grit my teeth and pull the trigger, the pain from my slashed forearm shoots up beyond my shoulder and into my ear. The gun goes off with a deafening bang and the back of Gazzara's head explodes like a smashed pumpkin, splattering brains, blood, flesh, hair, and bone across the back of the booth. He falls forward, blood pouring onto the table like spilled soup as his soul plummets to hell— or wherever in God's name it was heading—leaving nothing but the stench of gore and gunpowder in its wake.

The tender's fumbling with the chamber of a gun, trying to load it in his shaking hands. Hector's got a pistol trained on Santi and he's inching backward to the door, his slimy hair hanging over his forehead. He's going to shoot Santi when he reaches the doorway but I can take him down before he gets there. I raise my revolver and squeeze, but my finger is numb and slips off the trigger. I hear a gunshot but it's not coming from my piece. Santi gets hit above his left eye and slumps to the ground.

I yell out Santi's name and my voice sounds as if it's coming from the far side of a canyon. The tender has his pistol in his fist and he's raising it toward me. Grabbing my gun with my left hand, I shoot at the tender and Hector, leaving my right arm to dangle and drip blood onto the floor. I squeeze off all five shots left in the cylinder. The third one plugs the tender in the cheekbone. Two shots later, I nail Hector between the shoulder blades as he runs for the exit. They both fall instantly, dead before they kiss the floor.

I rush to the champ, who is still out cold from Hector's blackjack. Johalis is slapping his face, trying to revive him.

When the champ finally comes to, Johalis kicks into gear. He runs around the club using a handkerchief to wipe down any surfaces we might have touched.

I can't take the noise another second. I yank the plug and put Fats out of his misery. The joint turns as silent as a monastery. Now Johalis is behind the bar, he's got his ear to a small safe and he's working the lock with his blade.

My father looks around and surveys the carnage. "What happened?" he asks, his speech as thick as wet cement.

"We got to get outta here," Johalis says. The safe is open and he comes over to me with a roll of cash in his hand. He shoves it into my pocket and then wipes my prints off the music box.

"Santi?" my father says, crawling over to my young friend's broken body.

I want to explain, but instead of speaking, I vomit, splashing twenty-three years of rejection, crime, and sin onto an ashtray standing next to the doorway.

And while retching, I weep. Tears run down my face as I look at Santi, lying on the floor. He was too young to realize what a misfit he'd chosen to champion. I've killed three men. I've shot a man in the back. I've got a pocket full of blood money.

And now I've got to go the Hy-Hat and tell one of the few angels of Harlem that I've brought his only son to his death.

CHAPTER 14
1906

*W*alter made his way through the streets of Hoboken, trying his best to blend in with the men who were congregating on the street corners. He was grateful for the cover—he knew Albright wouldn't be happy when he got hold of the day's paper.

Walter's story had finally appeared in ink and it was hot news. Not only was the morning edition stacked up at corner newsstands, it could be found in every populated intersection of Newark, clenched in the extended fist of a screaming newsboy. Walter had made it—he'd landed in bold type on the front page of the *Evening-Star*. Better yet, the article brandished the byline, "Walter J. Wilkins," which meant that he'd finally graduated from the slapdash sports page.

Thanks to Louis Hoenig, Walter had remained a step ahead of Albright. He'd fleshed out his exposè on Richard Canfield in the protective refuge of the old supply room in Glenny's office, pecking away at his boss's Underwood typewriter, the one that rarely saw the light of day due to its sticky *Y* key. Walter worked for hours, imprisoned in the windowless room, surrounded by old newspapers, notebooks, carbon paper, and typewriter cartridges. He left the *Evening-Star* only to check important details with the records at city hall. And he'd dodged Albright, knowing his story would blow the lid off of the phony commission. Now, so many eyes would be on Albright, the crook would have to think twice before making Ernie his patsy. The only way Higgins would get the title would be to strap on his gloves and beat Ernie in the ring.

Walter strode down Grand Street, making his way past the boys loitering outside the public house and arriving at the cigar shop underneath Ernie Leo's room. He had the collar of his topcoat hiked up and a copy of the *Evening-Star* tucked under his arm. He realized Ernie couldn't read the paper, but he figured the boxer would enjoy hearing what it said.

Ernie sat on an iron bench in front of the shop; he filled out a maroon blazer and had a cigar poking out from between his lips. He puffed the stogie and carefully flicked its ashes into an empty bottle of pop that sat on the bench beside him, seemingly oblivious to the winter chill that had begun to set in throughout the Northeast.

"Ernie!" Walter shouted as he crossed the street.

When Ernie looked up, Walter's stomach tumbled. The right side of the champion's face looked as if it had gone ten rounds with a nightstick. He had a gash under his eye and the dark brown skin on his temple was puffy and tinged with purple.

"What the hell happened?" Walter asked, knowing full well.

Ernie puffed at his cigar. "I got in the ring with the wrong guys."

Hoenig had been right: Albright's boys wanted a rematch and they weren't going to take no for an answer.

"This was the Higgins gang, wasn't it?" Walter asked.

"I'm done talkin'," Ernie said.

"I'm on your side, Ernie." Walter meant it, even though he'd started this mess.

"I said I'm done talkin'."

"Then I'll talk. Albright's thugs showed up and they forced you to take a rematch."

Ernie didn't say a word but his glare told Walter he'd hit a nerve.

"I know it's true, Ernie," Walter said. "I've got the goods on these thugs."

"It doesn't matter," Ernie said. "They're never gonna get a rematch, not from me, not the one they want. You want to print somethin'? Print that."

"I already did, or close to it," Walter said, holding up the morning's headline, *Crooked Commission Linked to Canfield*. If Ernie could read, he surely would have appreciated seeing it in print. "This blows the lid off the whole thing."

"All that means is when they come back, they'll be lookin' for you, too."

Walter took a look at Ernie's temple. If that's what they'd do to a boxing champion, he could only imagine what they'd do to a newspaper reporter.

"So let's say they don't take no for an answer," Walter said. "What are you going to do?"

"Already doin' it," Ernie said, rolling the stogie between his puckered lips with his thumb and forefingers. "When they come, they come. But this time, I'll be ready."

Walter thought about reasoning with Ernie. Even a champ couldn't outfight a pack of armed men, and if the police got mixed up in it, they'd undoubtedly arrest the Negro. But Ernie had made a decision and Walter didn't bother trying to undo it. In fact, he admired Ernie for standing up against the bastards—and felt too responsible for Ernie's mess to let him do it alone.

He walked into the shop and bought himself a Tansill's Punch. Then he came back outside, dumped his copy of the *Evening-Star* into the wooden garbage receptacle, sat down next to Ernie, and lit up.

And that's where he stayed, puffing his Punch cigar, waiting with Ernie for Higgins's roughnecks to show up and demand a rematch.

⊰⊱

Saint James the Less Catholic Church was empty. Father Stafford sat with Dorothy in the front pew, mere feet in front of the altar. His face took on a greenish hue as it bathed in the glow of the stained glass mural that hovered over the tabernacle.

Stafford was a short, skinny man of about thirty; his black shirt hung loosely from his wide shoulders. He had light skin and small teeth, the bottom row stained from coffee. Powdery dandruff speckled the wiry hairs that sprung from his ears.

Meeting the priest alone in the church made Dorothy feel special, like she did when she was fourteen and her teacher, Miss Madigan, started lending her books after she'd made the honor roll.

"You haven't changed your mind, have you?" Stafford asked, his collar biting into his clean-shaven neck and leaving a series of looping red lines around his Adam's apple.

"No, I'm going through with it," Dorothy said.

She had been hoping for some other advice, but Father Stafford had echoed the feelings of Father Jennings: God would not allow her to rid herself of the child. Father Stafford also told her, in no uncertain terms, that it was a sin to carry a Negro man's seed inside of her. So by keeping the baby, she was sentencing herself to the lesser of two evils. She would live in holy disgrace for five more months instead of cleansing herself of the child and facing eternal damnation.

"And you've contacted the orphanage?" Father Stafford asked.

"Yes, I spoke with them. They're taking the baby."

This was the first lie Dorothy had ever told a priest, but handing her baby over to the Sisters of Charity would be the harshest punishment she could face—and she still wasn't sure she'd have the strength to do it.

"Good," Stafford said. "Only then will you have set yourself straight with God. Free the child to grow in the Lord's world. Your humiliation will be punishment enough for you. There's no reason to punish the child."

The air inside the church carried a hint of incense that lingered from a funeral that morning.

"Are you sure I shouldn't go see the child's father?" Dorothy asked. "Just to let him know?"

"Visiting hell is no way to rid yourself of the devil," Father Stafford said.

Like every priest Dorothy had ever known, Stafford couldn't help but sound as if he were giving a homily, even in a private conversation.

"Forget the Negro," he said. "Just worry about God."

When he said the word "God" he nodded toward one of the stained glass windows. The church had fourteen of them, each depicting a different station of the cross. Father Stafford had picked the fourth, the one in which Jesus meets his mother, Mary, and Dorothy started to cry.

"The punishment that comes with sin always breeds tears," Stafford said. "Let them flow. And let your child be what it will be." He patted his knobby knees and nodded his head, indicating to Dorothy, in his way, that she had to leave.

"Don't worry, Father. I'll follow God's way."

"I'm pleased to hear it," he said. "When in doubt, look to the Bible. That's where you'll find your answers."

Dorothy walked out of the church and sat on the front steps in the shadow of the steeple, weeping right out in the open on Aisquith Street. The Baltimore sun was succumbing to the chill of autumn, no longer strong enough to take the sting out of her tears.

⚜

Walter had never heard a lock get picked, but he knew the sound of metal on metal. He stood with Ernie inside the boxer's room; the lights were out and their eyes had become accustomed to the dark. He'd convinced Ernie to come upstairs, but now he questioned whether they'd be safer out on the street. He kept his eyes on the doorknob as he listened to the clinking sounds coming from the keyhole.

As the lock popped and the door inched open, Walter held his breath and clenched the fingers of his right hand around the heaviest weapon he'd been able to find: a cast iron frying pan. He wished he could handle himself as well as Ernie—and he wondered why he had ever gone after a front-pager when the sports section had treated him just fine.

The hinge squeaked as a figure crept into the room, shadowed by the silhouette of a thin, broad-shouldered man whose head was topped by a homburg. When the first figure passed the window, the light from the streetlamp hit his face—he had a large nose and tiny chin under a wide-brimmed felt hat. Walter recognized him as a roughneck named

Henry who had a scam going at Luna Park. The glint of a gun barrel twinkled in his hand.

Ernie didn't wait for a hello. He planted himself and drilled his left fist into Henry's gut. The roughneck doubled over, but quickly uncoiled and whacked Ernie below the ear with the butt end of his six-shooter. Ernie took three steps back before steadying his legs against his daybed. Then, while clutching his neck with his left hand, he raised his right fist, ready to brawl, even though he was one-armed, hobbled, and outmanned in the weapons department.

"Alright, calm down," the crook in the homburg said. Walter knew the voice. It belonged to Albright.

"Drop the gun and we'll go one-on-one," Ernie said to Henry.

The roughneck didn't move a muscle—he kept the weapon pointed straight at the boxer's bruised forehead.

"He's not dropping it, Ernie," Albright said, "So sit down. You too, Wilkins, I'll deal with you later."

Ernie stayed on his feet, but Walter leaned against the windowsill, a cool draft chilling the sweat that was running down his spine. He held the rusty skillet at his side with no intention of letting it fall.

Walking over to Ernie, Albright said, "We have a problem."

Walter heard his own heart beating so loudly he was surprised the others didn't notice.

Albright took off his homburg and ran his fingers along its rim. "We've put a considerable amount of money into Higgins," he said, "and you're going to help us make him a world champion."

"Higgins can't even win Jersey," Ernie said.

"Like I said, we have a problem. And we're not leaving here until we come up with a solution."

Walter couldn't take Albright's cat-and-mouse game any longer. "What's your deal, Albright? You gonna kill us like you killed Caroline Barker?"

It was a guess, the only thing Walter knew of Caroline Barker was that her name had been carved on the tombstone that had brought Albright to his knees.

Albright's eyes narrowed, but Walter couldn't enjoy the moment. Just then, Henry socked him square in the breadbasket, a blow so hard that Walter thought he would crap his pants. He dropped to his knees, the frying pan clanging on the floor beside him. Unable to catch his breath, he wrapped his arms around his midsection and panted through his nose. His eyes stung as he fought off the impulse to cry.

"Leave 'im alone," Ernie said. "You wanna go a round, go with me."

"The big nigger's going to fight for his master?" Henry said, mugging at Ernie, taunting him to take a swing.

"Shut your ignorant mouth," Albright barked at Henry and the mocking expression dropped from the goon's face.

Albright rested his homburg on the worn seat cushion of Ernie's armchair. "Ernie, one way or another, you're going to give Higgins the Jersey title. If Walter here had left things alone, then we'd all be going about our business. But now you've got the belt and we want it. You see our predicament?"

Walter lay on the floor, his knees pulled to his ribcage and his arms clamped around his shins. Henry had been right, he needed his big brother to take on the town bully. He wished he'd taken the job at H. Grant's and left the newspaper business to bolder men. Everybody involved would have been better off had he never written a word.

"I see your problem," Ernie said to Albright. "You need me to lose to your white boy."

"That white boy cost me a lot of money and he's going to become the champion."

"Good luck to you."

"We're willing to pay you for your services," Albright said.

Walter managed four words between short breaths. "Don't do it, Ernie."

Albright shook his head. "Wilkins, you really have to learn to keep your nose out of my business."

Henry picked up Walter by the lapels of his sack coat and flung him against the wall, then pounded him with a relentless combination of rights and lefts to the body and head. Walter was as helpless as a marionette—he held his forearms in front of his face and squeezed his eyes shut. He felt as if he were tumbling down a mountain, rolling over rock-hard boulders.

Ernie grabbed Henry's shoulder and spun him around. "I said deal with me."

He tucked his head into his chest and charged at Henry, throwing hooks and haymakers. Henry wrapped his arms around Ernie's head and the two grappled like kids in a schoolyard, kicking over an ashtray and tumbling on top of the side table, sending it in splinters across the room. Walter's right eye was swelling so quickly he felt as if he were looking through a keyhole, but he could still see Albright pull a .38 from the pocket of his topcoat and aim it at Ernie, who had Henry's shoulders pinned to the floor with his knees.

"Get off him, Ernie," Albright said.

Ernie stood up, but not before slapping Henry across the face, an open-palmed smack that let out the spanking noise of flesh on flesh when it hit the roughneck's cheek.

Albright pressed the barrel of his gun up against Ernie's ear. "You may be strong," he said. "But you're stupid."

"If anybody here is stupid, it's you. I already told the commission they can have the belt, so long as I keep the prize money. You're tryin' to fix a fight with the champ, and I ain't the champ no more."

Walter couldn't believe what he was hearing. He could only guess that Ernie had given up the belt because it hadn't brought him anything but misery.

"That may be the smartest thing you've ever done," Albright said. "Although you could've saved us all a lot of trouble by letting us know sooner."

"How do we know he won't change his mind?" Henry asked, obviously itching to go at Ernie one more time.

"We have a deal then?" Albright asked Ernie.

"It's no deal. It's just the way it is."

"Then I owe you one," Albright said, putting his pistol back in his pocket. "You stay out of the way and I won't forget to repay you."

"You don't have to repay me nothin', because I ain't doin' it for you."

"Just the same," Albright said. "Come see me if you ever need a favor."

He picked up his homburg and nodded to Henry. The two walked out of the room and Ernie locked the door behind them, as if that would stop them from returning.

Walter's eye was swollen shut and blood trickled down his throat. His knee throbbed and he felt as if a cold, steel knife had slit open his gut. But just when he thought he wouldn't have the strength to walk out of Ernie's room, he looked out the window through his bleary left eye and remembered why he needed to get back to his typewriter. There, underneath the streetlamp in front of the cigar shop, a newspaper boy was hawking the *Evening-Star*.

CHAPTER 15
1930

I'm sitting with Old Man Santiago in my booth at the Hy-Hat, the tall one by the back window, telling him that his son is dead.

I got here fifteen minutes ago—I let myself in with the spare key behind the iron lamp and then double-locked the door to be sure I was safe. I found Old Man Santiago in the kitchen; the top of his balding head was glazed with a coat of sweat as he made sandwiches for tonight's Christmas party. When he looked up, a smile crossed his face and he wished me a Merry Christmas. Now he's staring out the window, his nostrils quivering and the dark, olive skin of his face drooping, almost as if it were buckling under the weight of the news.

I can't spill the straight facts onto the one man who has always opened his arms to Harlem's teenagers, so I spew a story about Santi defending Tommy Sudnik. He doesn't need to hear that his son died protecting a hopeless misfit.

He covers his watery eyes with his hands. I want to hug him, but my forearm is wrapped in thick, stiff gauze and bound in a blue and white cloth sling. Doc Anders cleaned me up at two in the morning, stitching up the three stab wounds left by the steel blade of Joseph Gazzara's knife. According to the doc, the muscle in my forearm was punctured down to the bone.

Old Man Santiago speaks but his voice is raspy. "His mother," he says.

I tell him I don't understand.

"We have to tell his mother."

"Okay, we'll tell her," I say. I've only met Santi's mother once, when Santi and I swung by his family's apartment to pick up his chess set and bring it to the Pour House. She barely spoke English and I didn't do much better in Spanish, but her face beamed when Santi introduced me as his boss. I'm ashamed that a much different memory is about to replace that one.

Old Man Santiago stares straight ahead as if there's a movie playing twelve inches in front of his face and he's afraid to miss a scene.

"Mr. Santiago?" I say.

His gaze is unmoving. "He never was a fighter," he says into the empty air.

"He wasn't looking for a fight," I say. "He stood up for a kid who had nobody protecting him."

Old Man Santiago breaks down, bawling into his hands, and I go to the kitchen to get him some water. I'll stick around as long as he needs me. The old man wouldn't leave me in the lurch and I'm not about to do it to him. Besides, I'm safe here. Johalis is down in Philly sorting things out as best he can. I'll stay with Old Man Santiago, and at some point later today, I'll go to the Pour House and hand Jimmy the blood money from Gazzara's safe. That'll settle our score and allow me to cross one mobster off my list.

On my way to the sink I hear the front door open. Very few people have the key, so I duck behind the arch that separates the back area from the game room and poke my head out. It's Pearl. A brown hat sits atop her tiny ears and a long black overcoat is draped over her full figure. She's weeping and a shiny stream of mucous is leaking out of her nose. I'm tempted to tell her to stay out of my sight until she can keep her tongue off of other guys' necks, but I swallow the urge. I step into the game room.

"Your father told me what happened," she says between sobs. "Thank the Lord you're okay."

She walks over and hugs me, sandwiching my wrapped right arm between us. Then she says into my ear, "I'm sorry."

Sorry for what? Sorry that I had to send a bullet through a man's skull to stay alive? Sorry that she led me on and then dropped me like yesterday's racing form? Sorry that she can't bring herself to fall in love with a zebra-nigger-lackey-coon?

Every cell in my battered brain is screaming at me to turn away, but I can't. As of this moment she's the only person in my life who isn't stained with blood.

"Santi's dead," I tell her. "So's Gazzara and so's Hector." I leave out the bartender because she doesn't know him, and I don't want to get into the whole story, especially the part about the bargain-basement hooker.

"I know," she says, her weighty top lip shaking. "Your father told me how you rescued that young boy."

Knowing my father, he stopped at Pearl's place this morning, a white bandage plastered across the back of his head, and told her I was a hero. He wanted to help, but it's too late for me and Pearl.

"He also told me you saved his life," Pearl says.

I'd love to take credit for saving the champ, but he wouldn't have even been in the cellar club if it weren't for me.

"I think it was the other way around," I say.

"How's your arm?" she asks.

It feels good that she's asking.

"I'll be okay," I say, rubbing my bandages with my left hand. "I owe the doc one. He cleaned us up, no cops, no hospitals, no paperwork."

I try pouring a glass of water for Old Man Santiago with one arm but Pearl has to do it for me. When we get back to the booth, the old man is just the way I left him—he's got his face in his folded arms, sobbing.

"I've got to tell my wife," he says again. He gets up and walks through the game room, wobbling from side to side, like a ginned-up rummy after a night at the Pour House. I walk him to the door, and when Pearl's not looking I reach into my pocket and pull out the blood money Johalis had earmarked for Jimmy. I put it where it belongs.

"Here," I say to him, slipping the wad into his hand. "You need it more than I do."

He nods and takes it. He'll pull that money out of his pocket in a day or two and not even know where it came from.

He leaves and I lock the door behind him—he'll never be back now that Santi is gone. I don't care that I've got nothing to hand Jimmy now. I couldn't live with myself if I didn't give the old man the dough to bury his own son.

I walk over to Pearl and she asks me what I said to Old Man Santiago.

"I gave him a couple of bucks," I say, knowing I'm screwed. Now I've got to face Jimmy with nothing. I might as well have put a gun in my mouth. Luckily, I'm getting used to the taste of metal.

⚜

Johalis swigs a shot of bourbon. We're sitting in cabin 11 at Gwendolyn's Cozy Cottages off Route 27 in New Jersey. Outside, a blue and brown sign says we're in a roadside family hotel, but it's nothing more than a handful of log cabins blanketed by a foot of snow and surrounded by frosted oak trees. The place should be called the Getaway because nobody would consider coming here unless they were running from something. The regulars seem to be truckers and hookers, and now they can add to their register a one-armed albino hiding from a stuttering bootlegger and his roster of crooked cops.

Our cabin feels no bigger than a telephone booth and looks like a cross between a cheap hotel and an abandoned ski lodge. The air smells like damp cedar and the brown carpet stinks of stale whiskey. The smoke from Johalis's Lucky Strike isn't helping.

"Right now every cop in Philly is out for our hides," Johalis is saying, sitting on the edge of the bed. "The clean cops are doing their jobs and the dirty ones are hunting us for Denny Gazzara. Either way, we're cooked."

I'm slumped in a tattered armchair across from Johalis, my bandaged right arm resting helplessly in my lap. My father is next to me, sitting on a worn orange couch.

"I'm only concerned 'bout the clean cops," my father says, no doubt wishing he could wash the blood from his hands and the guilt from his soul.

"Squaring it with the clean ones is easy," Johalis says. "It's not like they weren't after Joseph Gazzara, too. I got some news on that creep."

He's holding a flask of whiskey and a Lucky in his right hand, the cigarette wedged between his first two fingers.

"Joseph Gazzara could've cared less about the devil—he was nothing but a two-bit thief. He worked the docks, lifting entire containers of Cuban sugar cane. He even went to Cuba and set up bogus shipments, so nobody ever knew the sugar was missing. At some point, when he was down there, he ran into a witch doctor with connections. He cut a deal to ship albino bones to Cuba for sugar, tobacco, rum, whatever he could get. He got a Santerian sicko up here—Hector—to do his dirty work, and he probably made some big bucks for a while. To him, it was nothing but another grift. But to the people in Philly, it was a lot more than that. Every albino in the city owes you one."

He tips his flask toward me, takes a healthy sip, and smacks his lips together as he swallows.

My father says the bastard had it coming, but I'm too nauseated to speak. I'm picturing my legs, hacked in half and packed in ice on a ship bound for Cuba. I grab the flask from Johalis with my left hand and down a double shot to settle my stomach. The image I've got in my mind is so gruesome I practically gargle with the liquor before swallowing it.

"So all we gotta do is find a squeaky clean cop," my father says.

I appreciate the champ's morals, but he's dreaming if he thinks we can walk away from three bodies.

"I'm not telling the cops that I murdered Denny Gazzara's brother," I say.

Johalis nods. "You're right, you don't know who to trust. We'll worry about the cops after we settle up with Gazzara."

"And that's an even bigger problem than you think," I tell him. "You two weren't at that tree farm."

"Don't matter," my father says. "We gotta sit down with Gazzara and let him know it was self-defense."

He shrugs as if there's no other solution, but his plan's got more holes in it than a watering can. One of them is too big to ignore.

"Denny Gazzara's not the talking type," I say, my voice getting louder. "What do we do when he pulls out his machine gun?"

Nobody says it, but we all know the answer is that we'd have to pull one first.

"We won't walk out alive," I say. "He's got too many triggermen."

"What about McCullough?" my father says. "He's got his money now. Maybe he'll take care of Denny for you. Let the two thugs fight it out."

I can't tell the champ or Johalis that I gave the money to Old Man Santiago.

"Jimmy could make things a lot worse than they are now," I say. "If he goes at Gazzara and misses, Gazzara will be on us twice as bad."

"Then we've got to sit down with Gazzara when his boys aren't around," Johalis says.

"Man to man," the champ says again, nodding in agreement. "No triggermen."

I get up and crank the window with my left hand to let in some fresh air and common sense. The snow is coming down again, and with it comes the germ of an idea. Tomorrow is December 22, a busy day, I'd imagine, at a Christmas tree farm. If it keeps snowing this heavily, we might have a shot at crossing the farm and reaching Gazzara's cabin without being seen by Frank or any of Denny's other triggermen. That would put us face to face with Gazzara, minus the bullets.

And if that happens, then maybe I can spend Christmas in Harlem, helping Old Man Santiago stumble his way through the holidays.

⚬⚬⚬

The Auburn slips and slides as we inch through the blanket of snow building up on Route 27. Inside the car, the only sounds are the howl of the wind, the squeak of the wipers, and the grunts coming out of the champ's mouth as he wrestles with the steering wheel.

To our right the frosty peaks of spruces and firs reach for the blue, snow-filled sky. If I didn't know I was staring at a camouflaged barrel-house, I might think the blizzard belonged on a holiday postcard.

"The shop is around this bend," I say as we ride alongside the tree farm. "The cabin is up ahead."

We're figuring Gazzara's boys will be holed up in the store until the snowstorm lets up, so we don't shoulder the car until we're about a quarter-mile past the shop and much closer to the cabin. Johalis runs through the plan, which takes all of ten seconds. He and I will make our way to the front of the cabin. We'll knock and hope Denny answers. The champ will go around back just in case any loose gunmen think about throwing us a surprise party.

I've got my revolver holstered on my right shoulder since I'm now forced to shoot with my left hand. I'm also carrying my brass knuckles in the left pocket of my overcoat. I tug my hat low, wrap my scarf around my mouth, pull on my leather gloves, and, to take the edge off the blinding snow, slip on my dark glasses. I step out of the car and my right foot sinks into a knee-high drift; an icy frost seeps down my boot and bites at my calf and ankle. The flakes whip my face—I feel as if a plague of chilled thumbtacks is pricking my cheeks. I pull my scarf up to my eyes and lead Johalis and my father through the rows of Christmas trees, each a powdery pyramid extending three feet over our heads.

The cabin was tough to find on a clear day and it's doubly hard in a whiteout. I stop to get my bearings. It can't be more than a hundred yards away—I'm just not sure which hundred.

Tapping me on the shoulder, Johalis points over his head and to our right. A trail of smoke is spiraling toward the sky. There must be a chimney below.

"Okay," I tell him, and then turn to my father. "Champ, you're around back."

My father lumbers forward—he'll keep going until he spots the cabin and then he'll circle around to its rear entrance. Johalis and I need to head toward the front. We squeeze between the trees, their frozen branches banging at our knees as we move to our right. We make it through the third row when a mound of snow slides off a spruce and pelts my face. As I shake it off, I hear voices. I motion to Johalis that I've found the cabin. We stop in our tracks and crouch behind a tree.

The steady hum of the swirling wind is broken by the sharp *rat-a-tat* of a machine gun. It's coming from the cabin and must be targeting my father because it's not shooting at us. I crawl forward, my body slithering in the snow with my slinged arm beneath me. I'm trying to spot the triggerman, but I can't see shit with these damned glasses on. Johalis pulls out his pistol, gets down on one knee and aims up at the roof of the cabin. He squeezes off two shots but the patter of machine gun bullets continues.

I hear hurried footsteps crunching in the snow—my father's two rows to our left and running back to us. The triggerman isn't letting up—he's spraying a row of trees as if he's throwing down metal grass seed. Bullets are ricocheting off stones and ripping chunks off spruce trunks.

The champ cries out in pain and I hear him hit the ground. I bolt to my left, stumbling through the manmade forest, not caring that branches are ripping through my clothes and flesh. Johalis shoots at the cabin but he's no match for that Tommy gun. I toss the fucking sunglasses so I can get a good look at my father.

The champ's lying on his back, moaning. He's clutching his left thigh with gloved hands that are doused in blood. A deep red circle stains the snow under his leg. The machine gun is still spitting bullets but now it's targeting Johalis.

Yanking off my sling, I grab the champ under his shoulders, and pull him toward a tree. A stabbing pang erupts in my right forearm and I can feel the stitches popping under the white gauze. I drop the champ, grit my teeth, reach down, and yank him again. This time my arm feels like it's exploding, as if a knife is slicing its way past my jaw and up into my right eye. I get the champ under a tree and drop him there.

"You okay?" I say, pulling his collar up to keep his head warm.

"I'll live," he says, but not with any conviction.

Johalis crawls on his belly to reach us. "I don't think they can see us if we stay low."

He reaches into my father's pocket and pulls out the keys to the Auburn. "I'll get the car," he says. Then he asks me, "Can you carry him to the road?"

"Yep," I say, my teeth chattering. I pull the glove off my left hand and grab my revolver. "Go, go, go."

Johalis makes a run for it and I take a couple of shots at the cabin to cover him. It's little help. The triggerman starts up again, showering the trees around Johalis with bullets.

I help the champ up and drape his arm over my right shoulder, keeping my left hand free to shoot. We run as best we can with only three good legs and arms between us.

The machine gun is on us and it's got company—now two of them are firing. They're each shooting in quick bursts and sound like dueling typewriters. We're being bombarded. Shards of bark and splintered wood fly off the trees and hit me in the neck and mouth.

I spot a car's headlights pulling onto the shoulder of the road. It's Johalis in the Auburn. We can't be more than thirty yards away and he's throwing the passenger door open for us. My father is leaning on me as we jostle our way through a row of trees. The triggermen keep shooting and I'm wondering if they'll ever run out of bullets.

A burst of pain rips through my right shoulder and I feel as if a gasoline bomb went off inside of my chest. I fall face-first into a snow-drift—my gun flies out of my hand and the champ lands ten feet away from me.

"Jersey!" he rasps. He scrambles toward me, his left leg dragging behind him like a tail. His round eyes are bulging under his fedora and his meaty lower lip is shivering. He's panicking, scanning my legs and arms to see how many times I've been hit.

"I'm okay," I tell him. "Get to the car, I'll follow you."

"You ain't okay, you're bleedin' right through your coat." He points at my left hand, which is clutching the exit wound below my neck.

"Can you walk?" he asks me.

"I think so," I say, getting to my feet. I feel woozy.

He hobbles a couple of steps toward the road and picks up my revolver. Then he leans back against a tree, the snow from its upper boughs raining down on his head like confetti, and he fires in the direction of the cabin.

"Go!" he yells to me.

I don't want to leave him but I know he won't listen to me. I run to the Auburn, the pain radiating to my forehead every time my right foot hits the ground. Johalis has the driver's door open—he's using the car as a shield and is shooting toward the cabin. I fall into the back seat, clenching the hole in my shoulder.

My father comes hobbling after me.

Johalis squeezes off a few final shots as the champ drops himself into the front seat and swings his leg into the car. Johalis gets behind the wheel and makes a U-turn away from the cabin. As we gain ground, the clacking of the gunfire peters out, but we've still got to pass the store.

Just as we're rolling by it, I inch my head to the window and see Frank and Freddy running out the front door, each holding a machine gun. They pepper the Auburn with metal—the hailstorm hitting the back of the car sounds like a blizzard of nickels pelting a trashcan. The rear windshield shatters in two places and I hear a taillight explode. I roll myself down under the rear seat as Johalis keeps driving. My father's down low in the front; he must be trying to cover the hole in his thigh with his hands because he's cursing that he can't stop the bleeding. I'm clutching my right shoulder, which feels like it just lost a bar fight to Hector's cleaver. Eventually, the machine gun patter fades in the distance.

"Can you make it to the doc's?" I ask my father from behind the seat.

"Yeah," he grunts out. "Can you?"

My vision is blurring, I'm seeing two of everything. "Don't think so," I say. "Maybe he'll meet us at the cabin."

No longer caring where I bleed, I lay my head down on the seat and close my eyes. A year ago today, December 22, 1929, I laughed my way into the holidays. Now, I'll be using the time to eulogize the people I've lost. Assuming I'm not one of them.

⚜

I'm looking up at Doc Anders. His horn-rims sit low on his nose as he clucks his tongue and tapes up my chest and shoulder. I recognize the water-stained tiles on the ceiling behind him and the brown cloth shade on the lamp next to me. We're back in cabin 11 at the Cozy Cottages, but I don't remember getting here.

Johalis is peering at me from behind the doc's shoulder.

"Welcome back," he says.

I'm groggy and I've got to piss. "What time is it?"

My words drag, I sound like I'm sloshed on moon. I've got a pounding headache—my right temple feels as if it's getting slammed by the butt end of a shotgun.

My father answers from the couch. "Tuesday, seven in the morning." He's out of my line of vision, but I remember how badly his leg was bleeding.

"Is he okay?" I ask the doc. I have to space my words to get them out clearly.

"The bullet lodged next to his kneecap," the doc says. "The one that hit you nearly pierced the upper lobe of your right lung. You're two lucky sons of bitches."

I don't feel lucky, but I don't tell him that.

He rips a six-inch piece of tape off of his roll and presses it over the bandage on my shoulder. Then he wipes the sweat off his forehead with his wrist and palms back the side of his frizzy white hair. "I hope you know what you're doing."

Again I ignore him. It's clear I have no idea what I'm doing.

"Santi's funeral," I say.

Old Man Santiago told me he'd be skipping the wake and burying

Santi today because he couldn't bear to have the funeral on Christmas Eve. If I'm to pay my respects, I need to do it this morning. The services are scheduled at Trinity Church Cemetery at nine. That gives me two hours.

"You can't go," Johalis says. "It's too dangerous, Denny Gazzara is sure to be waiting there."

The doc nods. "You shouldn't get out of bed the next few days," he says. "And that's optimistic."

I picture Pearl at Old Man Santiago's side, helping him stay on his feet as they throw dirt onto Santi's coffin. Then I picture a pair of machine guns behind her.

"I'm going," I say. The second I raise my head off the pillow, a wave of nausea charges up my throat and I fall back onto the bed.

"Hero," the doc mutters.

My father shouts out from the couch but I'm too woozy to move my head to look at him. "I'm comin' with you," he says.

"We'll stay out of sight," I tell Johalis, my head pinned to the pillow.

"You're a goddamned albino with a bullet hole in your shoulder," Johalis says. "You can't stay out of sight." He fumbles for his cigarettes and calms down after lighting one.

He has a point—I don't have a face for undercover work. But I do know the cemetery. It's in a valley east of Riverside Drive. I used to pick up shipments of moon from Jimmy's truckers behind the mausoleum. If we stay to the west of the graveyard, we could watch the funeral from the edge of the roadway.

"I'm going anyway," I say. "We'll stay on the hill. If things get hairy, we'll be out of there in seconds."

"Goddamn it," Johalis says, his lips curling downward. "I can't let the two of you go alone."

I can tell he wishes he never got sucked into this mess, but I guess he's going to see this through until it ends, one way or the other. I give him credit for living up to his word. He's more like the champ than I thought.

"We won't even get out of the car," my father says, before letting out a yelp of pain. He must have tried to move his leg.

The doc looks at my father and then at me. He doesn't say anything, but by the way he's muttering under his breath, it's obvious that he doesn't like where this is heading.

—❧—

An hour later, I'm in the Auburn with my father and Johalis. We're on the hill above Riverside Drive, looking down on Santi's funeral. An elderly priest in his all-black getup is delivering a sermon to a small crowd gathered in front of an open grave. I can see a wooden coffin resting on a metal stand and long-stem red roses lying on its lid. Pearl is exactly where I'd pictured her: standing behind Old Man Santiago and his wife. I've never seen the old man in a suit, but he's in a black one today. His gray overcoat is unbuttoned and he seems oblivious to the cold that's needling my skin. His wife is draped in black with a dark blue hat.

I can't hear the priest, so I get out of the car, leaving Johalis behind the wheel and my father in the front passenger seat. Grabbing the branches of a frozen bush with my left hand, I make my way around the car to get a better vantage point. My boots slip on the snow and I land in a frozen drift at the trunk of an oak about twelve feet from the Auburn. My overcoat is barely protecting my rump from the chill of the frosty ground and the white landscape is stinging my eyes. My shoulder feels as if the doc stitched me up with a knitting needle.

The priest circles the coffin and shakes a tin canister of incense. I still can't pick up any voices, but the clinking metal of the incense chain echoes all the way up the hill as it rings its final goodbyes to Santi.

I spot a light blue necktie and a head of shiny, waxed hair behind Pearl. It's Jimmy. He's standing next to Diego, holding his white hat in his hands and looking around as if he's admiring the scenery. I know better. Jimmy's not stupid; he figures I'm here somewhere. I'm hoping the tree is camouflaging me and making me look like some kind of yellow-haired weed, but Jimmy keeps on gawking. Then he fixes his stare in my direction and our eyes lock. He's onto me for sure. I'm ready to crawl back into the Auburn, but Jimmy doesn't react. He turns and looks back to the priest. This is why I was able to work for Jimmy: he may be a crook but he respects the few people he cares about—and he loved Santi. We've got a truce until after the burial.

A black Nash glides to the gravesite from the east side of the cemetery. It comes up the main drag and then loops around the mausoleum. I can see it's Gazzara's boys, Frank and Freddy, and my guess is they've got a couple of machine guns with them. They must want me pretty bad if they've driven all the way up here. They get out of the car and circle the mourners, no doubt looking for the yellowy-green eyes of a zebra-nigger-lackey-coon, but finding, instead, the murderous glare of Jimmy McCullough.

"Uh oh," Johalis says, leaning out of the car window.

"They got some nerve," my father says from the passenger seat. He's right, but he doesn't realize that Jimmy will handle this for us. Jimmy's got more venom than the three of us put together. I just hope things don't get so far out of hand that Old Man Santiago can't put his son to rest without a torrent of bullets raining down on his family.

Jimmy walks with Gazzara's boys to the back of the Nash. Diego follows them, unbuttoning his overcoat. When they're a good distance from the priest, Jimmy starts barking, his cheeks turning crimson as he pokes his finger in Frank's face. I have no idea what he's saying, but I'll bet it involves their lives and the speed with which Jimmy will take them. Jimmy opens the door of the Nash and pushes Frank in, slamming the door shut and nearly clipping Frank's ankle in the process. Freddy gets behind the wheel and drives off, back toward the mausoleum. I can't deny that I'm delighted to see Jimmy throw his weight around. If I weren't in his doghouse, I'd pour him a shot of moon the minute I started my next shift.

He walks back to the gravesite, looks up toward me, and nods. The heat is off for now. I've got the day to grieve for Santi. It's not much, but I'll take it.

The Nash is in the shadow of the mausoleum when its brake lights shine. It makes a U-turn, drives around the site and climbs the tree-lined service road that curves like a coiled snake. Gazzara's goons must have spotted me because they're headed our way. And even Jimmy can't stop them now.

I get up in a hurry and scramble to the Auburn. The snow feels greased beneath my boots and my right foot slips beneath me. I stick out my bandaged arm to break my fall but I slam the ground with my right shoulder. I feel as if I've landed on a live grenade.

"Jesus," Johalis says.

He jumps out of the Auburn, plods through the snowy embankment, grabs my left arm and helps me to my feet. The Nash continues up the hill as we get back in the car. I collapse into the rear seat, clutching the stitched hole in my shoulder, and Johalis takes off down Riverside Drive.

By the time I look out the back window we're a half mile south of the cemetery. The Nash is on us and we're about as hard to spot as a white face on 125th Street. Not only is our taillight shattered, the trunk is branded with eleven fresh bullet holes.

Frank leans out the passenger window of the Nash, a machine gun in his arms, and opens a round. The patter of gunfire rips through the air and is echoed by the ping of bullets striking the back of the car.

"Son of a bitch!" my father barks.

I reach for my gun, but before I can get it out of the holster, Johalis is rolling down his window and shouting for us to hold on. I grab the back of the driver's seat as he slams on the brakes and makes a U-turn, the Auburn's tires skidding in the snow and the engine whining under the stress. Then he pounds his boot back onto the accelerator. We're speeding directly at the Nash.

"Grab the wheel," Johalis yells at my father and pulls his pistol from the sun visor.

The champ starts to protest but he stops in midsentence with his mouth hanging open.

"Grab it!" Johalis yells.

Trying his best not to put any weight on his ravaged leg, my father holds the wheel and steers the car from the passenger seat. We're still aiming at the Nash, but now we're teetering from side to side.

Johalis's boot is pinned to the accelerator when he reaches out the window and squeezes off six shots, four of which hit the Nash's windshield. The Nash goes in a tailspin and winds up in a frozen snow bank on the east side of Riverside Drive. We race past the dead car, quickly passing the puffs of black exhaust that pour out of it.

"This is gonna end once and for all," the champ says, more to himself than to me. "I got one move and I'm gonna take it."

Johalis doesn't say anything and I don't either. We just let the champ grumble. As we loop around and speed toward the Cozy Cottages on the other side of the river, I wonder if the champ actually has a plan. If he does, it better call for hitting Denny Gazzara with some serious muscle, because at this point—what with the champ's leg plugged and my shoulder torn up—I don't have any choice other than to jam my revolver into Gazzara's stuttering mouth and blow his brains to the sugar pop fucking moon.

CHAPTER 16

1907

*S*unlight streamed through the *Evening-Star*'s office windows as Walter dug out his file on Barry Higgins. Now that he was rid of sports, he was more than happy to hand off his notes to Crager.

"You think the Higgins–Spurlock fight is dirty?" Crager asked as he took the stack of notebooks.

Walter didn't need to be working the bout to know it reeked. Once Ernie had given up the title, the commission had handed the belt to Higgins, telling him, in an effort to save its own face, that he had to defend it against a Negro, Jack J. Spurlock. Yet Albright had already booked Higgins to fight Tommy Burns for the world heavyweight championship in two months. Spurlock didn't stand a chance.

"Albright wants to get at Burns for the world title," Walter said, sipping his second cup of coffee. "He's not going to let fair play get in his way."

Crager walked back to his desk, opened the first notebook, and pinched his lips as he studied Walter's scribbles. Looking at Crager, you'd think sports suddenly got important because he was on the job.

"Nothing here seems too bad," Crager said, scratching the stubble under his chin.

"Keep reading," Walter said, rolling up his shirtsleeves and going back to his research. *And pray you don't cross Albright or you'll wind up spending a month at the dentist's office, like I did.*

"Wilkins!" Glenny called from his office.

Glenny probably wanted an update on Walter's latest story, but Walter had little to share. He was working off a tip from an old high school chum, Jimmy Farley, who said the 107th Street mob was behind the body found earlier that week in Newark Bay. Walter was getting closer—he could sniff it—but he hadn't yet found anybody who'd talk.

"Wilkins!" Glenny shouted again.

Walter shot down his last inch of coffee and scooted past the other reporters to Glenny's office. Poking his head inside, he found his boss in his usual pose: seated in his high-back chair, reading through a pile of newspapers, and waiting to yell at someone. His wireframe spectacles rested on the bump of his pointed nose.

"Sit down," Glenny said, nodding toward the pillowy armchair in front of his desk. The chair was covered by the day's proofs, so Walter dropped the ink-stained sheets to the floor and took a seat.

Glenny straightened his desk, first arranging his pens and then stacking a pile of loose carbon papers.

"Boss, I'm still chasing leads on the floater," Walter said. "I'll have something soon."

As Glenny shuffled through his desk drawer, Walter knew something was wrong. Nothing bothered his boss more than one of his reporters coming up empty, but Glenny's typical barrage of curses never came. Walter would have to wait this out, but the clock was ticking. He checked his timepiece; he had fifty minutes to get to the station and meet up with Farley.

"Listen," Glenny said. "The paper's in trouble. Circulation is down. So is advertising."

Horseshit. The paper was doing better than ever, thanks in no small part to Walter, whose front-pagers were keeping the newsboys busy. It certainly wasn't due to Crager.

"I've got to, umm, let some people go," Glenny said, yanking at his collar as if it had suddenly become a size too small.

Walter got the message. He was fired. He should have seen it coming. His piece on Canfield had knocked the *Evening-Star* on its ear. The publisher had had no choice but to pull Werts off the commission—so the slippery reptilian bastard had probably exacted his revenge and taken Walter down with him.

"You're a good newspaperman," Glenny said. "But you've got to learn to handle the politics."

Walter didn't stick around to hear the rest. He got up and walked out of Glenny's office, leaving his boss talking to an empty armchair. He had believed in Glenny, especially once the editor had gone ahead with the piece on the commission. Walter couldn't sit there and watch the man stumble over his words, trying to come up with an excuse that would make sense. He walked past the bullpen to his desk, grabbed his jacket, his derby, and his notes on the Newark Bay floater. Then he left the building, a newspaperman in search of a newspaper.

❧

Ernie had been pushing Dorothy out of his mind since she'd left his dressing room ten months ago. If she'd shown that she had any feelings for him, he would have fought off a lynch mob to be with her. But he was finally coming to see what had been obvious all along: Dorothy couldn't handle the heat that the world was capable of dishing out. So when he walked out of the Grand Street cigar shop at closing time on a summery evening in May, the last person he expected to see was Dorothy.

"Ernie!" she called out through a wide smile.

Ernie's face turned hot when he saw how her milky skin still glowed; she was a stark contrast to the sweaty Hoboken street vendors who were grooming their horses behind her.

"Dorothy!" he shouted back, thankful that he was wearing a pressed suit and freshly shined shoes. He sucked in his gut and pulled back his shoulders, the same way he did at weigh-ins and photo shoots.

As Dorothy came closer, Ernie could see that her dark eyes lacked the confident shine they'd had back in Camden. She was carrying a blanketed bundle and lifted it; a baby peeked its white head out from the thin cloth, its cheeks as round and dimpled as Dorothy's. Ernie had a million questions but thought better about asking any of them.

"I've been busy," she said, nodding her head toward her baby, who was now drooling onto Dorothy's stiff, lacy collar.

Ernie struggled with a surge of jealousy that somebody on earth was smart enough—and white enough—to build the life he wanted. "Yours?"

She nodded. "His name is Jersey." With that, she handed the kicking bundle to Ernie who cradled it in his left arm, letting his broad round bicep serve as a pillow.

"Why Jersey?" he asked, moving the cloth off of the child's forehead to get a good look at the tiny boy. The baby was as white as the cotton that cocooned him. His eyes were light blue and a handful of platinum hairs sprouted out of his head.

"I named him after his father, in a way," she said.

Ernie's throat turned as dry as leather. She must be lying, or mistaken. This boy was whiter than any mulatto he'd ever seen. Against Ernie's fingers, his face was a cube of sugar floating in a cup of black coffee. Then Ernie remembered his own grandmother, an albino who'd been ghostly white since the day she was born.

The baby looked up at him and gurgled. Ernie knew the infant was too little to recognize who was holding him, but he tried to convince himself otherwise. In a flash, he fantasized about raising the boy, keeping him safe, and giving him the kind of life he himself never knew.

"He's good lookin'," Ernie said, his eyes stinging as they welled up under his lids. He looked at Dorothy—her beauty, her character, his Achilles' heel.

"Why'd you bring him here?" he asked.

"I'm not sure," Dorothy said as teardrops formed in the corners of her dark eyes. "I'll have him baptized. A priest I know has made arrangements for me to give him to the Sisters of Charity."

"Don't I get a say?" Ernie asked. He wasn't sure what he would add but he knew he didn't want his kid taken away from him just yet.

Dorothy didn't answer, at least not verbally. She just bit her bottom lip and shook her head, clearly too choked up to form words.

"Why let me see what I can't have again?"

Ernie's bitterness stained his words. He fought the urge to run off with the newborn—the beautiful, gurgling, freakish boy—and hide him away from Dorothy and the rest of the world forever. Instead, he gave his child back to Dorothy, even though his arms nearly betrayed him and pulled the baby back to his chest.

Dorothy took Jersey and cradled him against her breast. Over her shoulder, the sun dropped behind the row houses that lined Grand Street, leaving the littered cobblestone road in shadow.

"I'm sorry," she said. "I thought you'd want to know."

Ernie didn't acknowledge her; he was already walking back toward his rooming house, trying to hold on to the image of the baby—his baby—murmuring in his arms. He trudged up the stairs to his quarters, away from Dorothy and Jersey, into a life that now seemed emptier than ever.

⊶✠⊷

No respectable young woman would be comfortable walking the streets of Hoboken alone at night. Dorothy didn't dare turn to look at the vagrants and prostitutes that loitered on the city's streets. Lifting Jersey to her shoulder, she hugged his weightless body with her hand. His back was no bigger than the size of her palm.

Jersey let out a wail that Dorothy was sure could be heard on both ends of Washington Street. She stroked his head and whispered into his ear. "It's okay now. You'll see."

The baby dribbled onto the front of her dress, his saliva forming a round, wet bubble on the cotton above her left breast.

After leaving Ernie, Dorothy had gone back to the Hoboken train station but had no intention of boarding a train. She'd seen the way Ernie held Jersey and knew she'd found her answer. Sitting on a wooden bench in the cavernous room, she'd waited until the sun had gone down before returning to Grand Street, where the knot of men still loafed on the corner, chomping on stogies and spitting tobacco juice onto the dirt.

Her plan was straightforward, and she didn't allow herself time to change it. She would walk up the stairway next to the cigar store and do something no confession could ever wash from her soul: abandon her infant son into the dark brown calloused hands of a professional prize-fighter—who also happened to be the only person she knew who could teach a motherless mulatto child to survive in a violent, hateful world.

CHAPTER 17
1930

My father walks two paces in front of me as we make our way down Weatherbee Road. He's swinging himself on a pair of crutches to avoid leaning on his bandaged left leg. It's half past two on Christmas Eve and light flurries are dusting the city of Hartford. We pass an elderly man and a young girl hanging Christmas lights on a red brick house and I wonder if they'd be interested in swapping places with a one-legged boxer and his one-armed albino son.

We stop at number 1116, a two-level Tudor with a conical slate roof that gives the house the look of a miniature castle. It's the residence of Edward Albright, the renowned gangster who runs just about every gambling parlor in the Northeast. I just found out that Albright's the button-pusher who stole the champ's title twenty-four years ago. I've also just learned that he's my mother's father.

For years, the champ has told me that he never met my mother's parents. I can't get angry with him because I know why he lied. He didn't want me coming here for favors, just like he's doing now.

"This is it," the champ says, his tone oozing guilt and misgivings.

Part of me is itching to meet Albright to help me figure out who I am. On the other hand, I'd be just as happy to get in the Auburn and head back to the Cozy Cottages and hatch a different plan. I've heard nothing good about Albright, not from my father, not from anybody on the street, not even from crooks like Jimmy. From what I've put together, Albright took over Richard Canfield's gambling parlors after Canfield was picked up by the New York DA's office. Apparently, Albright had a flair for the business. Once he took control, he brought in more muscle, put more cops on his payroll, and opened more casinos. Even hammers like Jimmy are afraid to cross Albright—they know he staffs the nastiest stable of hatchet men north of DC.

"You sure this'll work?" I ask my father. I'm not in the mood to cross another gangster. The champ and I are running out of working body parts.

"The man said he owed me," my father says, as if Albright has been sitting at home, waiting to live up to a promise he made more than two decades ago. "Besides, even he can't turn his back on his own grandson."

The champ makes his way up the front walk, his crutches leaving an asymmetrical pattern of two dots and a single footprint in the snow behind him. When we reach the door, he rests his right crutch on the iron railing and raps at the knocker. I stare at the door, shivering, as the falling snow bites into my ears and the back of my neck.

A small, sixtyish Negro woman opens the arched wooden door. She's carrying a bucket of dirty water and the cotton handkerchief wrapped around her head accents the bright whites of her eyes. Her cobbler's apron is grimy around the knees, and when I picture her scrubbing Albright's floors I'm ashamed to be of his blood. If I were in Albright's shoes, I'd give her a wad of my dirty money to buy herself an evening dress. Of course, my pockets are now as empty as the pouches of her smock.

She scans my raw face, my green eyes, my yellow hair. Then she takes a gander at our worked-over bodies. She steps backward, and I don't blame her. The champ and I look as if we crawled off a battlefield, which, I suppose, we did. She asks us what we want.

"We're here to see Mr. Albright," my father says.

"Who are you?"

"I'm an old friend of his." The champ flashes a warm smile at the maid, but she's not buying it.

"Just a minute," she says. She goes back inside and shuts the door behind her, leaving us in the cold.

Time stretches as we wait in silence, the snow powdering our heads and shoulders. My cheeks are burning, but I ignore the pain and try to figure out what the hell I'm going to say to Albright.

The door opens and a tall white-haired man stands in the foyer. He's wearing a red plaid bathrobe and brown leather slippers, and despite the fact that we've obviously gotten him on an off-day, he's clean-shaven and has his hair slicked into a smooth helmet. The lids over his blue eyes sag and a wad of loose skin hangs down from under his chin. He's giving off the scent of fresh tonic and his cheeks are a healthy, rosy red. I can't help but wonder why, if this is my grandfather, I couldn't have inherited his pigmented genes.

My father looks him square in the eye. "Edward Albright," he says. It sounds more like an accusation than a question.

"Ernie Leo," Albright says back.

He's either got an excellent memory or the champ is in better shape than I thought. Either way, it's clear from the look on Albright's face that he doesn't view this as a long-awaited homecoming. "I never expected to see you again, especially not at my front door."

My father shuffles for balance on his crutches. Albright doesn't help him.

"I'm not happy about bein' here either," the champ says. "But we need your help."

Albright's got his arms across his chest—he's already saying no. "So the upstanding champ winds up needing a scum like me."

Knowing my father, he's itching to walk back down the snowy steps, but he's standing strong because Albright could be my last chance at licking Gazzara. I'd tell the champ to walk away with his dignity intact, but we've got nowhere to turn after this.

"I'm collectin' a debt," the champ says. "I gave you the Higgins title, remember?"

"I remember. The title, that is. Not the debt."

The champ shakes his head. "A man's only as good as his word. I think maybe you said that, too."

"I'm not saying I'll break the deal," Albright says curtly. "I'm saying I don't remember making it."

Leaning forward on his crutches, the champ looks Albright dead in the eye. "You told me to come callin' and that's what I'm doin'."

Albright puts his hand up to stop my father from going on. "If I owe, I'll pay," he says. Then he opens the door and motions for my father and me to enter.

The champ hops into Albright's home using his crutches to swing his legs into the entry foyer. I linger behind, wondering how in God's name we ended up here.

Albright sees my hesitation. "You too, Snowball," he says, pointing into the house with his thumb.

I don't know where the hell he heard my name but one thing is clear: I'm the worst underground operator to grace the streets of Harlem since the invention of moonshine.

⧓

My father and I lean back in dark brown leather club chairs as Albright splashes some brandy into twinkling crystal snifters. Just watching him tip the bottle makes me miss the simplicity of pouring moon for the Joes back at the Pour House.

Albright's house is more impressive on the inside than it is from the street—and considerably more comfortable than the Cozy Cottages. The walls are lined with bookshelves and a stepstool sits nearby, no doubt to help Albright reach the encyclopedias near the coffered ceiling. There's a small bar and a burgundy-felted pool table on our right. Strips of garland wind around the curtain rods, and between the windows is a lit fireplace that gives off the scent of burning pine. If Christmas has a smell, this place has it in spades.

My father refuses a drink—which doesn't surprise me—but I take one of the crystal goblets. I sip the brandy and it's smooth enough to wash any of my misgivings away. In fact, if I knew for sure that Albright wouldn't blow our heads off, I could learn to like it here.

"I've been hearing your name a lot the past couple of weeks," Albright says to me. "You've got a knack for tripping up the wrong people."

"When you're in my position," I tell him, "everybody's the wrong person."

He nods as if he's got the same problem and pats my shoulder. Then he takes a seat in a club chair opposite my father and me, puts a shine on his lips, and tilts his head back as he swallows.

"Smooth as butter," he says. Then he examines his brandy through the side of his glass.

I do the same and return Albright's smile. It's hard not to like the man when he's pouring liquid gold.

Albright leans forward and rests his forearms on his thighs, his snifter in his palm.

"You've got some big guns out for you," he says. "The Gazzara brothers, Jimmy McCullough. I don't know the whole story, but these aren't penny-ante crooks. They're big spenders at my parlors. They've got muscle."

I imagine he already knows that he can scratch Joseph Gazzara's name off his revenue sheet.

"That's why my father brought me here," I say, my mouth going dry as I gear up to ask the favor. "He doesn't need your help. I do."

Albright tips his glass toward my father, acknowledging that the "upstanding champ" wasn't here for a favor after all. He'd shown up to help his son.

My father turns to the fireplace to avoid eye contact with Albright. "Figured you might wanna help," he says. Then, continuing to look into the fire, he adds, "Snowball's your blood, too. He's your grandson."

I'm expecting Albright to whip out a gun and plug my father in his forehead for deflowering his daughter. Instead, he looks at me and sizes me up. I try to offer a lovable face as my heart races and my eyes shimmy.

Albright chuckles, as if he'd been expecting a mulatto albino to show up on his doorstep and call him grandpa.

"I figured you were my grandkid the minute I heard about your run-in with Denny Gazzara."

For the first time since we entered the house, my father looks at Albright head-on. "You knew Dorothy had a son?"

"I haven't seen my daughter in twenty-four years, but that doesn't mean I don't keep tabs on her," Albright says.

The laughter drains out of his face and he shoots down a healthy slug of brandy in one shot. I've been around long enough to know when a guy's downing booze to make his pain go away and this qualifies. He might as well give up, though, because there's not a drink in the world that can replace a daughter.

"But how'd you know it was me?" I say.

He gets up and takes a framed picture from a bookshelf. It's a chewed up photo of a woman about twenty years old. I can see from across the room she's albino. He puts the frame on the table in front of me.

"Caroline Barker," he says.

"Albino," I say, a little confused.

He nods. "Your grandmother."

I look at the photo of the young woman, her white hair falling onto her shoulders. She's smiling, posing for the picture. I can tell that behind those pale, dimpled cheeks, a soul is crying out for acceptance. Looking into her colorless eyes makes me feel as if I've found my homeland, except it's not a place, it's a gene.

My father shakes his head. "Dorothy's mother was Harriet Albright."

"Dorothy's mother was Caroline Barker," Albright says. He's annoyed with my father for butting in. "Trust me, I was there."

"It makes sense," I say, remembering that the doc told me it took two carriers to make someone like me. I already knew my father's grandmother was an albino. If the photo in my hand is my mother's mother, it's clear why I am what I am.

"I didn't even know Harriet when Caroline died," Albright says, the creases around his eyes getting deeper as he continues talking. "The Ferraro gang killed Caroline. She was standing in front of a jewelry store and they gunned her down. Said they got the wrong woman, but that's horseshit. The Ferraros hated anybody who wasn't like them," he says. His eyes glisten as he pours himself another shot.

"That's when I turned," he says with disgust. "Now they're gone and I'm still here."

I nod because I too was pressured into pulling a trigger. Albright is cut from a different cloth, though. He did something I could never do: he kept on shooting. And he has paid a steep price, because when the smoke from his gun finally cleared, he found himself in this big house, alone, with nothing to comfort him except a bootleg bottle of brandy. I can only hope I land in a homier place.

"Albright?" my father says. "How's Dorothy?" The champ's jaw is tight. I hope for his sake she's okay.

Albright stands by the fireplace and gazes out his window. "She's teaching at a school outside of Chicago."

The champ smiles even though Albright never really answered his question. I let it go—neither my father nor Albright is ready for an alternate version of the story.

Albright drops another splash of booze into my snifter.

"To family," he says, raising his glass.

My first thought is that our family belongs in a carnival, but then I see the edge of his lips twist in sarcasm.

"To family," I say.

I hoist the crystal and take a hearty swig without the ritual I gave to my earlier sips. I feel my cheeks flush as the syrupy sweetness coats the back of my throat.

Albright settles into his chair and I color the picture for him, starting with how I bought the bogus moon and finishing with my father insisting we show up at 1116 Weatherbee Road. I give all the important details, except the one about the money from Joseph Gazzara's till. Albright doesn't know Old Man Santiago and he may have a tough time understanding why I'd hand that money over to anybody but Jimmy. When the time comes to tell him, I will. But that time isn't now.

I stop singing and Albright leans back, staring at the ceiling as he thinks things out. He reminds me of Santi sitting in the Hy-Hat, and I do my best to bury my shame.

He shifts forward in his chair. "You need to stop Denny Gazzara," he says, as if I needed help figuring that out.

"I know that," I say. "But I need muscle to get at him."

He laughs and the skin under his chin joggles. I get a glimpse of the cocky criminal that my father spent his life trying to avoid.

"You won't need muscle because you're not going at him," he says. "We're going to let him come to you. Just like his brother duped you into coming to him."

"I don't get it," I say.

"Did I mention that he's a regular at one of my parlors?"

I have no idea what Albright's got up his sleeve, but I can tell by the way he's swirling his brandy that he's already come up with a scheme. And I'll bet my bottom dollar that it involves lies and threats—the same stuff that he spent the last hour claiming to regret.

I grab my snifter and put a fresh coat on my lips, silently toasting my father for knowing enough to knock on grandpa's door.

CHAPTER 18
1930

I've known my grandfather, Edward Albright, for all of four hours, but here I am, an invited guest at his Over-Under Club on Bleecker Street in Greenwich Village. The joint's got two floors: a speakeasy on the street level and a gambling parlor in the basement. Both are hopping and I'm not surprised. It's Christmas Eve and anybody without a home is out looking for one.

The minute the champ and I walked into the place, I could see Albright wasn't hurting for money. There are maroon fabrics hanging on the polished red plaster walls—it's an old speakeasy trick to deaden sound, but these drapes are made of thick, heavy velvet and have a gold trim. A curved mahogany bar runs the length of the room along the right wall and three tenders in white blazers are working the counter, telling jokes, lighting cigarettes, pouring moon.

As impressed as I was with the speakeasy, I didn't get the full picture of what Albright had built until he led us down a curved iron staircase. The gambling parlor is a bettor's dream. There are four roulette wheels, three blackjack tables, and a lineup of slot machines surrounding the three craps tables that fill up the middle of the room. Waitresses in silky, hip-hugging black dresses walk the floor serving drinks. A piano player is working his way through "Puttin' on the Ritz"; the tune is drowning in a din of tumbling dice, shuffling cards, and cursing gamblers. The place is filled with crooks, but they're unarmed—the bouncers working the front door pat down everybody who walks into the joint.

I'm watching the action from the manager's office with Albright and my father. Albright was smart enough to sneak us into the club before it jammed up with customers. If we showed up now, the bouncers would drag us out onto the street and toss us around like dice on a craps table. It's bad enough that I'm an albino, but my father and I are the only Negroes here, aside from the valets.

The manager's office is even more luxurious than Albright's home study. The champ and I are resting our mangled bodies on an over-stuffed couch. To our left, Albright is relaxing behind his carved wooden desk in a leather wingback chair, and we're all monitoring the casino through a two-way mirror on the wall next to him. Behind him, standing in silence, are a couple of triggermen dressed in similar dark gray herringbone suits with white shirts and blue ties. It isn't hard to imagine Albright sitting here alone, controlling the action, avoiding chance, and smashing the dreams of every unsuspecting customer who's foolish enough to shake a pair of dice on the other side of that mirror.

Albright's got his eye on a group of customers at the second roulette table. A cloud of tobacco smoke hovers over their heads as they watch the wheel spin. A bald gambler with a pile of black chips sits in front of a heavyset, pockmarked galoot. They're both screaming at the bouncing marble as if they can scare it into landing where they want. That gambler is my long-lost friend, Denny Gazzara, and I'm guessing the acne-pitted goon behind him is his new muscle.

Gazzara is dressed to the nines. A white starched collar hugs his bloated neck.

"C'mon, t-t-twenty-two," he's yelling as the marble bounces around the wheel.

The ball ricochets and plops into the twenty-two slot. Gazzara lets out a whoop as a fortyish blond croupier slides three stacks of black chips to his spot on the table. As soon as the croupier lets go of the stacks, Gazzara reaches forward and pulls them closer to his chest, a smile stretching his waxed Vandyke to the center of his round cheeks. Even his gloating irks me.

Albright reaches across his desk, pushes an intercom button and calls for the pit boss.

A broad gentleman dressed in a black tuxedo hustles into the office and stands in front of Albright's desk waiting for instructions. His mustache is so thin it looks like he painted it on with a fountain pen. His shoulders are pulled back and his spine looks about as relaxed as a broomstick.

"Pump Gazzara up, then bring him down hard," Albright says. "When he complains, tell him I'm back here."

The pit boss gives a quick mechanical jerk of his chin, and then heads back to the parlor. I don't see him speak with the croupier, but I'm sure he flashed some kind of signal to relay the message across the room.

"I hope this doesn't get messy," Albright says, the toothy smile on his face indicating the exact opposite.

"What do you mean 'messy'?" my father says. I'm sure he's remembering how things turned when Albright wanted to free up the Jersey title.

"That's up to Gazzara," Albright says. "He's about to lose an awful lot of money."

Albright grins at me and raises his glass to toast Gazzara's impending financial doom. I hate to disappoint my father but I hoist my glass toward Albright and slug down a gulp of whiskey. The man is nailing Gazzara and I couldn't ask for more.

"What's next?" I ask Albright. "How will I get him off my back?"

"You'll see."

I have no idea what's coming but the snicker in Albright's tone is answer enough for me. Gazzara slides his pile of black chips onto number twenty-two; the croupier starts the roulette wheel and rolls a small white marble around the edge of it in the opposite direction. As the glass ball ricochets on the twirling numbers, I lean back on the couch, resting my damaged arm on one of Albright's plump sofa cushions. I'm going to enjoy this.

The croupier's a master. Over the past hour, he's put Gazzara on an extended hot streak and plunged him into a financial sinkhole an inch deeper than his pockets. Now he's got the mobster on a string, allowing him to hit every four of five spins, but never letting him get on a roll large enough to pull himself out of debt. I can't figure out how the wheel is rigged, but there are some questions I'm smart enough not to ask.

Gazzara is banging his fist on the table and screaming for more chips. Nobody is standing near him except his hired goon. The gamblers who were sharing his table have moved to other games, obviously preferring to lose their money in peace. Gazzara's collar is soaked, his necktie is undone, and his hairless scalp is dotted with beads of sweat that glitter under the casino lights. The croupier slides four stacks of black chips toward him. Gazzara wraps his chubby fingers around the little towers and shoves them onto the table chart, stopping when they're all on red. When the wheel spins, he watches, his eyes bulging as he bites his lower lip and holds his breath. His flunky stands behind him, barking out curses at the dancing marble, begging it not to land on black.

Albright is standing next to me as the marble skips around the spinning wheel. "Fun, isn't it?" he says.

My father doesn't answer but, to me, there's nothing more delightful than watching Gazzara regress into a stuttering infant. I guess I did inherit some of Albright's genes, after all.

The marble lands on black and Gazzara screams at the croupier. "You're ch-ch-cheating!" he yells out. "This w-w-wheel is rigged."

The pit boss walks over to the table and whispers into Gazzara's ear, flipping his thumb toward Albright's office.

"W-w-where is he?" Gazzara yells, his spit flying into the air. "D-d-damned right I want to speak to him, you p-p-p-issant."

The pit boss leads Gazzara and his buddy out of the parlor and into Albright's office. I can't stop myself from being a wisenheimer.

"Hiya, Denny," I say, sipping my whiskey, which is as smooth as his bald head.

Gazzara comes at me like a Rottweiler charging a piece of raw liver. I back away on the couch, afraid he'll land on my gimp arm, but the pit boss grabs him from behind. The goon's staring me down but he's too outmanned to make a move.

"You n-n-nigger freak," Gazzara screams at me, "I'll rip y-y-your head off."

Albright's triggermen pull their guns. The younger one points his pistol between the goon's greasy eyebrows. The other one trains his on Gazzara's chest. His eyes are as steady as his hands—he's got them fixed on Gazzara as he cocks the hammer on his pistol. I'm ashamed to admit I hope he pulls the trigger and we all get to watch Denny go down once and for all.

"Have a seat, Denny," Albright says. He couldn't be calmer if he were lounging on a hammock.

Gazzara doesn't move; neither does his goon. They just stand there and glare at me. I watch from the corner of my eye as my father shifts his weight, getting ready to swing if Gazzara comes at me again. It's nice to know the champ is in my corner, but right now his only weapon is a crutch.

"I said, sit," Albright barks, stabbing his index finger toward two chairs in front of his desk.

They sit, but Gazzara's shooting me a look that could load a Tommy gun.

"What's he d-doing here?" Gazzara says, pointing at me. He wants to pounce on me so badly his leg is twitching and he's squirming on the edge of his chair. I wish I had two working arms so I could get up and sock him across his stuttering mouth. If he comes at me, I'm going to kick him square in the giblets, just like I did to Hector.

"That's Snowball," Albright says, walking around the side of his desk and leaning on the edge of it with his hip.

Gazzara lunges at me and I spring to my feet, but Albright pushes him back into his chair.

"You owe me money, Denny," Albright says.

"I'm not p-paying you. That w-wheel is r-rigged."

"You owe me money," Albright says again. "And you're not walking out of here unless you pay me tonight."

With that, Gazzara's eyes widen. For the first time since I laid eyes on him, I spot fear on his smug face.

"We're talking thirty l-l-large!" Gazzara says.

"That's right, and I want it tonight. Cash."

"This is a j-j-oke."

"It's no joke," Albright says. "I hear you're lousy at paying your bills."

I look at the champ and wonder if he's getting any satisfaction out of watching Albright square his twenty-four-year-old debt.

"Who said th-that?" Gazzara asks. "I've never had a t-tab I didn't pay."

"Snowball here told me," Albright says. "He says you crossed him. And when you cross Snowball, you cross me."

Gazzara's mouth opens, but nothing comes out. I can practically hear his thoughts stuttering.

"He says you owe him seventy cases of sugar pop moon," Albright says. "He bought eighty, but only ten were any good. Are you saying he's lying to me?"

"He k-k-illed my brother," Gazzara yells out as his back slumps. His agony is so palpable I think he might break into tears. He should only know how guilty I feel about pulling that trigger. I killed a mother's son.

If Albright is moved by Gazzara's pain, he's not showing it. "Your brother was going to chop him up," he says. "I think Snowball's reaction qualifies as self-defense."

He waits for an argument but Gazzara is mute. "So you're on the hook for seventy cases of sugar pop moon to Snowball. And thirty large to me."

"I d-don't have the thirty large n-now."

"Okay, you don't have to pay me now," Albright says, shaking his head to convey he's a reasonable man. "You can stock Snowball with sugar pop moon until your debt to me is paid off."

Denny's lips twitch and the vein running up his forehead bulges and turns blue. He stammers, but not one word comes out of his arrogant, stuttering mouth.

"I'll take that as a yes," Albright says. "Of course, if it's a no, you'll be dead by midnight. And it would be a shame for you to miss Christmas."

I feel juiced with power over Gazzara. Still, as the piano player bangs out "Deck the Halls" in the parlor, I find myself wishing I'd never worked at the Pour House, never gone down to Philly, and never run into the Denny Gazzaras of the world. I'd gladly give up the joy of watching Gazzara beg for his life if I could run through my teen years again. This time around, I wouldn't be here. I'd be at the Hy-Hat, watching Santi decorate the Christmas tree with a string of popcorn and his painted chess pieces.

Albright claps his hands and rubs them together as if we're all excited about the free moon. "So where do the cases get delivered?" he asks me.

"The Pour House," I say.

"McCullough's already been paid," my father says.

It's time I came clean. "I never gave Jimmy the money," I say. "I gave it to Old Man Santiago so he could bury Santi."

I'm braced for the worst, but my father smiles at me as if he just found out that his years of preaching have taken hold. Maybe's he's forgotten that we're sitting in a gambling parlor, strong-arming a stuttering mobster for free booze.

"So seventy cases to the Pour House?" Albright asks again.

The street doesn't have many rules but it does have a few, and I know I can't leave Gazzara's bill at seventy cases. I've got to bring the hammer down on him or I'll be his patsy for the rest of my living days.

"And seventy cases to a speakeasy at Juniper and Vine in Philadelphia," I say.

"Okay," Albright says. "Seventy cases every two weeks to the Pour House and the joint in Philly."

My father shakes his head, confused. "Every two weeks?" he says. "For how long?"

Gazzara didn't ask and neither did I. We both know the answer.

Albright shrugs. "For life," he says, as if he's not asking for much.

"I don't need all that moon," I say and my father grins again. "Just seventy to the Pour House and the same to Philly."

Albright looks at me, his thin lips turned downward, probably disappointed that I don't have his killer instinct.

"Okay," he says. "Two deliveries. Seventy to the Pour House. And three hundred to Philly."

"Three h-hundred?" Gazzara asks.

"And another seventy cases to me," Albright says. "I hear it's good stuff."

Gazzara looks horrified. "If I'm spilling all that b-booze, then y-y-you and I walk away for g-good," he says to Albright.

I'm actually hoping Albright agrees because Gazzara's ready to go off like a Roman candle. At this point he's so humiliated he'd probably welcome the bullet that would rub him out.

Albright nods. "That'll square us. And it'll square you and Snowball."

I walk over to Gazzara and extend my good hand.

"Shake his hand," Albright says.

I don't know if I'm proud or embarrassed that the man's my grandfather.

Gazzara grips the tips of my fingers and gives a quick tug, as if he's afraid he'll become an albino by touching me. His hands are hot and his nostrils flare when his fingers hit mine. Our score isn't settled.

"Wonderful," Albright says. "When can we expect delivery? I'm thirsty."

Now I know where I got that wisenheimer gene.

"It's a lot of m-m-moon," Gazzara says, his jaw tight.

"Tomorrow morning's perfect," Albright says, smiling and slapping the side of his thigh as if it were Gazzara's suggestion. Then, he adds, "Deliver to Philly first."

It's a shrewd move. Philly's the big delivery, he wants to be sure it arrives.

Gazzara gets up and his shadow does the same.

"You'll get your f-fucking m-m-moon," he tells Albright.

Then he and the goon walk to the door. The pit boss follows, along with Albright's triggermen, who have holstered their pistols but still have their herringbone jackets unbuttoned.

Albright pours a round of whiskey and this time my father takes a glass. His hands are shaking, but he downs a hit of booze and steadies them. Albright does the same—minus the trembling fingers.

"Meet with McCullough before the shipment arrives," Albright says to me. "He needs to know why he's getting it, and he needs to hear it from you. Settle up with him, man to man."

I nod and slug a shot of Albright's whiskey. Then I rest my head on the couch and wait for the liquor to dull the pain radiating from the hole in my shoulder. Albright is looking at me, smiling, obviously happy with himself for saving me. He raises his glass to toast our success and I put yet another glaze on my tongue so he can relish the moment. But I already know this is the last time I'll call on him. Albright is a shark, same as Gazzara, and I don't have the genes to swim in their waters. All I want to do is walk away—no guns, no cleavers, no triggermen—free to go back to the simplicity of my old life.

CHAPTER 19
1930

*I*t's Christmas morning and I'm in cabin 11 at the Cozy Cottages rubbing cream over my blistered jaw. My father is asleep on the couch; I'm sitting on the edge of the bed as Johalis squeezes his gloves and boots into a packed leather bag. His work is done, but he's still not buying that Albright got Gazzara to bury his grudge so easily.

"Gazzara will never completely walk away," Johalis says.

I don't disagree, but I need at least seventy cases of liquor to arrive at the Pour House to shake Jimmy off my back.

"You don't think he'll cough up the moon?" I say.

"He'll deliver because he wants to even up with Albright," Johalis says. "I'm just not convinced he's done with you. But I suppose we've got to take him at his word."

"I hope his word is strong," I say. "But just the same, I won't push it. Once Jimmy's got his booze, I'll stay out of Philly."

I'm disappointed because I find myself missing the dim lights of the Ink Well. I was hoping to drive down and visit Angela before New Year's, just to see if she was still checking coats and soothing souls. She had a way about her that made me feel hopeful, which is not something I could ever say about Pearl.

"Too bad, because you're a hero down there," Johalis says, flipping me a folded copy of the *Philadelphia Inquirer*.

I read the headline that stretches across the front page. *Son of Former Boxing Champ Saves Kidnapped Boy*. There, below the big block type, next to a photo of Tommy Sudnik standing in front of his row house on Chatham Street, is my mug.

"Your father put me in touch with the reporter, a guy named Wilkins. I gave him the story the day after we went to Saint Mark's. Wilkins said he owed your father but I had no idea he'd go hog-wild. He caught up with Sudnik's mom and even chased down Father O'Neill at the church. I'm surprised he didn't find you at Albright's casino."

The champ has cashed in on a lifetime of goodwill and I wonder if I'd ever be able to do the same in return. I look at him on the frayed orange sofa—his stitched-up leg hoisted onto the coffee table as snores come from his proud, scarred face, and I smile, surprised I remember how.

"So no more worrying about cops?" I ask.

"The clean ones love you," Johalis says with a shrug of the shoulders. "Gazzara still owns the dirty ones but that'll always be the case. The investigation is officially closed."

"And your debt is paid," I say to him, nodding toward the champ.

He dismisses me with a wave of the hand. "Call me any time," he says. "This isn't about debt." His voice is as thick and rich as ever. I'm telling you, those pipes could woo a dog off a meat wagon.

We shake hands and he grabs his bag. Before he leaves, I tell him I want to keep the paper so I can bring it with me to the Pour House. If Gazzara delivers the moon and I can square things with Jimmy, I just might hang it up behind the bar.

⬥

I step into the Pour House a few minutes before noon. It's hard to relax knowing Jimmy's still after me, but the familiar smell of the joint—a combination of beer, steak, and moon—seduces me as easily as Pearl's outstretched arms. Diego runs over to me and clutches my good shoulder in both of his hands. He's looking behind me, nervously twitching his neck back and forth to see if he's been set up.

"Relax, Diego," I say, stomping the snow off my boots. "I'm not going anywhere."

My tone seems to calm him down, but he's still jumpy. "Sorry, Snowball. Jimmy keeps telling us to bring you in."

I'm ready to tell him there's a difference between grabbing me here and "bringing me in" but I let it slide.

He keeps hold of my arm and leads me past the pocket doors as if I need help finding Jimmy's office. The kid's so keyed up he doesn't even pat me down. If he'd given it a moment's thought, he'd have realized I'd never show up here without packing heat. My revolver's tucked inside my sling and my chesterfield's draped over it.

We circle behind the bar. There's a good-sized crowd singing along with Guy Lombardo as the radio plays "I'm Confessin' that I Love You." It's Christmas, so my guess is they're all confessing it to somebody who's not here.

Larch is in the group, not in uniform, but probably still on the precinct clock. He smiles at me, the bridge of his red nose wrinkling up like the snoot of a bulldog, and holds up his glass. It's half-empty, probably a dry Rob Roy, light on the ice. Diego should be filling it, but he's more concerned about leading an armed man to Jimmy. I nod at Larch but can't pour for him now.

When we get downstairs, Diego knocks on Jimmy's door and then opens it. We walk in and Jimmy looks up from his green leather high-back chair, his heavy eyelids rising in surprise.

"Snowball," he says. "I've been wondering when I'd see you."

I've always managed to respect Jimmy, but seeing him now, after what's gone down over the past two weeks, fills me with nothing but contempt. My father's been right all along. An honorable man works for a buck—Jimmy bankrupted his soul for a thousand.

As usual, he's wearing a shirt and tie; his shirt is starched so smoothly it looks like white butcher paper. He has his gabardine jacket hanging on the back of his chair. The three bookcases behind him are filled with ledgers and old newspapers; a fourth holds rows of books but it's only there for show—it doubles as the emergency exit to the ratacombs.

He motions for me to take a chair and tells Diego to leave the room and shut the door behind him. Knowing Jimmy, he's already worked up new ways to torture me. I lower myself onto one of his hard wooden side chairs and keep my right arm as loose as possible in its sling. If he takes one step toward me I'm going to pull out my revolver and start shooting. My left hand's not accurate, but it can still squeeze off six shots pretty quickly.

"I won't be staying long, Jimmy. I'm just here to tell you that you're getting your moon. It's coming today."

Jimmy leans back in his chair and folds his arms across his chest. "I heard you made quite a commotion getting it back, but I wasn't sure whether to believe it. That Philly story stunk as bad as Sister Hannigan's twat."

He's staring at me, no doubt trying to spot a glitch somewhere in my expression. I'm trying to stay calm but my heart is pounding its way up my throat. Every time I exhale I let out a long, slow whistle. When my eyes start to shimmy, he turns away. Jimmy could never stand it. On the day he hired me he told me that my pupils made me look like some kind of magical coon sorcerer.

I can't take the charade any longer so I get up and head for the door.

"The story's true," I say. "But I didn't do it for you. I did it for me. I couldn't let Gazzara kick me around."

I'm hoping he'll agree with me but I hear his desk drawer slide open. When I turn around, he's got a pistol trained on my gut.

"I'll believe you when the moon gets here," he says. "If it doesn't, I don't have much choice. How would it look if I let you take my money and walk away?"

I can't say I didn't expect this. I sit back down and plant my feet on the floor. I don't miss the irony that I'm now waiting on Gazzara to save my ass after he tried so hard to shoot it clean off my albino legs. I cross my arms so that my fingers are touching the butt of my gun. If Jimmy fires I'll get off a shot or two myself. In all likelihood, neither one of us will leave the room alive.

Jimmy keeps his pistol on me as he grills me on the fine print: the tree farm, the cellar club, the Cozy Cabins. He's all ears when I talk about Denny's operation, but I can tell he's having a tough time swallowing the part about Hector.

"He was out for my legs," I tell him. Even I hear how outlandish it sounds.

"It's not adding up, Snowball," Jimmy says. The look in his eyes says he's going to rub me out right now.

I grip my gun and start talking a mile a minute. I'm telling him about Tommy Sudnik, not that he gives a damn the kid was nearly butchered. The revolver's curved wooden handle is warming in my palm and I'm rattling on about Tommy—readying myself to put a hole in Jimmy's forehead—when Diego rushes in and says that Denny's crew is unloading palettes of moon from a truck out front. Jimmy slips his pistol into his waistband and walks to the door, so I relax my trigger finger.

"They're dumping the cases onto the street in broad daylight," Diego says.

Gazzara's boys may know Philly, but they sure don't know New York. Our cops don't mind if you open a speakeasy, but they don't want you advertising it.

"I told you they weren't geniuses," I say to Jimmy, wiping the sweat from my palm on my pants leg.

We walk through the Pour House and Jimmy tells Diego and Antonio to grab the cases off the street and run them into the ratacombs faster than Sister Hannigan can flash her tits. Then he walks me to the bar and shakes my good hand.

"We're square," he says to me.

I exhale from the bottom of my gut. I feel as if I've been holding my breath since the bogus shipment arrived two weeks ago.

Diego and the boys have their jackets off and are piling the cases by the staircase before bringing them downstairs. If it were up to me, I'd have them in the ratacombs already.

"Hey, Diego," I say, "Why stack them here?"

Diego looks confused, not sure if I'm back on the job or about to be rubbed out.

"He's right, Diego, get them downstairs," Jimmy says, patting my good shoulder. "But first, fill a couple of glasses."

Diego smiles. He pulls a bottle of sugar pop moon and pours two double shots.

Jimmy holds his in the air. "To Snowball, back at the Pour House."

I clink his glass, but it hits me that I wouldn't work here again if he tripled my pay. I'm done with Jimmy. Still, I like knowing we're jake so I swallow the fresh moon. It goes down as smooth as I remember it.

"Gazzara makes some damned good moon for a stuttering lowlife," I say.

I feel the cool touch of metal on the back of my head. "F-fuck you, S-snowball."

I don't bother turning around. Every Joe at the bar is staring behind my head in silence. Diego's black eyes are also trained over my shoulder; he can't help me because he keeps his gun in his jacket, which is sitting on a case of moon next to the staircase.

Jimmy looks behind me. "What do you want, Denny?"

"Th-this is b-between me and S-snowball," Gazzara says. "Y-you've got your s-s-seventy cases, so sh-sh-shut the f-f-fuck up."

If I reach for my piece I'll be dead before my hand touches metal. I keep my head still, afraid to move it.

"Snowball works for me, Denny," Jimmy says. "If you take him down here I've got a problem." I don't know that I've ever seen him calmer.

I spot Larch out of the corner of my eye. He's slowly reaching under his jacket, so I start talking, trying to buy Larch some time to pull his revolver.

"I thought we were square, Denny," I say.

He doesn't have time to answer. The crashing sound of a battering ram comes from the front room.

"Raid!" Diego screams out from behind the bar. Everybody in the place is scrambling to take a powder, but there's nowhere to go—cops are spilling into the place through the front and back doors. Only Jimmy and I know the escape routes, and we're tied up at the moment.

Gazzara takes the gun off my head. He doesn't have any influence here and he's not about to take a murder rap. If we were in Philly, I'd be dead.

Jimmy makes for his office in quick strides, dodging panicked customers. I'm hustling down the stairs behind him and Gazzara is on my heels. I'm not sure if he wants to kill me or tail me out of the joint.

We're about to step into Jimmy's office when I turn and see Larch grab Gazzara's right forearm and yank the gun out of his hand. "What's with the rod?" he says.

"It's n-not m-mine," Gazzara says. "You've got n-n-nothing on m-me."

I finger him for Larch. "Officer, this is Denny Gazzara, a business acquaintance from Philadelphia."

Larch's eyes widen, as they should. Gazzara is wanted in every state in the Northeast and Larch knows he's just been handed a nice collar. And he probably also realizes he's inherited a good-sized shipment of sugar pop moon. At least fifteen cases of the stuff are still stacked in front of the staircase.

Larch calls over a beat cop and I don't wait for a thank you. I hear Gazzara stammering that he wants his lawyer as I run into Jimmy's office. I find Jimmy sliding the bookcase away from the wall. We cross the threshold and cover our tracks by sliding the wooden stack of shelves back into position. We step down into the cold, safe, dank air of the ratacombs and cross the basement. Jimmy takes out his keys and unlocks the steel fire door.

"This is getting tiresome," he says. He's lost some of his freshness, his eyes are drooping lower than ever before and he has a sweat stain the size of a pancake under each arm of his starched shirt.

A rat circles his feet and he kicks it out of the way.

He opens the door and we enter the basement of 321 West Fifty-Third Street. I'm surprised to see a healthy supply of liquor; there must be two hundred and fifty cases down here. Even in my panic, I'm steamed at what I had to go through to get him moon that he didn't even need.

We make our way through the row house in the dark, which isn't too difficult because the place doesn't have a stick of furniture. Walking out the front door, we stay behind the hedges and stroll the path where I ran into Hector only a week ago. The icy Manhattan wind is still racing across the city and I pull up the lapels of my overcoat to blanket my neck. If I had my cream with me, I'd be lathering it on my burning cheeks.

Jimmy cuts across Fifty-Third Street in his suit pants and white shirt. He'll lose himself in the crowd that's gawking at the paddy wagons from across the street.

I walk up the block with my back to the action and tug on the front of my fedora. I've got one more stop to make before starting the holiday season. I stroll to the traffic light at the corner of Broadway, my boots crunching the newly fallen snow as Jimmy McCullough, the Pour House, and Denny Gazzara fade into the distance.

CHAPTER 20
1930

*T*he snow is coming down in lazy flurries. There's a wreath on Pearl's door, so I knock above it with the knuckles of my good hand. Out of habit, I take a quick look over my shoulder. It just goes to show how your anxiety can rise when a crime lord puts a price on your head.

The instant Pearl opens the door I remember why I used to love her. Her doughy cheeks roll into a beaming smile that belongs on the top of a Christmas tree.

She invites me inside but I tell her no. I've finally figured out that chasing a moving target is as fruitless as being one. Besides, I can stand the cold for a while longer. I'm wrapped in a memory of Angela that's got me so warm I'm surprised my boots aren't melting the snow beneath me.

"You're a hero," she says, her eyes twinkling as she holds up the *Philadelphia Inquirer*. I should have known she'd have a copy of the paper— my father's been handing them out to anybody who'll take them.

"Looks like everything's jake," I say, nodding my head. "I'm square with Jimmy, and Larch threw Gazzara in the wagon. He'll nail him with plenty."

"I knew you'd figure things out," Pearl says.

"Yeah, well," I say. I'm not here for a pat on the back. Since Santi's funeral Pearl's been helping Old Man Santiago clean out the Hy-Hat. He wants to close the club but I've got another idea.

"About Old Man Santiago," I say. "I know you've been there for him."

She shrugs as if it's nothing, but that's not the case. She did me a favor just by showing up at the Hy-Hat while I was busy with Gazzara and Jimmy.

"I appreciate it," I say. "But I can take it from here." She looks hurt and I almost apologize. I didn't mean it as cold as it sounded.

"So this is how things end?" she asks.

I want to tell her they never started, but it's not worth the trouble.

I'm surprised to see her eyes watering. She must be crying over the hero on the front page of the *Inquirer*, because she's certainly not interested in the real me, the albino she left in the lurch just when he needed her most.

"You'll be fine," I say and I'm sure I'm right.

I walk back to the car without turning around, not wanting to see the woman I thought I loved in tears. I know what it feels like to be left alone, and the last thing I expected was to do it to Pearl. My neck is hot with shame, but my plans no longer include chasing after her.

When I get behind the wheel I spot the guy who was necking with her last week. He's walking to her place and he's carrying a red box with a gold bow. My guess is that Pearl's tears will dry up in about fifteen seconds.

I start the engine and head up 124th Street. Once I cross the river, I'll pull onto Route 25 and drive down to Philly as fast as the Auburn will take me.

Working in a speakeasy at the corner of Juniper and Vine is a woman who doesn't care about the color of my skin. I'm itching to see if she's still in the coatroom, standing under that clump of mistletoe, waiting to talk to the albino with the funny name. This time, I won't let her slip away. I'll put her in the passenger seat and race her back up here to Harlem to help me run the Hy-Hat. Maybe I'll even find a retired boxing champion to give the kids some lessons and teach them the discipline it took me so long to find.

I'm finally free because for the first time in my life I'm not hiding from who I am: an everyday Joe who's doing the best he can with the hand he's been dealt.

I pull onto the highway and jam the stick into fourth gear. My arm smarts in its bandage but the doc told me it will heal in time. I don't bother checking the rearview mirror because there's nothing behind me I need to see.

I've got the radio on and Rudy Vallee joins me as I make my way to a place I've never been before.

I'm on my way home.

ACKNOWLEDGMENTS

*I*t's hard not to feel as if you and I are at the Pour House, nursing one last round before they close up for the night. The stools are empty, the radio's off, a mound of stained aprons are piled atop the ice cooler. Let's stay 'til they kick us out.

In the meantime, join me as I raise my glass to a special group of people.

Dan Mayer at Seventh Street Books had enough faith in Jersey Leo to bring *Sugar Pop Moon* to press. And my agent, Elizabeth Evans of the Jean V. Naggar Literary Agency, put the deal together.

Fellow writer Alex Jackson, also Ellen Neuborne, helped me build a novel out of a few meandering pages of prose. And many sciencey friends shared their time and advice along the way—here's to doctors Greg Plemmons, Dave Page, Tim Doran, and Brian Burnbaum; geneticist Lenore Neigeborn; and the inimitable, irreplaceable optometrist, Arnelda Levine.

Two automobrothers, Larry and Jeff Trepel, gave me the keys to Jersey's Auburn, along with the other vehicles that rolled through these pages. And speaking of brothers, my own, Bill Florio, eagerly knocked down drafts as quickly as I served them up.

The clock is running out and our glasses are nearly empty. It's time I head home to my wife, partner, first reader, and biggest fan, Ouisie Shapiro. She believed in Jersey, believed in me, and kept me believing in myself. For that, I offer a humble thank-you and a bottomless heart.

The lights are out, so I'll say farewell for now. I hope to see you here for Jersey's next adventure. I'll be at the bar with the rest of the gang, waiting to pour you a shot of moon.

ABOUT THE AUTHOR

*J*ohn Florio is a freelance writer whose work has appeared in print, on the web, and on television. He is also the author of *One Punch from the Promised Land: Leon Spinks, Michael Spinks, and the Myth of the Heavyweight Title*. He lives in Brooklyn, New York, and is at work on the next Jersey Leo novel. Visit him at johnfloriowriter.com.